# The Last Love of
# CAMILLE

## Works by Frances Winwar

### Novels

THE ARDENT FLAME
THE GOLDEN ROUND
PAGAN INTERVAL
GALLOWS HILL
THE SENTIMENTALIST
THE EAGLE AND THE ROCK
THE LAST LOVE OF CAMILLE

### Translations

THE DECAMERON OF GIOVANNI BOCCACCIO

### History

PURITAN CITY: THE STORY OF SALEM
THE LAND OF THE ITALIAN PEOPLE

### Biographies

FAREWELL THE BANNER (Coleridge and the Wordsworths)
THE ROMANTIC REBELS (Byron, Shelley and Keats)
POOR SPLENDID WINGS (The Rossettis and Their Circle)
OSCAR WILDE AND THE YELLOW NINETIES
AMERICAN GIANT (Walt Whitman and His Times)
THE LIFE OF THE HEART (George Sand and Her Times)
THE SAINT AND THE DEVIL (Joan of Arc and Gilles de Rais)
THE IMMORTAL LOVERS (Elizabeth Barrett and Robert Browning)

### Art Monograph

RUOTOLO: MAN AND ARTIST

# *The Last Love of* CAMILLE

A NOVEL BY
FRANCES WINWAR

HARPER & BROTHERS PUBLISHERS
NEW YORK

# DEDICATION

---

TO

LENORE AND JERRY

*whose pursuit of the good, the true and the*
*beautiful has been an unending source*
*of inspiration to their*
*devoted mother*

# Contents

viii    CONTENTS

Ascolta, ascoltami! In questo silenzio
Palpita la mia storia
Di dolore e di gloria
Poiché nulla tramonta, e van per l'aria
In un eterno ciclo, insiem coi venti
E gli echi delle sfere, i moti e l'onde
Dello spirito; e qui, nella mia notte,
La mia carne disfatta avviva il seme
Per la gloria del fiore. . . .

—GIUSEPPE TUSIANI, "Ode al Tempo"

# The Last Love of

# CAMILLE

# 1. The Great Man

BOWING slightly the great man made for his traveling carriage, cutting through the crowd like a swimmer against the current. The autumn wind ruffled his long light brown hair as if it, too, were enamored of that famous profile which at this moment stirred unlawful longings in many a woman's breast and jealous rage in every husband's heart. Yet they were all cheering in a discordant but exciting symphony, the feminine voices rising in shrill flutes against the sustained bass of their male companions.

The sound thrilled the great man more than anything audible except for the voice of a princess saying "I love you" and the music he called forth with his magical hands. They were carefully gloved, those hands, in ginger calfskin and he held them clasped protectively against his breast. The German concert tour had been a triumph.

He took the two steps into his carriage at a bound. The ladder was pulled up after him, the gilded door closed and the ivory profile appeared framed to advantage behind the crystal of the window. The crowd raised a parting shout, making the six white horses shake their manes and rear. Decidedly Berlin, critical Berlin, was his, won by the power of his art.

In the morning sunlight the carriage dashed away with a jangling of harness bells. Thirty coaches, each drawn by four horses, followed, together with an escort of students in costume singing university songs. From the window of one of the royal palaces a Prussian monarch leaned out and watched this popular demonstration till it disappeared. Never had he awakened such enthusiasm. Times were changing.

Unaware that he had roused the envy of a king Franz Liszt leaned back, suddenly tired, and closed his eyes. His face was thin, almost ascetic, and of an extraordinary spirituality. It was the forehead which dominated it by its loftiness and by the lines of strength springing up from the powerful yet delicate nose. The mouth had a sensual fullness even though he held it compressed. The chin, rounded in profile and deeply dented under the lower lip as if the sculptor had sought to leave his thumbprint there, gave to the full face an almost feminine piquancy. But its character changed when the eyes opened. Then the whole countenance lighted up in their blue fire and spirit suffused what had been flesh. He was like some disturbing Giorgione youth with the eyes of a prophet and the lips of Pan.

At every town and hamlet the population, hearing that the famous pianist was to pass by, lined the roads for a glimpse of him. Liszt would stop the carriage and for a few clamorous minutes he would show himself at the door, his tall, spare figure bent, his arms folded across his chest and his head bowed. At one place the burgomaster presented him with a laurel wreath which a golden-haired Valkyrie laid upon his brow. At another a group of girls sang him verses to one of his own *études*. At the first change of horses a delegation of workmen with broad red ribbons across the breast and banners flying honored him with a speech and a parchment hung with seals as large as saucers. They had not forgotten that when Liszt had last come to Germany he had given concerts to help the strikers' families. Liszt was deeply moved and for the first time he spoke.

"I thank you, my good friends," he said. "You tell me that you won your strike. Good! I am happy not only for your sake but because, like you, I helped to deal a blow against injustice."

The words, uttered in a harsh yet vibrant voice, seemed incongruous coming from that aristocratic young man. But they had sincerity and a ring so unmistakably republican that it would have confirmed the Prussian king's concern over the changing times.

The delegation cheered with enthusiasm. The men harnessed themselves to the carriage and insisted on pulling it for the next half mile, while the horses pranced on behind, happy at their unexpected freedom.

It was dusk when Liszt's student escort left him at the inn where his friend and secretary, arrived from France, was waiting. From the balcony Liszt waved to the gay cavalcade till the echo of the songs faded away and the pale carriage lamps reddened in the gathering dusk.

Marcel Arnaud had already arranged the correspondence on a table when Liszt re-entered the room. All the letters were open but for two, on mauve paper sealed with a device in white wax.

"Ah, letters, letters!" sighed Liszt. "What a blessing, Marcel, to receive them and never have to answer them!"

"But then I'd find myself without employment," answered Marcel, humorously lifting his graying brows like circumflex accents. "And who would engage Marcel Arnaud, ex-fencing master, ex-littérateur, ex-adventurer and ex-lover?"

"As for the last, we find ourselves in the same galley, *mon ami.*" Liszt picked up the mauve squares. "I sometimes wonder whether it wasn't the coat-of-arms that made Marie go back," he said, passing his fingers in a rapid run over the ornate seals. "Is Paris still talking about the great reconciliation?"

"You know that nothing is interesting for more than three days in the capital," replied Marcel, "though I must admit everyone found the Count d'Agoult magnanimous in forgiving the prodigal wife even though he would not live with her. But then, she has her own charming rose-pink house on the Champs Élysées and a salon and freedom. Of course the Jockey Club joked about Helen leaving her handsome Paris, but they gave a novel reason."

"For our parting?"

"They said the Countess d'Agoult was mad with jealousy over your other mistresses, especially when Lola Montez came on the scene again. They blamed you, of course. A man may be unfaithful to his wife, but to be unfaithful to his mistress— that is unforgivable."

"It's absurd! The whole thing is absurd!" cried Liszt. "I

was never in love with Lola. It was Byron I loved in her, the divine Byron—"

"What would the Jockey Club make of that?" said Marcel.

Liszt ignored the quip. The flashing eyes assumed an inward look and the harsh voice softened as he went on, "When I touched her it was like clasping Byron's hand. I felt the living warmth of the poet. I saw the smoldering imagination behind her marvelous eyes. I loved her eyes, Byron's eyes—"

"But the whole world knows she is not Byron's daughter, though she's honest enough to qualify herself as illegitimate. Doesn't she also claim the Spanish bullfighter Montez as her father? She's nothing but an adventuress. She can't even dance. They hissed her off the stage not so long ago at the Porte Saint-Martin."

"I know, I know. But she gave me moments of illusion, of spiritual ecstasy."

"Spiritual?"

"Yes, spiritual," Liszt repeated. "I did not go to her for any other kind."

"Forgive me, *cher maître*. It is a commonplace that fire melts ice. The contrary would be a miracle. The stories that reached us in Paris, the tales Lola herself told—"

"I know, and they were all true. I did lock her up in the hotel rooms, but only to flee from the ardors I did not want. I did pay the hotel for every piece of furniture and the bric-a-brac, knowing that she would wreck everything in her rage."

"And all for the loss of your spiritual love?"

"You would not understand, *mon ami*," said Liszt without anger. "Long ago I fell in love with a woman so old that I could scarcely find in her the shadow of what she had been. But Goethe had once loved her and found her beautiful, and I loved Bettina von Arnim for that beauty which neither time nor infirmity could take away. I'm no great admirer of Musset," he went on, going to the window and looking up at the sky, "but he is a poet with a poet's gift of divining truth. *Aimer est le grand point, qu'importe la maîtresse—Qu'importe le flacon, pourvu qu'on ait l'ivresse. . . .*"

"Still, people say you would prefer the *flacon* etched with a noble crest. Your compositions, dedicated to duchesses, countesses—"

"Bah! It is because my art throws me among them. I would have loved Marie d'Agoult if she had been a milliner's apprentice." Suddenly he burst out laughing, and Marcel joined him, at the thought of the cold, haughty Marie d'Agoult as a Paris *grisette*. "Yet there might be some truth to what people say," he added gravely. "I was only a boy when I went to her salon. She was a woman of thirty, sophisticated, surrounded by luxury and the flattery of great men. I thought her a goddess and being young and foolish I had to have her."

"A Frenchman is no longer young at—was it twenty-five?"

"Twenty-four. But you forget, Marcel, I'm Hungarian. I was also a prodigy, which means that from the age of nine it was tours, concerts, salons, kisses on the brow. Even Beethoven kissed me. Did you know that? I remember a smell of snuff and age and stale linen in a cluttered room. But I did not wash my forehead for a week, and every night I prayed God to make me as great as Beethoven. I had no time for anything but music and God. When I was fifteen I even thought of taking religious orders. But why am I telling you what you already know?"

He turned away from the window and sat down at the table. The lamp cast its light upward so that the flame was reflected on his moist forehead. Marcel was disturbed by it and moved the lamp to one side. Liszt was about to open the letters but changed his mind.

"You had better order dinner, Marcel. I've had nothing since morning and I feel one of my famous hallucinations coming on."

Marcel went out, leaving Liszt at the table, his eyes fixed on the lamp's crystal globe where a restless flame was trying to split in half. Two flames had once joined and burned together in a light intended to be eternal. But what is eternal? A moment may hold all eternity and ten years fleet away as an instant. How bravely they had set out, he the ardent poet of the piano and she golden, beautiful and proud, to teach humanity love and freedom. They had taught it nothing. The world called their freedom license and their love adultery. They themselves learned that even a free union on an altitude from which all levels are visible is not immune to jealousy and petty irritation and finally boredom, and that it too can become as prosaic as marriage.

The seal snapped like a fingernail breaking and he flinched. Why did Marie insist on writing to him? For years, though their love had been long dead, she had kept on thrusting herself upon his awareness. Was it still to keep alive the myth of their romance? It had been beautiful when, in the intoxication of their daring, they had scaled the forbidden mountain and stood at the peak, for all to see. But would it have been as intoxicating if no one had noticed? Their reflection in the eyes of the world had offered the deepest exhilaration. Not so much to him who had been a popular idol for more than a decade, but to her who had found her salon too small. She wanted the world for her mirror and he, Liszt, had given it to her.

Then, too soon, he discovered that Marie herself was only a shining surface capturing the reflections of others. At first he was amazed to hear his own thoughts echoed as her own, to see charming affectations he had admired in others adopted by her. Her very love, her resolve to join her life with his, had found its first impulse in George Sand's novel, *Léone Léoni.* "I am nobler than Madame Sand's Juliette," she told him. "Besides my social position I sacrificed my husband and my children for our love."

How jealous she had been of George Sand! Yet how shamelessly she had tried to win the affection of that forthright, simple George, so honest and loyal in love and friendship, in spite of the chaos she had made of her life. He could see Marie, striking her most seductive attitudes to deflect to herself the admiration George had for him, till the puzzled and flattered woman dedicated a novel to her. Marie herself was now writing and, like George Sand, she used a masculine name, Daniel Stern.

In fact the letter Liszt opened was chiefly concerned with a novel in progress and a catalogue, like Don Giovanni's, of the important men who were flocking to her salon to lay their hearts at her feet. There had been a time when the thought of another man kissing her hand had given him almost physical pain, yet now he felt not the least pang of jealousy. What was this apathy? Was he getting old? He had loved Marie. He had loved her deeply and passionately because of her very faults. For what merit is there in love that spends itself on virtue, nobility, beauty? Everyone can love noble qualities. Real love is Christian charity. It belongs to the sinner. He still remembered something George Sand had said on the subject long ago, and its truth even now made him nod in affirmation. "When you, O righteous man, can feel a noble passion for a miserable fallen creature, then you can be sure it is love."

He was reading the Countess d'Agoult's second letter when Marcel returned. "It's all about her writing, Marcel," said Liszt, "a novel she has very nearly finished and which she hopes I shall like, whatever evil tongues may say. Why evil tongues? Have you heard anything about it in Paris?"

"Not a thing," answered Marcel, a little too quickly. Liszt darted him an incredulous look. "Not a thing?" he repeated.

"Really, *cher maître,* not a thing. Unless you'd have me repeat the gossip of the boulevards."

"By all means! If there's anything unpleasant that I shall be hearing in Paris I had better be prepared for it. Well?"

"It's nothing, really. Musset has been saying on the authority of Sainte-Beuve, who said he had seen the manuscript—"

"As a matter of fact she mentions Sainte-Beuve. Yes, here it is."

"—that it is about a much wronged heroine and a fascinating villain who bears a close resemblance to yourself, *cher maître*. But Musset draws most of his inspiration out of a bottle these days, so—"

"Thanks," said Liszt, rising.

For a while he paced about the room, his eyes on the carpet. "Charity," Marcel heard him say, "charity."

At dinner Liszt ate little and immediately excused himself.

"Order the carriage and horses for five o'clock tomorrow morning," he said. "Don't bother to wake me. I know I won't sleep tonight."

Nevertheless he undressed, his lean yet muscular body borrowing a glow from the lamp which he quickly blew out. In the dark he went to the window and pulled aside the curtain. The sky had few stars, so large and low in the sky that they seemed caught in the half-denuded branches overarching the balcony. He shivered. There was a touch of winter in the air, though it was still early October. Drawing on the fine linen nightshirt which in the lamplight had revealed the work of loving feminine hands, he threw himself upon the massive bed.

He hated to lie in strange beds yet he had never had a sleeping place of his own except as a child. All his years with the Countess d'Agoult had been spent in rented houses and borrowed couches.

Who had slept in this bed? What casual intrigues had gone on under these brocaded hangings? What passions, what crimes, perhaps, had been enacted on this most important of life's stages?

These thoughts, mingling with a stirring of sensuality,

forced him to his feet. He put on a dressing gown and after walking about the room took a cigar from his traveling case and sank into the armchair near the balcony. In contrast to the darkness within, the window now framed a pale sky filigreed with black branches. Gusts of wind shook them, loosening the last dry leaves which scraped against the glass like sharp talons. Again he felt the unpleasant sensation as when he broke a fingernail on the piano keys, a recurrent torture whenever anything troubled him.

Yet he had everything even the most ambitious man could wish: an unparalleled career, wealth, admiration and a trunkful of ribbons and orders. In his field he feared no rival, not after vanquishing Thalberg in the famous battle of the pianos. Someone had dared say, "Thalberg is the greatest pianist in the world," and instantly the retort had thrust: "But Liszt is the only one."

He was the only one, the Napoleon of the keyboard. That's why he had had his traveling carriage built on the model of the conqueror's. All over Europe, where Napoleon's blue-green chariot had left the ruts of its crimson wheels, his own carriage had followed, even to Russia. But there he had been more fortunate than Napoleon. He had made his conquest and held it.

How thrilling that first recital at St. Petersburg, where three thousand Russians had gathered to hear him in the Salle de la Noblesse. What a triumph when he, alone with his art, had held captive so vast a throng! For hours he played and they wanted more. Men and women fell at his feet. "Fortunate are we to be living in 1842 in the same age as such a genius!" cried a Russian poet. "Have I indeed heard Liszt, or was it the god of music?" Idolatry, but he loved it.

Yet that year of glory, three years ago, had been one of his unhappiest. He had won Russia but he had lost love, for it was then he discovered what Marie d'Agoult with her feminine instinct had learned much earlier—that they were tragic comedians playing a role which had grown stale. As the queen of poses Marie kept up the pretense, but he plunged into debauch, seeking in others what he had lost in her. He tried to exhaust himself with playing, giving twenty concerts in a single month. He fasted as in his adolescence, and spent hours kneeling on the cold stones of the churches. But the void in his heart remained. He was a Casanova incapable of either love or enjoyment, an amatory snob, a frequenter of aristocractic boudoirs.

What had become of the pure youth for whom his father had to wrestle with a host of angels? He could still hear the rasping voice of Adam Liszt: "You belong to art, not to the Church, my son! To art! Art!"

The angels had very nearly conquered, or rather, his patron Saint Francis de Paule, who had appeared to him in a vision. By closing his eyes as he did now, he could see the saint again poised upon the waves, his cloak spread at his feet. In one hand he held a glowing coal, but it was in his eyes that the true fire burned as he gazed toward heaven where shone the one word, *charitas*.

"*Charitas*—love," Liszt said aloud.

# 2. The Blue Coupé

PARIS was buzzing with a new scandal. Wherever Liszt went someone was sure to rush up to him. "Have you heard the latest? George Sand and Chopin are not the cooing doves any more. *On dit* there will soon be a break. Imagine, after six years!"

Why the news should grieve him he did not know. Perhaps because he had brought them together. What a friendship theirs had been, his and Chopin's. They were inseparable, glorying in each other's success, playing each other's compositions. "Pearls on velvet," they said of Chopin's runs. "Pearls on hot velvet," they said of his.

How young they had been, in love with love, in love with beauty. Then Marie d'Agoult had come into his life and he, another Galeotto, had brought George Sand and Chopin together, never dreaming that *la grande amatrice*, heartsick and disillusioned, would fall in love with the consumptive youth. As for him, Liszt, he had to give up both Chopin and Sand. Marie could not tolerate the loss of an admirer, especially to the woman she envied. That had been long ago.

Yet never had he been so lonely and unhappy as now,

since his return. Although a record number of women had fainted at his last recital, he felt something wanting. He had been away from Paris too long, and Paris, the fickle, soon forgets. Like a woman she had to be wooed anew. Yes, like a woman.

At the echo of the phrase he realized that for the first time in his manhood he had no woman to woo. Always before there had been a discreet apartment to go to, with Marie waiting. Now she was a stranger in the crowd that came to hear him. Twice he had seen her with a different escort. Her face was cut in marble and harder still was the look in her eyes. Was it possible he had ever held that statue in his arms and felt it warm and pulsing against his heart?

He had also seen Chopin. The chair beside the youth was empty, but he was not alone. Chopin was already in the clutch of the mistress whose hold is for eternity. He, Liszt, could hardly endure to play the rest of his program before that an-guished face, rather, that skull covered with wax, whose eyes smoldered with genius and a desperate questioning. How much longer still? A year, two or three, when a century would not suffice to give voice to the music in that brain?

The concert over, he looked for Chopin among the men crowding the antechamber. He was not there. That night he went to Chopin's rooms. The servant said his master was not at home. "Say that Liszt called, then. Better, let me leave my card." On it he wrote his motto, *Génie oblige*, adding, "and so does the friendship of your old Franz." As he was leaving he thought he heard a muffled fit of coughing. The servant quickly shut the door.

Chopin never answered his card. Liszt saw him again later, leaning back in a carriage, his features set in that proud aloofness which, as a young student eager for all sensation, Liszt had remarked on the faces of the dead in the hospitals. He had an impulse to stop the carriage and force Chopin back to the old friendship. Something held him back. Why break the peace of the dead? Wasn't he himself leading a kind of posthumous life? There could be no human emotion in ghost meeting ghost. He said good-by forever to Chopin and to old friendship and to dead love.

"If I were to die now! If some revolutionist were to throw a bomb at Louis Philippe and kill me instead? I'd be remembered as I am, at the height of my youth and glory. Ah, to die and to die young—what happiness! Chopin doesn't know how lucky he is. He'll always be remembered with regret. They'll build a myth about him, the victim of fate and of a heartless woman. Poor George!" he sighed. "You and I will probably live to an unromantic old age, our hearts have grown such a thick crust from all our buffetings!"

Along the tree-lined Champs Élysées all fashionable Paris was passing in contrary currents at that hour of the promenade, Louis Philippe with the rest. The men lifted their enormously tall hats as they passed him, heavy, old, almost obsolete in his antiquated stock and wig and the inevitable umbrella. Recently he had stopped wearing the tricolor cockade on his hat. It might revive dangerous ideas. Although it was customary for the young Romantics to ignore the king, Liszt raised his hat. Louis Philippe glanced up, looked again and stopped. The guards who followed at a discreet distance stopped also.

"Ah, *bonjour,* Monsieur Leets," he said cordially. (No one in France called Liszt anything else. The challenge of the consonants was too formidable.) Liszt bowed. "Your last concert was superb! Are we to have the good luck of keeping you with us a while this season?"

"Through the winter and spring, Your Majesty. Except for a few recitals abroad."

"Then we are indeed fortunate, Monsieur Leets. That word *recitals* that you adopt—pardon the curiosity of an amateur philologist—it has always puzzled me. You do not recite at the piano, you play, *n'est-ce pas?* Yet you say *recital.*"

The promenaders slowed their pace to enjoy this encounter and equipages halted along the drive to give the occupants a chance to look at the great Liszt in conversation with the king.

Liszt spoke with animation. "I must contradict Your Majesty. I *do* recite at the piano. What are my *études* and *pièces* but musical soliloquies in different moods? It is the same with the pianoforte rhapsodies, the legends, my own work and the music of greater men. I do not play for the ear alone. I strive to reach the heart and the imagination."

"Which you admirably succeed in doing, Monsieur Leets, though—permit me!—sometimes with distressing results. Those incidents among the ladies, brought on by excess of emotion . . . When I was young music did not make us faint. We marched to it, to the glorious victories of Valmy and

Jemappes. Yes, Jemappes. I was there, Monsieur Leets. I fought side by side with—"

The king did not have a chance to recount the story of his one memorable feat as an uproar of shouting coachmen, lashing whips and clattering hoofs drew all attention to the drive. Instantly the king's guards surrounded him. But there was nothing alarming, only a carriage jam caused by a speeding coupé in the lane headed for the Arc de l'Étoile.

The rebel vehicle was blue, gilt and fashioned with the exquisiteness of a jewel box. The coachman, who had jumped down from his high seat, was quieting the two magnificent bays who were shaking their manes, their nostrils quivering at the commotion. Although against the window of the closed carriage one could see only the head of an English greyhound, the people were saying, "La Duplessis! It's Mademoiselle Duplessis's carriage."

At the name all attention shifted to the coupé. Eagerly men and women pressed forward to the dismay of Liszt whose fascination had never before yielded to another's. Mademoiselle Duplessis? He had heard the name since his arrival. Was she an actress? A singer at the Opéra? He had been too long away. New idols rose quickly in the capital. With the rest he and the king watched as the carriages were disentangled and the currents began to flow again. Mademoiselle Duplessis's coachman leaped upon his seat and was about to crack his whip when the door of the coupé opened. A gasp of anticipation came from the crowd but it turned to a sigh of disappointment when a very familiar figure descended and made straight for Louis Philippe.

"Well! If it isn't Korff!" exclaimed the king. "What were *you* doing in La Duplessis's coupé?" he asked jocularly as the doctor made the crossing with the strut of a hurried peacock.

"Your Majesty! My apologies! My client's apologies for the regrettable incident—Monsieur Leets, a most unexpected pleasure!" He clasped the pianist's hand but returned immediately to royalty. "I trust Your Majesty was not startled? May I take the liberty?"

He leaned over before Louis Philippe could answer and pressed his ear against the royal heart. "Regular as a clock. Your Majesty's pulse?" He took the king's thick wrist. "Good! Good! Still, it does no harm to quiet the nerves." Thrusting two fingers into the pocket of his waistcoat he drew out a silver pillbox. "Now, Your Majesty, your mouth." The royal mouth obediently opened and the doctor laid a small comfit on the tongue. "Let it melt, Your Majesty. And now, with Your Majesty's permission, and yours, my dear Monsieur Leets—"

He bowed and was about to leave. "But you haven't answered my question, Korff," said the king. "What were you doing in that charming coupé?"

"A professional visit, Your Majesty. Purely professional."

With that he removed his hat, bowed once more and hopped back nimbly into the coupé, which started off at once. The crowd, cheated of its glimpse of the Duplessis, drifted away. Liszt too felt a pang of disappointment. Who was this woman who could draw attention away from him?

He wanted to escape the king before he could return to the

battle of Jemappes but etiquette forbade his making the first
move.

"That devil of a Korff," said Louis Philippe. "Would you
believe it, Monsieur Leets? He was already famous under
Bonaparte. I am sure he is older than I am yet he looks no
more than forty. He hasn't changed a hair." He laughed.
"Perhaps he is Cagliostro, as they say. *Au revoir,* Monsieur
Leets."

"Your Majesty!" Liszt placed his hat over his heart, inclined
his head and left the king to his guards and his umbrella.

Duplessis. A charming name. Aristocratic, no doubt. Of
course; would Dr. Korff attend her otherwise? He was a
notorious snob, Korff—and Liszt repeated to himself the doggerel someone had maliciously printed not so long ago:

> For queens alone he saves his skill;
> Each royal migraine, every ill
> Yields to his mighty art. . . .

But what could be the matter with the Duplessis? Probably
nothing more serious than the vapors which would respond
readily to the doctor's treatment. Everybody knew that his
amusing gossip was as effective in his cures as his nostrums.
Certainly nobody ever died of it. Duplessis. Decidedly an
intriguing name. Was she young? Old? Young, of course, or
Louis Philippe would not have made his insinuating jest, nor
Korff his equally suggestive answer. Ah, well! What did it
matter? Young, old, it was all one to him. He had had enough
of love. It was only his vanity that was piqued to curiosity.

Yet why should he be thinking of love when only a few

minutes earlier he had been pitying himself for his heart's hardened shell? He was conscious of feeling tired although he had barely walked half the distance from his hotel near the Place de la Concorde to the Arc de Triomphe de l'Étoile. There it rose, massive yet immaterial between the converging lines of trees, like a gateway opening onto heaven and immortality. It thrilled him whenever he walked under its arch, as if indeed he were passing from one state of existence into another. Grandeur, tragedy, death: they haunted his imagination, particularly now that he had gone back to a work begun long since, when his whole being had been shocked to creativeness by some paintings in the Campo Santo of Pisa.

The frescoes reappeared, as vivid in his memory as the day he had seen them—rather, the weeks, for he had gone back to haunt them like one of their own uneasy phantoms. The "Dance of Death," the "Triumph of Death" they were variously called, but the impact was the same, shattering the nerves and making the soul reel.

Like an Italian of five hundred years ago, when the colors had been fresh on those painted walls, he had stood before the pictures, penetrating and becoming part of them. He was one of those youths returning from the chase with falcon on wrist and the hounds at his feet. Those lovely maidens in the April of their beauty had listened to his songs as they were now listening in this enchanted garden to the amorous duo of a minstrel and a singing girl. All was joy and beauty in the luminous dusk filled with flights of Loves waving torches.

The youths and maidens were so entranced by the loveliness about them that they were unaware of the vengeful harpy tearing toward them through the air. They did not see her glaring eyes, her clawed hands swinging the scythe. They did not hear the hum of her batlike wings nor the death cries of the victims at her feet where cardinals lay in their blood-red robes, and kings in purple and queens with golden hair richer than their crowns. Warriors and conquerors who helped to people the domains of Death were now themselves Death's prey. For she spared no one, not the great, not the humble, not youth nor beauty. Only those who implored her to end their misery she cruelly ignored—like that crowd of wretches in their rags, those cripples with their crutches, the leprous, the plague-ridden.

The scene shifted. But even where Death was not she left her horrid traces. In a flowery glade another group of merry-makers sported with horses and hounds. The men were conversing gaily. The ladies, lovelier than ever, smiled in the pride of their beauty. But what was the horror at their feet to which an ancient holy man was pointing with his crutches? Three graves lay open before them, and three corpses revealed to the day the devouring work of the worm. Their moldy raiment, their panoplies, bespoke their exalted state. Corruption had devoured them equally with the beggars' rags. If the men had glanced at those open graves they had turned away unheeding. For what had youth to do with the dead, whether pauper or emperor? So they returned to their sport and their lightsome talk. The ladies' smiles still trembled on their lips. Only one, the fairest, lingered on the sight, her face leaning on her hand, her eyes clouded with sorrow. For the dead princes? For herself?

That sorrowful face became an obsession. Often Liszt would go to the Campo Santo to gaze on the simulacrum of someone loved long ago when he, Liszt, a Florentine, had set sonnets to music to restore the delight of life to those eyes that had looked on death.

In turmoil of soul he had begun to compose the "Dance of Death" in a new musical idiom, fantastic, shocking, full of crashing chords and eerie effects on the piano, while the somber theme of the *Dies Irae* dominated the orchestra like the fearsome presence of Death. He had been working on the score for nearly seven years. Meanwhile he had planned and finished other compositions and still the "Dance of Death" demanded more and more. Sometimes as he sat at work it seemed as if the Death of the fresco were in the room, urging him on and beating out the macabre rhythms with her bony hands on his aching skull.

The rhythms never left him. He heard them now in the clop-clop of the horses along the Champs Élysées. They echoed in the light tripping of the women on their high heels, in the scampering steps of the children teasing their nursemaids. The wind through the trees became the whirr of Death's wings, and the swishing of carriage whips the rush of her falling scythe. All Paris was joining in the inescapable dance.

At the Étoile Liszt did not turn back but passed the arch and went on toward the Bois de Boulogne. New themes were running through his head. He even thought of a stirring resolution for an ineffectual chord which had long troubled him. As if his mental activity had communicated itself to his body

he quickened his pace and breathed deep, enjoying the
warmth of the sun and the vividness of the grass still untouched by autumn.

Little boys in wide hats were floating toy boats along the
edge of the lake, to the shrilling of their governesses warning
of wet feet and ruined clothes. Groups of women dotted the
lawns. Their bright dresses, the color of hortensia, rose and
iris, gave them the look of overblown flowerbeds. Liszt recognized ladies of his acquaintance but not wishing to inter-
rupt his thoughts pretended not to see them. Along the drive
the unoccupied carriages were lined up, the coachmen chat-
ting in groups or shouting their greetings across to one another from their high seats. In the liveliness of the scene
Death suddenly became incongruous.

However, he was in a propitiously creative mood. Hiring a
fiacre he left the more frequented part of the Bois. The long
narrow lake with its wooded islands on his right was agitating
itself into futile whitecaps that lapped the shore and died. On
his left the islands of tree-shaded lawns grew less populated.
Rounding the southernmost tip of the lake he directed the
coachman toward the Route de la Vierge aux Berceaux. The
name had a gentle sound and the image of the Virgin of the
Cradles completely dispelled the presence of Death.

He had the path to himself although he could hear the
sound of wheels from the nearby Allée des Acacias, and the
occasional barking of a dog. Taking off his hat he shook his
head as if to clear it of extraneous thoughts and walked
through the woods in the direction of the waterfall. His whole
being was like a sensitive instrument in a state of extraordinary

receptivity. He saw without looking, heard without listening, everything converting itself to musical symbols on five parallel lines. Occasionally he caught himself humming. Once he shouted an exultant theme, answered by the alarmed barking of a dog.

As he emerged on the alley of the cascade, the dog itself came bounding toward him, its tail contradicting the reproof of its bark. It was a handsome animal, slim, high on its legs, long-muzzled and of a subtle sandy shade brushed to a sunlit gloss. Liszt was fond of animals. He looked round for its owner and, seeing no one, began talking to it in a cajoling tone.

"Come, boy, enough of that noise! You don't like my voice? I can't blame you with your sensitive ears. But there's really no need for such din, my good fellow!"

The dog leaped about him playfully, then stretching out its front paws on the ground, placed its head between them and reared its haunches in a canine bow. Liszt noticed its gold collar studded with topazes.

"Well! So you want to make friends. Do you know how to give a man your paw?" He reached out his hand. To his amazement the dog put its paw into it, gazing at him with eyes of the same dusky gold as the stones on its collar.

Just then a voice came ringing down the alley. "Dash! Dash!" it called, high-pitched and true.

The greyhound pricked up its ears, the tail motionless. For a moment it hesitated between obedience and its new friend. Obedience won. As Liszt gazed after it he saw, at the turning, the blue coupé. The door was open, the steps were down, but there was no one in its rose velvet interior. Suddenly he remembered the head of the greyhound he had seen behind the window as he stood talking to Louis Philippe.

He found himself walking eagerly after the dog which bounded ahead to the end of the path and turned into the Allée des Acacias. Passing the empty coupé it made for the trees a little distance away and leaped about teasingly, wagging its tail.

"Naughty, naughty Dash!" The voice was now soft, low and velvety. "Where did you go, naughty? Come, now, fetch the ball!"

In a moment Dash came leaping out and dropped the ball at Liszt's feet. He picked it up and turned toward the wood. Against the trunk of an acacia whose last feathery fronds almost touched her head stood Mademoiselle Duplessis. The young man felt his heart beat so violently as to cause him pain.

She was tall and slight and graceful, with long narrow hands and slim feet encased in white velvet with jeweled clasps. Her dress was of a lustreless heavy white silk. Her pelisse which came down to her waist was also white, but of a fur that had the patterns of watered silk. She had hung her hat on a low branch and her hair, parted in the middle with classic simplicity, fell in dark curls to her bosom.

It was her face that held him, with its challenge of revelation and mystery. Where had he seen it? For he had seen it before, a face of flawless beauty in feature and expression. The arch made by the line of her hair was answered by the curve of her brows. But her eyes—it was her eyes which gave her an almost unbearable beauty. They were large, widely spaced and slightly elongated, with the longest lashes he had ever seen and pupils the color of those pansies that capture the gold of the sun and the darkness of night in their tawny petals. Her nose was straight, her chin delicately rounded. And what an exquisite mouth, the upper lip finely cut, quivering upward at the corners, the lower moist and full. Where did her smile come from? And her strange melancholy? Leonardo's women had those smiling-sad eyes and equivocal lips and that angelic purity. It was a face of the Renaissance, preserving its disturbing mystery.

Liszt was too much moved to speak and his eyes wavered before her unfaltering gaze. Was it boldness or innocence?

He threw the ball at her feet with the gesture of Paris bestowing the apple. Then, holding his hat against his heart, he bowed and left her, walking backward as from a queen.

Pacing rapidly he reached the Avenue de la Grande Armée. Where had he seen that face? In a flash he remembered. It was the face of the compassionate woman in the Campo Santo of Pisa. Suddenly exhausted, he signaled a hack and sank back with closed lids against the cushions. But the image did not leave him.

# 3. At the Jockey Club

MADEMOISELLE DUPLESSIS was no angel of purity, as Liszt found out at the Jockey Club, where horses and women, and their price, were commonly discussed in that order.

"Oh, yes, the Duplessis is expensive, but she's worth it."

"*Ravishing!* Absolutely!"

"The rage of the season! She has only to wear some silly hat or shawl for every lady of fashion to adopt it. The uglier and more virtuous they are the more they ape the Duplessis. Alas, if sin could make them more *attractive*, I'd almost suggest it to them. That is, if I didn't have to initiate them."

"Have you noticed the great popularity of the camellia, Monsieur Leets? It is her flower. She has discovered it. In fact at Madame Barjon's they call her the Lady of the Camellias, she buys such quantities of them. Now the name has become even more famous than the flower."

They spoke with authority, those bright young men with their loud waistcoats and tight trousers and their smattering of English, which was the language of the fashionable world. By their inflection, even more than by their words, they sought to suggest intimacy which in most cases existed only in imagination and unfulfilled desire. Liszt, who had introduced the subject, sat among them with assumed indifference, apparently absorbed in the game of chess that he was playing against himself. Still, he could not help remarking: "Strange, she does not look what you seem to imply."

"Imply! Everybody knows the fame of the Duplessis," said a tall blond youth hotly. "*Mon Dieu,* Monsieur Leets! Any man who succeeds in getting an invitation to—to supper at the Boulevard de la Madeleine would be the first to shout it all over town. It's—it's a title of honor!" he stuttered excitedly. "It's—it's like having a winner at the races."

"Stop boasting, Perrégaux," said Nestor Ronceval, *flâneur,* observer of humanity and journalist whose tongue was as redoubtable as his pen. "Just because you were the incumbent for a while, a very short while, as I recall . . . As a matter of fact, Monsieur Leets, it may very well be that I was the first to have the honor of knowing her in her salad, or shall I say in her green apple, days?"

Édouard, Vicomte de Perrégaux, flushed to the roots of his hair, which curled in ringlets *à la Titus.* His girlish face tried to register anger, ineffectually. His golden-brown eyes— like a greyhound's, Liszt thought—were too gentle, and his lips lacked firmness. But he clenched his fist so tight that his whole arm trembled.

"You and—and your nasty little stories!" he flung at Ronceval. "Someday I'll make you swallow your words and then you'll—you'll die of poisoning!" With that Perrégaux tore out of the room.

"Besides seducing the poor fools the witch drives them mad,"
said Ronceval with the lumbering slowness of the pachyderm
he resembled, yet with pity in the look that followed Perrégaux
out of the room. The small eyes sunk in the folds of flesh had
a piercing, exploratory stare, however, when they turned to
Liszt again. "Frankly, I don't fancy her kind of beauty, Monsieur Leets," he said. "I prefer women with more flesh on
them. I have a horror of the skeleton, maybe because when I
was a student some pranksters put one in my bed."

"She is very beautiful," Liszt answered quietly.

"You wouldn't have thought so had you seen her—let's
see, how many years ago? It was in thirty-eight, the year of
the Chopin-Sand affair, as we reckon epochs in our lively
metropolis. I was just going up the steps of the Pont Neuf
one evening when my nostrils were assailed by the smell of
sizzling fat. I had just come from a good dinner and found the
odor obnoxious. Not so the lanky girl who was standing a few
feet from the fried-potato vendor, staring at the bubbling
caldron. I noticed her unusual face, white, thin and angelic.
I noticed her rags, too, and the green apple she had been
munching which had suddenly become unpalatable."

"Poor child! In this rich city!" interrupted Liszt, rejecting
the picture but pitying the ragged girl.

"You should have seen the yearning in her eyes! No saint
in ecstasy ever gazed so raptly on her vision as that girl on
those sizzling potatoes. They were the impossible dream, the
ultimate of desire. Well, I made her dream come true. When
I handed her the paper horn filled with those golden chips,

her mouth dropped open. But then she helped herself to one piece after another, eating silently and greedily."

"Last time you told the story, Ronceval, the girl fainted and you brought her to by dipping your hat in the Seine and splashing her face," said one of the youths.

With a scornful hand Ronceval brushed aside the interruption. "The tale is a *feuilleton* novel, Monsieur Leets," he went on. "It has another installment. Time passed, as they say. Have you been to the amusement park, the Ranelagh? It's not so popular as it used to be a few years ago. Well, I used to frequent it with the rest, in search of pleasure, in search of something to write about. One evening, as I was wandering among the merrymakers, I felt someone tapping me on the shoulder. I turned and there was the young Duc de Guiche, proud and triumphant, with a very alluring damsel on his arm. She was his first mistress and he had decked her superbly, you may be sure. Feathers, jewels, flowers. He did not say a word. He merely smiled and turned to gaze at her as if she were his own creation. As for myself, I was struck dumb too, for there in all that finery was my gourmande of the Pont Neuf. I said before that I don't care for that kind of maladive beauty, but the girl has a face one can't forget. 'Mademoiselle,' I began. She looked at me and beyond, without a flicker of recognition. Mademoiselle Marie Alphonsine Duplessis, supplied the duke, thinking I sought an introduction."

"Extraordinary," said Liszt as if to himself.

"You may well say that, *cher maître*," said the youth who had contradicted the journalist once before. "Ronceval, you're

a fraud. Last time you told your Cinderella tale it was a
Russian prince who—"

"Oh, the prince came after the duke. It was Guiche who
launched her and the Russian prince who later took the helm.
I must say he carried her far. Mediterranean cruises, Switzerland, the spas. He also did what the duke had no time for in
his newly discovered ardors. The prince gave her an education.
Am I boring you, Monsieur Leets?" he broke off at the other's
abstraction.

"On the contrary, Ronceval. I was thinking of the girl on
the Pont Neuf and of another, long ago . . . in Pisa."

"Ah, our Childe Harold would have much to tell, if he
would honor us," said Ronceval with no intention, however,
of yielding the floor. "As I was saying, the prince hired pro-
fessors from the Sorbonne, dancing masters, teachers of de-
portment from London. Thalberg gave her piano lessons—"

"But you said it was Chopin!" said the youth.

"Chopin too," proceeded Ronceval. "They say she doesn't
do so badly though I've never heard her myself. A touching
picture, young Aspasia learning to inspire her admirers as
well as to excite them. The Duc de Guiche invented her, the
Russian prince brought her to perfection. Indeed, Prince
Stacklyn put his whole soul into the work. But then he had
little else of—what shall I say?—of a compelling nature to
distract him. He must be very nearly eighty-five. They say
she reminded him of someone he loved long ago."

"She has that kind of eternal look," mused Liszt moving
his queen.

"Oh, you have seen her then?"

"Only briefly, at the Bois. She does not know who I am—"

"But she does, cher maître, she does indeed, if it's my beautiful client you're talking about," said Dr. Korff who had come in on his habitual call.

It was as much a professional visit as a pleasant interim in Korff's day for the opportunities it provided for acquiring and dispensing the stuff of intrigue that was his stock in trade. More often than not the agonizing migraine for which a worried husband summoned him had no origin but the suffering wife's anxiety to arrange for an assignation with her lover. In such cases Korff served as Eros. He was also the unofficial banker for titled spendthrifts waiting for their inheritance. In the giving and taking much of the gold stuck to his fingers. Yet though he loved money, scandal was his passion. He followed it as the hunter follows the spoor, till he came to the fascinating prey. Often it proved as profitable as his banking transactions. But even where he gained nothing by it he had the exhilaration of knowing and the sense of power that the knowledge gave him.

Liszt was too much startled by Korff's intrusion to conceal the repugnance which that porcelain-smooth countenance, frozen into its sinister youthfulness, always caused him. The doctor was like some character out of Hoffmann, an automaton given the semblance of life by some intricate mechanism. At any moment one might expect it to break down and leave in place of the man a heap of bolts, springs and stuffing and, on top of it all, that head of a China mandarin, still young, with the graying brows and hair suddenly become a film of ancient dust.

"Forgive me if I startled you," said Korff, misinterpreting Liszt's look. "I hope I've not interrupted one of your delightful stories, Ronceval. As I was saying, *cher maître,* my lovely client has done nothing but talk about you. Of course she knew you at once. One does not have one's portrait in the papers for nothing, Monsieur Leets. Besides, she had seen the king talking to you."

"You mean the great Leets talking to the king," corrected Ronceval.

"She asked me a hundred questions," Korff ignored him. "You know how curious women are, *cher maître,* especially when the gentleman is young, celebrated and handsome. I also took the liberty of saying—unattached." A fan of crafty lines appeared like fine cracks at the corners of his mouth and eyes.

"Attached or not, what difference does that make in the Duplessis's profession?" Ronceval broke in.

Korff glared as if his honor had been impugned. "I beg pardon, sir, but I will not have my client spoken of as a member of a profession. She is incomparable. She is unique. She is sublime." At each adjective he touched his fingers to his lips and blew a kiss heavenward. "She is the reigning queen of beauty, a Cleopatra worthy of—" the brittle fingers searched the air for a word, caught it and tossed it at Liszt's feet— "worthy of an emperor."

"Bah! It's pleasure and luxury she wants like all her kind," said Ronceval as the musician looked from one to the other through the veil of his own thoughts. "She'll take them wherever she can find them. Perrégaux has been spending his fortune on her, the lovesick calf—double his fortune because he's not of age and borrows on his expectations. At what rate of interest you, my dear doctor, should know."

"I have the honor of being his confidant," Korff bowed. "But spare the boy's feelings," he said softly with a glance toward the door where, as if summoned by his name, Perrégaux was standing, his eyes roving uneasily from group to group. On catching sight of Korff he gave him an almost imperceptible nod. The mandarin head acknowledged it, so deftly that only he and Perrégaux were in the secret. "The poor youth had the bad luck of falling in love," he went on the moment Perrégaux left the doorway. "He has even offered to give her his name. Imagine! One of the oldest names in France!"

"All I can say is that he's a bigger fool than I took him for!" cried Ronceval. "Why, he'd be ostracized from society—he'd be expelled from the Jockey Club! Who ever heard of a gentleman marrying his mistress? I can see how the Duplessis would jump at it to have a grand title, armorial bearings on the equipages and all that—"

Korff drew himself up. "My client has her own prestige and title—"

"Yes, indeed, of her own making. Bah, Korff! Whom do you think you're fooling? For queens alone he saves his skill. . . . Do you take the doggerel seriously? Everybody knows she was Alphonsine Plessis, daughter of a drunkard and granddaughter of an unfrocked priest. A poor waif from the provinces—"

"You lie, like all your tribe!" shrieked Korff, his voice creaking like a rusty hinge. "If it weren't that I'm an old man I'd—I'd challenge you. I'd—I'd—"

"Sit down, Korff," said Ronceval. "Stop making a spectacle of yourself or we'll really believe what they say about your own antecedents."

"Gentlemen, gentlemen!" Liszt tried to appease them. "I'm afraid I've come to a stalemate," he added, brushing the pieces off the board.

"Don't we all, in our particular games of chess?" said Ronceval, rising. "It has been a pleasure, Monsieur Leets, one that you have not given us for many years. By your leave . . . No hard feelings, Korff. But I think Perrégaux's relatives had better get the king to approve his appointment to London. An ambasssador more or less, what does it matter? But it might keep the boy from ruining himself. Again, no hard feelings. Blame my rudeness, Korff, on my ungentlemanly profession—which you've already done, now I think of it."

"A dangerous fellow," said Korff the moment Ronceval was out of hearing. "I'm sorry I must go about my own affairs too, *cher maître*. But first—that devil nearly drove it out of my head—I have a small request, if I'm not too impertinent. At your concert the day after tomorrow my client—"

"Mademoiselle Duplessis will be there?" asked Liszt.

His eagerness was not lost on Korff. "She will indeed. You see, she missed your recent concerts. She was not well—a change of season cold which settled in her chest. But it's nothing that a few weeks at Bagnères or a little happiness can't cure. Anyway, she has been like a child about your recital. What will Monsieur Leets be playing, she asks? Do you think he will play the 'Invitation to the Waltz'? And she would go to the piano and strike those few meditative notes of the introduction. How beautiful and sad they are, she would sigh, breaking off. If you would play for her your arrangement of that piece, *cher maître* . . . ?"

"I shall play it as an encore for Mademoiselle Duplessis," said Liszt.

"You are as noble as you are great, Monsieur Leets." Korff bowed deeply. "Mademoiselle Duplessis will know how to be grateful."

"The indebtedness will be all on my side, Korff," said Liszt gallantly. "Her beauty will assure my success."

"Graciously turned, Monsieur Leets. Her beauty will assure my success. I will remember to tell her that. But now I must really tear myself away."

Liszt watched him striding jerkily toward the door where Édouard de Perrégaux had reappeared with a look of desperation in his eyes. The youth and the doctor went out together.

# 4. *Flowers from Monsieur Leets*

THE afternoon sun streaming in through the windows of Mademoiselle Duplessis's dressing room had been allowed admission only a few minutes earlier when Delphine, after preparing her mistress' bath, went to awaken her. Mademoiselle Duplessis had had little sleep that night even though she had spent it alone. An inexplicable restlessness had kept her wandering from room to room. Now she arranged the flowers trailing up from lacquered vases along the antechamber walls, now she would stand by the rosewood piano in the salon, her fingers gliding silently along the keys. Then she would sit down with a book in her hand, in a light too dim for reading, and lean back with a sigh against the brocade of the chair. Again she would rise, go to the window facing the boulevard, and peer into the night, listening to the sound of hoofs afar off. Whenever her mistress could not sleep Delphine too had a *nuit blanche*.

"I shall look dreadful tonight," complained Mademoiselle Duplessis, as she pulled her nightdress over her head.

"For me those worries are over. I don't know whether to say thank God," said Delphine, pouring the last pitcher of scalding water into a large silver-gilt scallop shell supported on the backs of four swans. "I had my time of ruling, like Charles the Tenth. I came in with him, I went out with him."

Indeed, for the five years following the death of Louis the Eighteenth, Delphine had been one of the reigning beauties. Old Louis had preferred male favorites, therefore during his reign the vogue of the courtesan suffered a decline. But with Charles the Tenth a new day dawned for the neglected belles. Delphine, then twenty-five, was at the height of a fascination strong enough to lure Charles himself from the *prie-dieu* to her boudoir. Now, at forty-five, she still preserved remnants of that beauty, though one had to look for them under the accretions of time.

Mademoiselle Duplessis clouded at the words. Delphine Prade had been, and still was, exceedingly helpful as her companion and agent, but she was also a living reminder of the passing of time and of beauty. However, Mademoiselle Duplessis's image in the water, as she tested the temperature with her foot, smiled at her fears.

She lay back in the great shell, her skin glowing to rose-tinted pearl in the steaming water. Her hair, piled up on top of her head, was held by a gold band crossing above the brow like a Grecian fillet. Even in the shallow basin her fragile body was wholly submerged but for the points of her breasts, pink and turgid, and almost insubstantial beneath the water. Instinctively she slid still farther into the basin as the doorbell rang.

"Oh dear, who can it be? Tell Julie to send him away, Delphine," she said. "But wait! It might be someone from—

it might be someone I should see. Tell her to have him wait."

"I wish I knew what's wrong with you these days," grumbled Delphine as she went out.

Mademoiselle Duplessis lay back, soothed by the water enveloping her like a garment. She had always been reluctant to show her nudity, ever since that time, back home, when her father had come upon her bathing in the pool under the waterfall. His rude fondling of her young body whose mysteries had only been revealed to her had made her suspicious of it, even afraid.

"There you go with your modesty!" cried Delphine as her mistress, startled by her entrance, drew up her legs. "It's only the Chevalier of the Sunflower, Édouard the Faithful."

"Again?"

"I told him to wait. But why are you huddling up like that? Goodness knows, I've seen you before."

"I can't help it," said the young woman. "It's that same terror, as when I saw my father lurching toward me."

"You're lucky it was no worse," said Delphine gently.

For a few moments neither spoke. Mademoiselle Duplessis lay so still that she might have been sleeping but for her fixed and thoughtful gaze. What was she thinking of in her past? Delphine, plunging her elbow into the bath, wondered.

"Time for you to get out," she said. "Too much hot water takes the strength out of you."

She unfolded a linen sheet and held it open in her outstretched arms. "If you'd only let them see you this way, Mademoiselle," she remarked, admiring.

"What an idea, Delphine!" She was shivering and quickly wrapped the sheet about her. "I'd die of shame."

"What's the difference whether you're naked in bed or naked in your bath? God made us as we are. I had a lover once who'd been to Egypt on the campaign. Out there, he said, it's their faces the women are ashamed to show. What are you giggling at?"

"Imagine going along the Faubourg Saint-Germain and meeting the old duchesses with their heads wrapped up and the rest as God made them! Ah, *bon jour,* Madame la Duchesse de la Tour. Or is it Madame la Vicomtesse du Pont? How odd! You have a mole in exactly the same spot."

Mademoiselle Duplessis's eyes twinkled with sudden mischief as she mimicked to the last asthmatic huff the relics of the old regime greeting the beauties of their youth.

Delphine chuckled appreciatively. "No wonder you turn their heads," she said, tossing her own in the direction of the salon where a reiterated note on the piano marked the growing impatience of the visitor. "Still, what you said wouldn't have been a joke, and not so long ago, either. In *my* time we glorified the body, maybe because we were still under the spell of the emperor who had a statue made of himself stark naked. Oh, he had a mantle, but it didn't do much good hanging over his arm."

"That's different. A statue is only marble," said Mademoiselle Duplessis, applying some patchouli with the tips of her fingers to the inside of her wrists and elbows. "It makes you think only of its beauty."

"What else do you think of when you see a fine body?

There's Mademoiselle George. How handsome she was, even in my time, though she must have been past her first youth. I could understand how Napoleon forgot even Josephine—"

"Mademoiselle George? I thought she died a hundred years ago! She was Napoleon's mistress?"

"For a while, but she never forgot him or his ways. Like him she took to having her levées in her bath. He did it to save time. She did it because—well, because when a woman loves she wants to be the thing she loves. That was the only way she could be like him, so she would receive her visitors covered only by the water and a gracious smile."

"Men and women?" asked Mademoiselle Duplessis.

"Of course, though she told me she was far more comfortable with the men. Oh, she was wonderful, as big as that statue without arms they have in the Louvre. She filled the bath like a nut in its shell and everything about her was beautiful."

"How could she? Before everybody?"

"Sometimes I wonder how you ever got where you are!" exclaimed Delphine with a sweeping gesture which included the dressing table glittering with crystal and gold, the bibelots, the Sèvres vases and Persian hangings and the Boule cabinet whose carelessly open drawers revealed a treasure in jewels. "Maybe that's your secret with your innocent face and your little breasts. Look at them, no bigger than a budding virgin's! In my time men wouldn't have looked at you twice. Those were the days, the days of the Delphines and the Georges! I can see her now talking, talking to her guests and lifting up her arms to fasten her hair with gold combs. You'd go from her hair to admire her breasts, as big as melons they were, but perfect and white as milk. Anybody could understand what made Napoleon crazy about her. He liked everything big, our little Emperor.—What are you laughing at now?"

"It must have been—" she choked with laughter—"like climbing the Alps again."

Delphine joined her with a heartiness that drowned the insistent pleading of the piano. "Yes, that's your secret," she said. "That naughty wit and that touch-me-not look. In my time men liked their mistresses big and healthy. I remember old Duc de M——," she reminisced. "The poor man had a wife so skinny you could almost hear her bones rattle. Do you know why it's good to sleep with you, Delphine? he'd say. Because when I wake up in the middle of the night and stretch out my hand, I think, This is Delphine, and here is more of Delphine, and still more of Delphine. . . . It gave the dear man comfort to know there was so much of me.—Now they like them thin and with a cough. How's the chest today, by the way?"

The piano note had given way to a knocking at the door. "Édouard the Faithful can't stand it any longer," said Delphine with a hint of disrespect which, in the servant, is usually a reflection of the mistress'. "Shall I let him in?"

"Yes. But first arrange the screen."

Delphine unfolded the Chinese panels of storks among iris and bamboo and concealed the bath, now filmed with iridescent bubbles. "Will you be wanting me?" she asked, her hand on the knob. Mademoiselle Duplessis, tying the sash of her lace negligée, shook her head.

At the door's sudden opening Édouard de Perrégaux was

surprised in an expression of anguish which swiftly changed to joy as he rushed into the room and flung himself at the Duplessis's feet.

"Alphonsine! At last!" he cried, clasping her knees.

"Get up, Édouard," she said gently. "You're too big a boy to be kneeling."

"But I adore you."

"I like you better on your feet or here, sitting beside me." She patted the cushion of the chaise longue. Still on his knees, he took her hands, laid them against his cheeks, then kissing the palms, released them and rose. His eyes swam at the fragrance of her skin and the sensuous humidity of the air.

"Why do you treat me like—like a boy?" he broke out, trying in vain to control his stammer. "It—it wasn't always so."

"I know. But things change. We change, *cher enfant*."

"Don't call me *cher enfant*! I ceased being a child the first time—the first time I saw you. What did you do to me my—my love? Ah, Alphonsine! Why have you changed? You loved me once. You—you said you did."

"Are you starting that again, Édouard? I loved you. I still love you but in a different way."

"I know. Like a brother. Don't say it. But I'm not—I'm not your brother and it's the last thing I want to be. Listen to me. In a few weeks I shall come of age. I'll have my inheritance. We can—we can marry—"

"Now I shall really be cross," she said, starting up. "We've gone into that a dozen times. In the first place I'm older."

"A few months, *mon ange*."

"My position will not permit me."

"But mine will. Once you're my wife who's going to remember? We'll—we'll leave Paris."

"I will remember, Édouard, and you will remember when your family disowns you and your friends turn away. You will be ashamed of me." She sat down before the jewel cabinet and began idly opening and closing the drawers.

"We'll go to England. I know, we'll—we'll spend the winters in Italy and the summers in Switzerland. We won't need company, no more than we did those—those heavenly weeks. We'll always be together—"

"Bored to death with each other. You'll be noticing other women's ankles and I'll be wondering whether the next man coming along will twirl his mustache for me. No, Édouard. That life is not for me. Besides, I love Paris, I need Paris. I'd be an exile anywhere else, even in heaven."

She spoke so vehemently that her cheeks flushed and she began to cough. He stood behind her chair, staring at her reflection in despairing incomprehension. At the look of sympathy she gave him he embraced her and with his lips close to her ear, pleaded: "Then take me as your lover again! Live—live as you please, darling. I won't be jealous—I'll try not to be. Only let me stay with you. I'll not be exacting, I promise. Only let us—let us be as we were."

"Édouard, my darling boy! When things change they can never again be what they were, alas! Life is like that. Now be an angel and let me dress."

"They can! They can! I have not changed. I'll—I'll make you love me, I'll give you everything. I'm going to be rich soon.—Oh, I nearly forgot."

He drew out of his waistcoat pocket a small jewel box of amber plush and laid it on the cabinet.

"Again, Édouard?" she said reproachfully. "I begged you never to give me any more costly gifts, for I can see this is one of Halphen's cases. I suppose you borrowed from Korff?"

"Soon I won't have to borrow any more," he said guiltily.

"Then take this back to Halphen's till you can pay for it with your own money."

"But it's—it's something that belongs to you."

"To me? I've sent nothing to Halphen's recently for re-setting."

"It's—it's something I stole," he said.

"Édouard, Édouard! When will you grow up?"

As she pressed the spring the lid flew open revealing a heart-shaped locket studded with emeralds. "But this is nothing of mine," she said. "I insist you return it to the jeweler."

He took the locket out of the case, opened it and gave it back to her without a word.

"My little cross!" she cried.

There, set within the lower half of the heart, was a plain inexpensive cross such as children receive on their first communion. "My little cross from the nuns," she said. "And all the while I have been wondering how I could have lost it. When did you take it, Édouard?"

"One morning, before I left you while—while you were still sleeping. You—I noticed you would always take it off when we went to bed. Now you may wear it all—all the time."

Her eyes filled with tears of shame, tenderness, regret.

"Adorable child!" she said, rising and throwing her arms

impulsively about his neck. But the kisses he gave her were not those of a child. He pressed her to him with the passion of his twenty years and his tormented desire till she had no strength to resist nor any breath to deny him. While his lips were still clinging to hers he lifted her up and carried her into the alcove.

It was dusk under the heavy canopy despite the sunlight streaming in through the windows. They could not see, though they tasted, each other's tears.

"Mademoiselle! Mademoiselle!" cried Delphine excitedly from behind the door. "Flowers from Monsieur Leets!"

# 5. Love and Witchcraft

"I T'S quieter now. Look again, Marcel, and tell me."

Liszt was twining and untwining his strong fingers till it seemed as if his gloves would split. It was not nervousness but an overflowing of impatient energy before each public appearance which made those moments of waiting intolerable. He was paler than ever in his dark dress coat and white cravat, over which he wore the Papal Order of the Golden Spur. He was also adorned with the Austrian emblem of nobility, bestowed by the emperor, and a cluster of honorary decorations hanging on chains from his lapel.

Marcel applied his eye to a slit in the curtain. A subdued conglomeration of sounds came from the other side, coughs, laughter, voices, footsteps, the scraping of chairs and canes.

"The house is packed, *cher maître*," said Marcel. "I don't see how they can seat any more. Every *strapontin* is occupied. The boxes are full. Even the Jockey Club has come early."

"Give the signal, then."

Liszt tossed his mane, a warhorse eager for the field. Every recital was a battle—with the pianos (there were always several), with the part of the public which his fame antagonized, and with his admirers who had to be reconquered by new strategies.

A rush of sound as of a dashing of waves rose with the curtain. He stepped onto the platform, stooping a little, conscious of his height, and closed his eyes before the glare of the wax lights in all parts of the Italian Opera House. His romantic pallor, his concentration, everything about him immediately stilled the audience. But between his entrance and his few paces to the nearer piano, an electric thrill communicated itself from the *fauteuils* and boxes to the very rafters. The ladies applauded, men rose and flowers began to shower upon the stage, bouquets, posies, wreaths and scattered petals.

With head inclined he let the storm descend upon him, but his eyes, open now, missed nothing as they scanned every part of the house. On the left, in the box nearest the stage, he saw her, white and still, in relief against the ruddy chiaroscuro of the plush interior. Her opera glass lay on the ledge of the box next to the bouquet of white camellias he had sent her. The red flower at the heart of it was gone. She was not applauding like the rest. She was not looking at him. Half shadowed by her hair, her face in profile bent in concentration on the red camellia she was clasping to her breast.

Bowing to the assembly Liszt spread his arms in all-embracing thanks. Before going to the pianos, arranged back to back, he picked up a single flower and slipped it into the buttonhole among the decorations on his lapel. The choice sent all eyes from him to the Duplessis. She was now facing the stage, looking like a disembodied spirit in the crimson glow of the loge. With the intuitiveness of its peculiar freemasonry the élite of Paris instantly thrilled to the same suspicion. A new romance was in the making, and what a romance!

The applause was still reverberating as Liszt slipped off his gloves and tossed them carelessly on the floor. How foolish his fears! Like Napoleon he conquered on his reputation. All the more reason to play as he had never played before. He might use the tricks of the mountebank to capture the attention of the public—so his enemies said!—but for him art was a holy thing.

He chose the piano on the left of the stage, his uplifted pupils and *profil d'ivoire* stirring a rustle of sighs among the women. Why was he not facing the Duplessis? They questioned one another with their eyes. Could they have been mistaken? At the idle wandering of his fingers across the keys the audience was electrified. It was the initial incantation, the tracing of the invisible symbol, which kept him and his music invulnerable and brought everyone beyond it under his spell. One man alone had wielded such magic before him, and Paganini was now fiddling for the damned in hell.

It was as if Liszt had evoked that demonic spirit when he plunged into a set of variations on a Paganini theme. The audience swayed as he swayed, carried away by the physical impulse of his playing. They almost heard again the trill of the bewitched violin and the Paganini eerieness in the *glissandi*. But with the next composition the mood changed.

For a moment his hands floated prayerfully over the keyboard and then plunged into Beethoven's C-Sharp-Minor Sonata. At the adagio his face, set in sorrow, was transfigured and, as the sublime elegiac movement floated over the audience like an echo from another world, it was as if Beethoven himself were playing and glorying in the music he had never heard in all its perfection on earth. When Liszt lifted his hands from the instrument no one applauded. The whole audience was trembling and in tears.

He would not leave them there, however. He played on and on, shifting the mood as if to reach every secret fiber in that hypnotized crowd. Somewhere a woman screamed. No one heeded. It was part of the witchcraft. He was sublime and grotesque, a poet in his own "Years of Pilgrimage," a demon in his musical descriptions of the macabre. Then the piano shook to the infernal thunder, Liszt's wild mane streamed, the hands trailed lightning. He was a man possessed who had to free his soul by his playing. Through the boards the mighty chords vibrated, entering the spent bodies like alien souls and shaking them in unbearable emotion.

He closed with his "Chromatic Gallop," which brought the house down and incapacitated the piano. The strings, broken and coiled, were still quivering as he rose, came forward and bowed to a frenzied ovation. More flowers rained down upon him, and pearls as a tribute to his *jeu perlé*, and even bracelets and brooches. Everyone was standing except the women who had fainted or pretended to faint.

The pianist glanced at the Duplessis box. She too had risen. One hand was resting on the back of a chair as if for support. The other still clasped the flower which she tore loose, fleetingly touched to her lips and threw upon the stage. Liszt did not pick it up. It would have been too obvious. Besides, she was no longer alone. The canvas in crimson and gold was now crowded with a circle of patrons round the central figure.

He could not understand why he should be annoyed. As if he had not known! Why, only the night before he had heard another of the many stories circulating about the Duplessis. Yet to see him sitting at the second piano, his hands folded and his brow uplifted in invocation of the muse, no one would have suspected how far removed were his thoughts from the sublime. Indeed, during his absorption he was wondering whether, as Ronceval had told him, Mademoiselle Duplessis really had a dressing table with seven drawers, the gift of as many admirers, each of whom had paid for a drawer and its contents. He did not glance toward her box, only a few feet away, so close in fact that he could hear the door opening and closing, but began playing his first encore.

It was not the composition which she had requested. He played another, and still another encore. Had he forgotten, or was he consciously taunting her by his refusal? The crowd, insatiable, clamored for more. *Génie oblige*—and Liszt obliged.

Mademoiselle Duplessis felt the blood rushing to her cheeks as he began each new encore. At last the charmed fingers went into the nostalgic opening of the "Invitation to the Waltz" and the whole audience sighed rapturously on recognizing the favorite which Liszt's arrangement had swept into immense popularity. Men and women floated on the sensuous melody, closing their eyes to recapture youth and love and illusion.

Mademoiselle Duplessis took her bouquet from the ledge

of her box and buried her face in it, gazing above it at the features which she saw fully for the first time. But was it his face or only a mask absorbing youth and beauty from the spell woven by his hands which seemed to have a life of their own? Why did he not look at her? Why was he not playing for her? Throughout the concert she had felt a communion between them and thrilled to imagine that among so many she was the center of his thoughts. Yet now he was playing her piece as if he were on another planet. She did not exist for him. In spite of the look they had exchanged in the park she meant no more to him than that fat old countess in the opposite box whom her gallant was trying to revive from the sensual coma into which Liszt had thrown her. She was sorry now that she had sent her admirers away. What was she doing here, alone in her box?

Liszt brought the "Invitation" to a close with his own brilliant cadenza, but before the audience could applaud he crashed his hands down on a set of chords echoing like doom through the auditorium. The wax lights shivered at the immense vibration which by some violation of nature gained substance and dimension and hung, an overshadowing presence, threatening them all.

What had possessed the pianist to bring Death into the gathering with these apocalyptic variations on the *Dies Irae*? He played on, oblivious of everything but a miraculous release as his "Dance of Death" took shape under his fingers. He was again in the Campo Santo among those youths and maidens with their music and their falcons. But Death had now caught up with them. The streaming hair hung limp about her shoulders, the bat wings lay folded, but she was even more terrible than in her flight. Her scythe flashed in the air. At every stroke one of his fair companions fell. But she only stared at him and passed him by, speeding toward the group by the open graves. One by one she cut them down. Now she was lifting her scythe toward the lady with the pitying eyes.

With a bang he clapped the piano shut and started to his feet. He was trembling but his audience was near collapse. When he turned to bow to Mademoiselle Duplessis he found her box empty but for the bouquet, forgotten on her chair.

The public, panting for the open air, had the dazed look of survivors from some incomprehensible cataclysm. The men tottered as from a prolonged debauch, leading on their arms hollow phantoms from a witches' Sabbath. They had enjoyed one of the supreme experiences of Romanticism.

Ronceval, leaning nonchalantly against the marble buttocks of a crouching nude, watched the people pass through the smoke of his cigar. The foyer smelled like a hothouse from the emanations of the excited crowd. He needed the honest tang of tobacco to counteract that dizzying effluence. He bowed to the women who stared at him but did not see him.

Odd, the effect Liszt had upon them! How often had Ronceval seen them picking up the ends of his cigars to preserve like precious relics. He even knew of an ancient dowager who had cut out and framed the brocade of a chair on which he had sat. At the Princess de B—— he once witnessed a curious scene when two Hungarian countesses threw each other upon the floor and wrestled like maenads to gain possession of his snuffbox.

"Korff! Arnaud!" he called to the two men pressing through the crowd. "Whither away in such a hurry, Korff? Aren't you always warning it's bad for the heart?"

The doctor wore a look of dismay. "Have you seen Mademoiselle Duplessis?" he asked. "We had an appointment after the music but when we got to her box she was gone."

"You're a better listener than I am—no reflection on your great master, Marcel," said Ronceval. "I suppose my journalistic sense keeps me on the alert and so preserves me from the general hypnosis. When I saw her get up to leave, something unprecedented I must admit when the master plays, my curiosity conquered my appreciation. I got here before she did and Venus," he stroked the statue's curves, "obligingly concealed me. But I don't think she'd have seen me anyway, she was in such a flurry. 'Come, my coach,' she said like Ophelia to the doorman."

"Where did she go?" asked Korff.

"You mean *they*. Perrégaux too was evidently impervious to the master's spell or maybe, poor fellow, he's still in the throes of a stronger infatuation."

"He went with her?"

"A thousand horses couldn't have torn him away. I must admit it was nothing prearranged. She seemed exceedingly vexed and tried to send him packing, but by the time her carriage came the public was beginning to stagger out, so she let Perrégaux ride off with her."

"Why this night of all nights!" Dr. Korff clasped his hands. "Sometimes I almost believe in her low origin! Pulling such a *malice de nègre* at a time like this! You don't know where they went?"

"A gentleman does not eavesdrop on such occasions," said Ronceval blandly. "How about coming to the Frères Provençaux for a bite of supper? Can it be the seat of the emotions is in the stomach, Korff? I'm always ravenous after . . . certain experiences."

"I must beg off," said Marcel as Korff shrugged and yielded. "Our Napoleon of the Piano has conquered and I must clean up the battlefield. Ah, the pianos, the poor vanquished pianos!" He heaved a mock-heroic sigh. "My heart always bleeds for them, cowering in corners, disemboweled, their broken strings coiling like nerves in agony."

At the Frères Provençaux Ronceval ordered a gourmet's dinner for Korff and was paid off with enough Parisian scandal to supply his paper for a week. But about the new amatory intrigue the doctor observed a cautious silence. There was evidently more to the thing than Ronceval suspected. The great Liszt and the little waif of the Pont Neuf! What a subject for a Murger romance! No, what a theme for Balzac, that anatomist of the human heart!

He offered Korff another brandy. "I am sure," he persevered, "everyone went home with the conviction that there was something to it—I mean, to the camellia in his buttonhole. It's not usual for the *cher maître* to hide his decorations under a flower, even the most expensive, to speak the language of the market place."

"Maybe there was, maybe there wasn't," said Korff, turning the glass contemplatively to the lamplight. "I saw dozens of camellia boutonnières."

"Which is hardly surprising. In her brief career the lady

has broken more hearts and run through more fortunes than Ninon de Lenclos—"

"That's not true! She's an angel of goodness," exclaimed the doctor, reacting for once with human warmth. "Is it her fault if those young fools falls in love with her? That's not part of the bargain. Take Perrégaux. You saw for yourself she can't get rid of him. It's almost as if—Aesculapius forgive me! —as if she had bewitched him."

"Perhaps she has. How do we know? It may be love is a kind of witchcraft. The language of lovers is certainly full of it. I'm under your spell," he mimicked in the outrageous style of the Porte Saint-Martin. "Your magic charms convulse my heart and twist my entrails. I languish, I die in the sorcery of your eyes! Oh, have mercy, my beloved—"

"For God's sake, enough," said Korff as an Academician, passing by, turned to give them a scandalized look. "Next thing you know they'll be saying I acquired bad habits at the court of the late Louis.—But seriously, witchcraft or not, Perrégaux's family wants none of it. They call me in every other day, as if I could do anything to cure him! All I advise is a tightening of the purse strings—"

"So that you can loosen yours at a profit, you devil!" laughed Ronceval. "He looked woebegone enough, the young fool. I couldn't help feeling sorry—for myself when I was his age. I'm afraid this time he'll find the competition too strong."

Korff nodded and shrugged in a fine balance of the noncommittal and set down his glass.

"To go back to witchcraft," continued Ronceval, "surely

there is no other way of explaining his remarkable fascination over the public."

"Whose?" asked the doctor, all innocence.

"Why, Perrégaux's rival's."

"If you mean the *cher maître*, I know nothing about the rivalry. But his effect on the public is easily explained," Korff smiled. "Mass magnetism or galvanism if you prefer, the animal contagion of hundreds of perfumed and perspiring bodies in a sultry hall, the flickering wax lights, the potent musical cantharides that the master dispenses—"

"Bah! I prefer to cling to the witchcraft theory. He comes of a mysterious people, Korff. Strange bloods mingle in him, the Magyar and perhaps the gipsy. How account for his wild, rhapsodic, yes, orgiastic music? It's not merely an expression of our delirious Romanticism or he would be more like our Berlioz. It's something—something—" He could not find the word.

"Demonic?" suggested the doctor.

"Yes, that's it, yet not quite. He is Lucifer caught in his fall somewhere between hell and heaven. I must remember to write that in my next article."

The night was still young when they parted. Since his rooms meant work and he was in a mood for amusement, Ronceval made his way to the Café de Paris. A wind had risen. High up above the solid wall of buildings on either side of the Boulevard des Italiens thin, ragged ghosts of cloud flitted across the moon. "The influence of the *cher maître* up there too." He smiled at his fancy.

At every step he greeted some acquaintance, fashionables—

they used the English word—in the sartorial perfection of Humann, with elegantly bonneted ladies whom they did not introduce; actors from the Boulevard du Crime; fellow writers, indeed, all the gaiety-loving world of Paris which bloomed at night.

The flower women near the pillar had almost sold out their stock. Their wicker hampers leaned empty against the stall, the remaining flowers wilting, disconsolate. Ronceval, who had little pity for the vendors, felt sorry for the flowers and bought a bunch of pansies. There would always be someone to whom to give it.

As he was about to leave, a poster on a pillar caught his eye. *Nélida,* by Daniel Stern, would soon be serialized in the *Revue Indépendante,* he read by the light of the lanterns slung across the avenue from the tall trees. "Hmm . . . *pauvre maître!!* We'll soon be having you plucked of all your glorious feathers and served up, done to a turn. . . . Ah, woman, woman! Beware of the idolized Beatrice when she takes pen in hand!"

Squeezing his bulk past the tangle of tables outside, he went into the café and toward his habitual corner.

"Ronceval! Ron-Ronceval!"

Simultaneously someone seized him by the hand and led him back toward a table near the entrance. "What the devil, Perrégaux!" he said as the youth dragged him along with all his strength. "I can walk without assistance, which is more than I can say of you."

The table was already occupied as he could see by the billowing of silks and the cascade of veils from the back of a bonnet. *Not* the Duplessis in so public a place!

It was not. But the lady needed no introduction. He had once known Laure Jeanne intimately and so had half of Paris, the male half, in her long if not honorable career. Now fathers of forty were sending their sixteen-year-old sons to her for initiation. But what in the world was Perrégaux doing here with Laure Jeanne after driving off with the Duplessis? And why drag him into it? The empty champagne bottles told him much. The youth's wild laughter and hurt-filled eyes told him more.

"Take him home, *le pauvre enfant*," Laure Jeanne managed to murmur as they were drinking together. "He thinks he can drive out one nail by driving in another."

Her once magnificent beauty was still more than a memory. Less provocatively dressed and without the lurid aura of her reputation, she would have passed for a handsome *bourgeoise* whose fruitful life was reliving its joys in the grandchildren about her knees. As it was, however, the man who publicly flaunted Laure Jeanne was either admitting his inadequacy in the courts of love, or was using her to affront another woman.

There was little conversation as Perrégaux's excitement gradually subsided to a glassy-eyed aloofness. As for Laure Jeanne, she had never cultivated the art in a profession where silence is a virtue. Ronceval made a screen of his hand and leaned toward her confidentially. "How did he find you?" he asked in an undertone.

"Such a question! Everybody knows where to find Laure Jeanne. As it was, I just happened to be around when the carriage stopped and he leaped out like a maniac. I didn't see the lady, but she was sobbing fit to break your heart. Near the church of the Madeleine it was."

"He came to you?"

"*Mon Dieu*, no! He didn't see me, he didn't see anything, he was so desperate. But when he bolted straight for the cemetery I made after him. You know these wild colts, Monsieur. They're as ready to leap down the precipice as after a filly. I was sure he meant no good to himself, and you know we have police orders to look after these young jackanapes."

"And so you remembered your duty." Ronceval's sarcasm was lost on Laure Jeanne.

"Yes, and I did it like a woman who's got a heart and not a cabbage in her breast," she said with the earthy simplicity of the south country speech which she had never lost. "I sat down on a stone with him and put my arms around him and let him cry his heart out."

Perrégaux made as if to rise but reached out for his glass and emptied it. "Who are you?" he asked blinking across at them. "Ah, Ronceval! Good old Ron-Ron-Ronceval. Pour me out another drink, will you? I've got a fire in my head. Good old Ron-Ron . . ."

The glass dropped out of his hand.

"Take the boy home," said Laure Jeanne. "The bitch! Doing that to him!"

"Are you sure it was—a bitch?" inquired Ronceval.

"What else? She was sobbing, it's true, but you may be sure it was for herself. The sex is like that," she said, contemptuous. "It's only a poor *fille* like me who knows what it is to patch up broken hearts. His, I tell you, is spilling its drops like the pomegranates in our old garden back home. *Mon Dieu,* how long ago!"

"I hope the fool didn't babble?" asked Ronceval tentatively.

"Like a hurt lamb he was, just crying and crying." She touched the tightly stretched silk above her heart. "It's still wet where he laid his head. But he felt better afterward. Laure Jeanne, he said—he knew me at once, Monsieur," she added with a hint of pride. "Laure Jeanne—and he kissed my hand as if I was a lady. I'm afraid he's touched in the head, though, the way he began to laugh without any reason. You must come with me to the Café de Paris, he said. Well, here I am, but where is he?" She shook her head at the unconscious youth.

"Look after him till I get a fiacre," said Ronceval. "Here, take this." He tossed her the bunch of pansies.

"As if I didn't have my fill of memories," she murmured.

# 6. A Midnight Fantasy

WHEN Marcel returned to the green room he found the master gone and no word to tell him where to seek him. Under the circumstances he felt justified in taking the night off. Too bad the meeting the master desired had not taken place. Yet the Duplessis was most anxious to meet Liszt. According to Korff she had ordered a supper *à deux* from the Maison Dorée and left instructions with the porter to admit no one. Well, the Duplessis had changed her mind and now Perrégaux would be enjoying both the supper and the lady. With a shrug the confirmed bachelor tripped toward the Boulevard du Crime swinging his cane and philosophizing on the foolishness of men who concentrate on one flower when they may have a garden.

The hours passed. The moon, freed of her cloud wraiths, circled above the city, dim but for the avenues of light where the pleasure seekers never slept. Under a greenish phosphorescence the Ile de la Cité lay hushed and withdrawn within the embrace of the Seine, which clasped that jewel of the past from the encroaching modernity that was making a new Paris on both sides of the river. The moonlight touched the square towers of Notre-Dame and lingered lovingly on the spire of the Sainte Chapelle, caressing every ornament on that filigree shrine set in the sky.

On Notre-Dame itself the stone population of saints, apostles, angels and devils came to life at the touch of the moon. The great rose window bloomed, faces flickered, wings fluttered and high, high up the gargoyles leered upon the nocturnal city and on the human beings who had made it and them.

It was easy to believe in the witching light that those monsters sometimes left their stony roosts and roamed about Paris. There were people who swore they had seen them. The story was always the same. A sense of oppression would rouse them from their sleep and there, filling the window, glowered a terrible face with flaming eyes and obscene lolling tongue. There was no record of a gargoyle's ever hurting anyone intentionally in these nightmare apparitions and nobody knew for certain the object of these visits. Perhaps there was something to the explanation of a certain learned doctor of the Middle Ages, when good and evil spirits gadded up and down the city in a St. Vitus's dance of activity. He said, the learned one— and he roasted at the stake for it—that God and the Devil were still struggling for dominion and that every day they would send out troops of angels and monsters to report the good and evil in the world.

Since the angels were all air and radiance gross humanity did not have the vision to see them, and so nobody except a few saints ever said anything about them. Hence it was the monsters who made the greater stir, scaring people half out of their wits and convincing gloomy folk that evil dominated the earth.

At any rate that was what the revolutionaries and the poets believed. How else could the uprising of 1830 have failed? How else could the evil breed of critics remain in power, slashing the throat of innocent poets with their sharpened quills? Certainly it was not just to admire the view, as they said, that Victor Hugo and Gautier and the rest of the Romantics would climb to the top of Notre-Dame's towers at midnight. For all their sipping of ices to make it look innocent they fooled nobody, least of all the cunning gargoyles who remained as fixed and stony as if they were really blocks.

This night the gargoyle who peered between scrawny uplifted shoulders over the balustrade facing the left bank kept his eyeballs rolling to follow the movements of the long-haired visitor, alone on the balcony. The man could not be planning suicide or he would have gone to the top of the belltower. Still he had a tortured look and kept pacing back and forth. Now and then he would stop short, give a harsh growl of several notes and run his fingers along the ledge, tossing his locks to the winds. He had been keeping this up for some time, but when he heard voices from the opposite tower he wrapped his cloak about him and made for the door.

The man's face and behavior roused the gargoyle's curiosity. Leaving his stone husk the gargoyle followed, invisible to all but God and the Devil. Down the stairs he went after him, out at a side door, and through the dark gardens behind the cathedral whose flying buttresses clutched its body on either side like huge skeletal hands.

Between the Pont Saint-Louis and the Pont de l'Archevêché the man passed with a shudder the Doric temple of the morgue where the drowned, the suicides and the murdered lay on marble slabs under white sheets, the cold water trickling, trickling to keep them from corruption long enough for some-one to claim them.

Suddenly the man, as if to avoid disturbing the peace of the dead, retraced his steps, crossed the parvis of Notre-Dame and skirted the island along the right bank, his shadow in the moonlight and the invisible gargoyle following. At the Pont Neuf he stood on the steps and looked about him thoughtfully. He was not waiting for a cab because he let one pass and they were not easy to find at that hour. For a while he walked along the Quai du Louvre, past the dark low buildings, to the deserted gardens. The moonlight playing on the naked nymphs, however, peopled the silent alleys with such beauty that the man stood still in wonder. He remained there so long that the gargoyle was about to leave when the man turned back and took a cab at the Pont Royal.

"To the Boulevard de la Madeleine," he said.

The gargoyle got in beside the driver, who felt a blast of chill air and pulled his coat about him. "Winter is coming early this year, Monsieur," he said.

The man made no answer. They drove through the square of the Concorde, past the obelisk between its fountains that sounded like wild cataracts in the stillness, and on to the Place de la Madeleine. The colonnade of the church caught the moonglow on its shafts, making the temple emerge from the dark like a thing of light and air that at any moment might melt away.

Dismissing the cab the man walked toward the row of houses which brought the luxurious elegance of the metropolis to a still verdant section of Paris. They were handsome buildings with carved doors and balconies and spacious courts. The man paced back and forth several times before Number 11. Although the neighboring houses were blank, a light slashed the heavy draperies behind the balcony. After a final hesitation the man pulled the doorbell.

The porter came with a promptness that showed he was accustomed to calls at that hour. *"Monsieur désire?"*

"I wish to see Mademoiselle Duplessis," said the man.

"Mademoiselle Duplessis is not at home to anyone tonight, Monsieur," he said.

"But she was, in a sense, expecting me," said the man.

"Sorry, Monsieur, but my mistress is not receiving tonight."

"But if you told her it's Monsieur Liszt?"

"Even if Monsieur were the Archangel Gabriel she would not receive you, Monsieur. She is *souffrante.*"

"I am sorry to hear it," said Liszt. However, as unmistakably festive sounds were coming from within he did not quite believe in the lady's indisposition. He would have commented on the fact but pride forbade and he left with a backward look toward the balcony. The gargoyle followed him. His supernal sense, however, had caught a sound of sobbing amid the laughter which he proposed to investigate later.

It was not far from the Boulevard de la Madeleine to Liszt's hotel near the Place de la Concorde, especially since agitation quickened his steps. He let himself in with his own key to a wing of the building set in a patch of garden, a privacy required by the caprices of his muse. But he did not go to bed. Instead, he went to the piano and began pounding out a volley of sound that sent the gargoyle off in a hurry. He had heard enough music from the organ of Notre-Dame, not to mention the great bells, to last him another seven hundred years.

"There is a man in whose life Art comes first," he reflected as he flew back toward the Boulevard de la Madeleine. "For it he would sacrifice everything but his glory. People are merely the servants of his Art, and his Art is only a dead thing that he calls to life from that black coffin at which I left him. Women can only fill his loneliness. They can never fill his heart."

In her bedroom Alphonsine Duplessis shuddered as a gust of wind shook the blinds and blew aside the hangings. She wrapped her quilted robe tightly about her, then trimmed the lampwick whose flame was still quivering. The gargoyle looked about him. There was no one else in the room, only an English greyhound which began to growl, its hackles rising.

"Hush, it is only the wind, Dash," said Mademoiselle Duplessis. Obediently the dog stopped growling, but it knew better.

The lady had been crying. The tears still stained her face, a dead white in the tangle of her loosened curls. Hairpins strewed the carpet and the bed where she had evidently sought rest in vain. Now she was pacing the room, clutching her temples and running her fingers through her hair. Her cloak lay on a chair where she had thrown it. Her gown was a silvery heap on the floor, with other wisps of mist and froth. She pushed them aside with her bare feet. Now and then she uttered a low moan, answered by a whimper from Dash whose eyes never left her.

All at once she fell on her knees and reached out for something under the dressing table. It was a crumpled concert program which she pressed to her lips as she rose and flung herself upon the bed.

"I love him! I love him!" she moaned.

Then why did she weep? Surely she had no lack of lovers, this lady who sold love. The gargoyle went curiously from one trinket to another, wondering why women were willing to sacrifice so much for them. The dog shook itself uneasily, went to the bed and gazed at Mademoiselle Duplessis with sad, wondering eyes. One hand was hanging limp over the side. Dash nuzzled it affectionately.

"Dash," she said, "I love him. Do you understand me, pet? I love him and he scorns me. He did not look at me once, not once while he was playing my piece. I'm nothing to him and I love him, I love him!"

As if the reiterated word pressed some spring of agony she buried her face in the pillows to smother her sobbing. The gargoyle waited a while longer, but it was the same scene repeated. Since he could feel no human sympathy, only a neutral acceptance, he left her for the sound of merrymaking which had broken into the bedroom through her weeping.

The dining room was a blaze of lights, caught and flashed back by Venetian mirrors and crystal goblets. Flowers filled the cloisonné vases in the corners, decked the place settings and strewed the floor in a profligacy of hospitality. Empty bottles and crumpled serviettes mingled in the disorder of unbridled enjoyment. There were four waiters from the Maison Dorée and four guests, but the extraordinary thing was that the waiters were drinking and laughing with the guests. These were Delphine, the maid Julie, the gardener and the porter, enjoying the banquet intended for Mademoiselle Duplessis and the friend she had turned away.

"I still don't understand what's wrong with her," said Delphine.

"Why bother to understand when we can enjoy God's bounty?" said the gardener, flourishing a breast of guinea hen on the end of a knife.

"God has nothing to do with it," said Delphine. "It's the devil that got into her, if you want my opinion. She's in love!" she snorted. "In love, if you please! What business has she to fall in love like a silly *midinette*?"

"Why shouldn't the mistress fall in love, Madame Delphine?" asked Julie meekly. "It's so wonderful when you're in love. You sing as you work and there's Sunday in your heart—"

"And a hole in your pocket and nothing in your cupboard if you're in our profession. It's different with you, Julie, working for your dowry and with a man from your village waiting for you. But with us, in our class, I tell you it brings nothing but ruin."

"If this is ruin," said the gardener helping himself to the truffles, "then let's enjoy it while we can."

"Delphine, do you know, Delphine, I had almost a mind to let this last one in," said the porter. "Rich as a Rothschild he looked and handsome, too, dressed like one of those Russian priests in a long cloak and hair down to his shoulders. Priests too, now, I thought to myself."

"*Mon Dieu!* It wasn't Monsieur Leets?" cried Delphine.

"That's his outlandish name. If he's come to convert the mistress, I said to myself, it's an odd time of day he's chosen. But she said, I'm not at home to anybody, do you understand? So what could I do? Do you suppose he's one of those missionaries passing through Paris?"

Delphine put down her glass and rose.

"What are you going to do?" asked the porter.

"Tell her, of course. I think it would make her glad to know he came calling."

"What is so special about this one?" asked the gardener. "Sit down, Delphine. Good news can always wait. You'll only get yourself into something—a tisane for her nerves, and this, and that. Sit down and don't spoil it all."

"Yes, sit down, Delphine," said the porter.

"I would make her the tisane," offered Julie.

"You stay where you are and drink your wine," said the gardener. "Here, let me uncork another bottle. Pop! What a jolly sound! Buc-buc-buc," he imitated the sound of the sparkling Burgundy gurgling and scattering bubbles through its liquid ruby. "This is living!" he shouted, staggering up. "Let their lordships drink the *cul-de-bouteille* for a change!" He tossed the not quite empty bottle into a hamper.

"I think I ought to tell her," said Delphine halfheartedly.

"Leave well enough alone," advised the porter. "She's quiet, isn't she? Don't worry, she'll ring if she wants you."

"Be grateful for what God gives you," said the porter filling her glass as if from him all blessings flowed.

Delphine let herself be persuaded. Julie, however, suddenly felt sad for no reason at all, but pretended to eat so that the others wouldn't notice her. Had someone opened a window? What was this cold gust behind her? The porter filled her glass and held it to her lips. "Drink, girl, drink," he roared. "That way you'll give your young man strapping sons."

Julie blushed and sputtered with embarrassed laughter.

The gargoyle returned to Mademoiselle Duplessis's bed-room. She was now sitting in a low armchair, her head tilted back and one arm round Dash's neck. She was talking softly to the dog, telling it things she could not confide to any human soul.

"You see God is punishing me, making me love a man who does not love me, whose heart is dead to love, perhaps, as I thought mine was. Ah, Dash, Dash! You have a cruel woman for a mistress. How horrid I was to Édouard! Because I was hurt I hurt him, and he looked just like you when I scold you, his big wet eyes full of pain, but he only kissed my hand as you lick it, *mon petit!* You know I would never strike you, but I struck him, Dash. With my words I struck him: For God's sake, leave me! How could I love you—you stammering fool? Dear God, what made me say it? He is so sensitive about the way he repeats words. But I was suffering too and he didn't see it. I was in despair and he thought only of his own misery."

On and on she babbled with a naïveté that would have

made it impossible for one to think of her as a *femme en-tretenue*. She was rather like a young girl suffering from her first love and her first heartbreak. There was no affectation about her innocence. It was something inward and deep yet also manifest in her look and manner which made the gargoyle feel an indefinable uneasiness before her.

"With my words I killed something in Édouard," she was saying, but the tears started from her eyes and for a while she could not speak. When she began again she was more composed. "It was like that time with the bird. But I was a child then and I did not mean to be cruel, yet whenever I've done anything wrong she comes to accuse me, that little bird.

"She had built a nest above our door—dear God, how long ago!—and I noticed it one day, a scraggly heap of grass and moss. I wanted to see if there were any eggs in it, that's all, just to see, and one day when she was not there I took a chair and stood up on it. But still I could not see inside the nest, so I reached up—I had to stand on my toes to do it— and I tried to lift up the nest, but she had fastened it to the ledge with mud. When I did get it the chair tottered, the nest fell out of my hand. . . .

"There had been eggs in it. When I looked on the ground they were only bits of shell and spattered yolk. I don't know why I did it, perhaps out of fright, but I threw the nest away in the old grapevines. It was so pretty inside, so soft.

"It was terrible when the mother returned. First she gave a frightened little shriek. Her treasure was gone!—and she flew away. But she came back as if she couldn't believe her eyes and began a heartbroken cheep-cheep, over and over.

Then she did what comes back to haunt me. She began fluttering her wings over those bits of moss and pressed her breast against them to feel with her heart if the eggs were really gone!

"What did the child know of right and wrong? Only what the nuns told her. She was good if she said her prayers, she was bad if she didn't. That day I knew I had done a very wicked thing. I hadn't meant to, but I had destroyed something.

"The bird flew away at last but she came to live in me. Cheep-cheep! Cheep-cheep! I hear that cry in everything that's hurt."

The gargoyle flying above the rooftops toward Notre-Dame reached it just as dawn was breaking. He was in such a hurry to slip back into his body of stone that he lost his head.

# 7.  An Emperor's Gift

AN INEXPLICABLE uneasiness had hung over the *beau monde* for the past few days, causing a peculiar unhinging of the customary mechanics of Parisian life. Louis Philippe showed neither his homely umbrella nor his Verdier cane on the daily promenade. His Majesty, said the court bulletin, was in bed with a cold. In vain did the strollers along the Champs Élysées look for the dashing coupé of the Duplessis. It remained in the carriage house, no reason given. At the Italiens, at the Porte Saint-Martin where a Dumas play had a *première*, opera glasses pointed unrewarded to the box nearest the stage. They saw no Duplessis, no flowers, no box of comfits—nothing. Something must be wrong for the Duplessis to miss a first night.

At the Jockey Club lethargy prevailed. Its shining ornaments by some peculiar accord failed to put in an appearance, leaving the lackluster idlers to dull by repetition the only piece of gossip that had turned up. Still, they had to pass the time. With each new arrival, therefore, the clubroom echoed to the selfsame dialogue.

"Ah, there you are, *mon vieux!* Have you heard the latest?"

"No. I've just come back from Chantilly. What is it?"

"It's Perrégaux, it's about Édouard de Perrégaux."

"He hasn't gone and married—?"

"Worse than that. He's going around with Laure Jeanne."

"Not *the* Laure Jeanne? *Our* Laure Jeanne?"

"He's flaunting her all over town, at the Café de Paris, at the play—"

"The Café de Paris? You can't be serious! At the Riche, even at Tortoni's, but at the Paris? He must be out of his mind!"

"That's what Korff thinks. Temporary aberration caused by an overexcitation of the emotions, or some such jargon. The Duplessis has given him his formal *congé*—"

"And Laure Jeanne is his revenge."

"Something like that. But it's not only Laure Jeanne. He's taking the pick of the Montmartre dives and decking them with camellias."

"*Ah, non!* That's a bit excessive, even if he's lost his wits. Laure Jeanne I can understand, it's like going back to one's mother."

"Hm?"

"I mean, for comfort. I've sometimes gone back to her myself when I had troubles of my own. I still remember the little homily she gave me the first time. I was going on sixteen. . . ."

The Boulevard des Italiens also felt the malaise. Somehow the champagne did not bubble, the waiters kept breaking the crockery, the *crêpes Suzette* turned soggy and the famous chef at the Café de Paris scowled all day long. For a week now not one of the patrons had come into the kitchen to compliment him on his culinary triumphs.

Outdoors it was the same. The paintings hung on the walls of the open-air galleries cracked and peeled for no reason at all. The flowers in the stalls hardly lasted the morning. "It's a phenomenon," the women sighed, shaking their heads. Was it also a phenomenon when the voice of the tenor broke on a high note at the Opéra? Or had it been caused, as he insisted, by the sorcery of a rival tenor who had smuggled into the theater the malefic charm of a sloughed-off snake skin?

At Les Halles, where feelings always ran closer to primitive sources, the market women had their own ideas of why the cabbages wilted and the eggs cracked if you so much as looked at them. "It's that devil at Notre-Dame," they said. "Last time he lost his head, in the days of l'Autre, it was, the world was full of wonders. Comets, bloody wars, defeats . . . It may not be so bad this time. The creature hurt nobody in his fall. He only broke his own ugly nose."

The sensitive organism of the artist in Liszt responded to the subtlest atmospheric waves, but it was something within him that gave him no rest—a soul hunger which he had not experienced, certainly not so powerfully, since his earliest youth. Then it had responded to music and beauty and God and the noblest ideals of man. He had sat at the feet of the Christian Socialist, Lamennais, his pagan god's face radiant with the lightning of thought struck by the prophet's craggy brow, his heart afire with dedication. Lamennais's battle cry of "God and Freedom" became his own. He set it like an

oriflame at the helm of his piano and every concert became a
call to liberty.

Friends warned him against the dangers of republicanism,
of sinking his patent leather shoes too deep in the proletarian
quagmire. With a rebellious toss of the head he continued to
give his benefit concerts, his smile slightly ironic as he bowed
to the clapping aristocrats whose francs were helping workers
to more humane conditions. He battled for his fellow artists,
too, against the prejudices of centuries.

But now, at thirty-four, the vital fire seemed to be banked
in his being. The smothered embers burned inward in self-
torment, not outward in warmth and light. Yet he was more
creatively alive than ever. It was as if he needed some gusty
wind of emotion to blow away the ash and liberate the flame.

Much of his unrest he attributed to the general uneasiness
which had hit Paris like a spiritual plague. He missed the
small routines that made the metropolis run like a faithful
clock. Most of all he missed the azure streaking of the Duplessis coupé.

Every day for nearly a week he had been going out at the
same hour, retracing the trajectory of that first encounter as
if it had been drawn with a compass. The Duplessis sent no
word to acknowledge his call. Korff could answer none of his
questions, for her doors were closed to the doctor also. She
admitted none but her dressmaker, Madame Elmyre, who
would arrive in a carriage laden with the fabulous fabrics of
East and West: the most luxurious cashmeres, gossamer
meshes from Brussels, *point d'Alençon, point de Venise,* all
those adornments which the ingenuity of man had devised to

throw an added aura over beauty. One morning Liszt, discreetly ambushed in a doorway, had watched Madame Elmyre's turbaned Blackamoors lend the magic of the *Arabian Nights* to the Paris street as they unloaded the shimmering cargo. But he was not granted even the comfort of a rustling curtain from the closed house.

Today, however, he was filled with inexpressible glee on seeing Dash come bounding toward him down the Allée des Acacias. The dog pulled short before him, wagging its tail as to an old friend and then leaped from side to side, inviting him to play.

"Ah, *bonjour*, Dash!" he greeted the animal. "Ah, *le beau chien!* Where's your toy? Go, fetch the ball, Dash!"

Dash started off, Liszt following with palpitating heart. He would see her again at last, and how favorably! Their first meeting repeated, canceling the thing that had come between them. He would apologize, try to explain. But what did it all matter? Beyond that clump of trees he would see her again.

The dog came back with the ball and dropped it at his feet. Instead of Mademoiselle Duplessis it was the coachman who followed, full of apologies for the *bête* who had dared to be so familiar. "He wouldn't have done it if the mistress was here," said the good fellow. "When the cat's away, as the saying goes."

Liszt was ashamed of the keenness of his disappointment. "I trust Mademoiselle Duplessis is not *souffrante?*" he inquired. "It is cruel of Mademoiselle to deprive Paris of its only sunshine these gloomy days."

"The mistress isn't sick, Monsieur," said the coachman. "It

isn't the chest, anyway. Who knows? Maybe a little malady of the heart. If it is, it's the only time she's ever had it," he added with the confraternity of male to male.

"Present my compliments to Mademoiselle Duplessis," said Liszt, ignoring the familiarity.

"*Oui,* Monsieur Leets." The coachman was immediately respectful.

"You know who I am?"

"Who does not know the great Monsieur Leets? Besides, Monsieur forgets that he was at this same spot not so long ago. The mistress was like a child returning from her first party all the way home.—By your leave, Monsieur."

"Wait," said Liszt. "Are you going back soon?"

"In a few minutes, Monsieur. Dash has had enough exercise."

"You can do me a favor, then, my friend," said Liszt.

The coachman drove him through the Bois to the address he gave. Inside, the carriage was permeated by a subtly feminine atmosphere, a fragrance which was also a glow that did not come solely from the rose upholstery. Dash, sitting up on the floor and looking out of the window, now and then glanced up at Liszt.

Who had been in this carriage before him? Perrégaux. No doubt also the Russian prince who had given it to the Duplessis, together with her horses and stables. And who else? Liszt, a stranger to jealousy, experienced its pangs for the first time. But then it was the first time that he had ever been the pursuer, the first time that a woman had not opened her heart —and her door—to him. Indeed, there was more truth than

levity to the name some gazetteer had given him: Orpheus of
the Nineteenth Century. From the age of twelve the Bac-
chantes had pursued him, first with motherly wiles and sweet-
meats and the kiss upon the brow. Then they had made as-
saults upon his adolescent senses, demanding what he was too
much frightened and too pure to give. It was as if they had
been contending with one another for his chastity. He was
still virginal in thought and deed when, just entered into
manhood, he stood by Adam Liszt's deathbed.

"My son, you'll now be left all alone. You have a great talent
and goodness of heart. Still I fear for you. Women will trouble
your life and try to rule it."

They had troubled it but they had not ruled it. Each had
taken something of himself, his faith in an enduring love, his
freshness of heart. Ah, no! Not his freshness of heart. His
presence in that carriage denied it, so did the restiveness of
his nights. Something had been happening to him, keying
up his senses to the point of pain. It was a resurgence of
youthful power, a tidal wave of feeling that sought some
wondrous shore on which to spend itself.

Could it be he was in love?

The unspoken question evoked an audible laugh, so bitter
that it brought Dash nuzzling at his knees. He patted the
dog reassuringly, thinking but not saying: "That's what it
must be." In love like a boy, he who had never loved with a
youthful love. Yes, once perhaps, when he had fancied himself enamored of one of his pupils, in a pallid romance composed of sentimental duets, stolen glances and an occasional
touch of the hand. Not even a kiss. But the aristocratic parents

had put a quick end to the aspirations of the youth, even if he was a prodigy. Their daughter must marry a title.

Then had come the great experiment in ideal love. With a shock he realized that was exactly what it had been, an experiment, the collaboration of two individuals fancying themselves the elect of the earth and demonstrating to the world their arrogant assumption of superiority. Well, they had suffered for it.

The carriage left the Champs Élysées and entered the section of the fashionable shops. As Liszt glanced out of the window the frown vanished from between his eyes. Wonderful Paris! Where else in the world could the gingerbread woman have set up her tray with such democratic confidence before the window of the most *recherchée* modiste, she herself wearing her shawls and homely cap?

"Go to the end of the street, then turn right," he directed the coachman.

Aucoc's atelier gave no inkling without of the wonders within, where the genius of a modern Cellini expressed itself in gold and silver, from massive table services to toys so fragile that a breath could have blown them away. Aucoc himself, clasping his fine, expressive hands, hastened to greet the distinguished buyer. "What an honor, *cher maître!* Something for yourself? For a friend? Everything I have is at your disposal."

"I should like some exquisite toy, something delightful and useless," said Liszt.

"For a lady, Monsieur Leets?"

"For . . . a young person very dear to me," he said.

Aucoc showed him one lovely trinket after another, per-fume vials, jewel boxes, a ringholder in the shape of a cupped hand in whose palm lay a violet with a diamond dewdrop sparkling in its heart. Liszt admired them all but they were not what he sought. Then, in a glass cabinet, something caught his fancy.

"Ah, that, *cher maître*," Aucoc hesitated, his gesture at once pleading and apologetic. "I would find it hard to part with that. It is by the great Biennais who made it for Napoleon. I will show you its exquisite ingenuity."

Like a knight approaching the Holy Grail, Aucoc took out a jewelled apple tree about six inches high. The blossoms and young leaves of spring were growing on its branches as in nature, and in a fork a nest of spun gold held four rosy pearls. On the edge perched a bird no larger than a bee, its throat and wings in the enameled blues and greens of a peacock's tail seeming to throb with song and quiver with flight, in a transmutation of metal into life itself.

Liszt exclaimed at the marvelous workmanship while Aucoc's fingers caressed the masterpiece as if it were indeed a living thing. "You have not seen all, Monsieur Leets," he said with selfless pride at another man's achievement.

With that he picked up the tree and began winding a concealed key. All at once the bird's throat swelled, the wings spread and fluttered, the ruby beak parted and a faint warbling like the ghost of song poured out of its little breast. At the same instant the pearly eggs broke open and four fledgling heads popped up to join in the song.

"Aucoc, my friend, you must let me have it!" cried Liszt.

"You must!" he pleaded as Aucoc shook his head. "I don't care what it costs—you know that. I warn you, I'll not leave without it."

"It's a delicate matter, Monsieur Leets. I promised Mademoiselle George—"

"What need has Mademoiselle George for such toys now?"

"It is not that, *cher maître*. It belongs to her. It was one of the gifts *he* gave her. She does not wish to have it sold out of the shop as a piece of merchandise, she said, and I gave her my word."

"Why did she part with it, then?"

"The bitter necessities of life. She needed the money. I gave her what she asked."

"I'll double the amount. As artist to artist, my friend!"

Aucoc shrugged helplessly. "You are as compelling away from the piano as when you bewitch us with your music, Monsieur Leets. I love this bauble as if it were my child." He reached out to fondle it. "It's foolish, I know, but I'll regret it when it's gone."

"Good! Then you'll let me have it?"

"Mademoiselle George will be grateful for the extra money. What an artist fallen on evil days, Monsieur Leets! The theater half empty, the magnificent lines that once made the Man of Iron weep bringing jeers from the young bloods. It was shameful, shameful! I could not bear it. Iphigenia it was, too, her finest role. Have you seen her lately, Monsieur Leets?"

"Not since my boyhood. But I've never forgotten her. A statue of flesh with a grandeur, a magnificence . . ."

"Don't go to see her, then. Remember her as she was. If

only the artist could remain changeless, like his art!" He picked up the tree and touched it reverently to his lips before giving it to his clerk to wrap.

Liszt borrowed a quill at the counting desk, wrote a few words and a musical phrase on a visiting card and added his signature. Outside he gave the package to the coachman. "For Mademoiselle Duplessis," he said. "Let Dash be my messenger."

He gave the man a pourboire that made him lend wings to his steeds.

MADEMOISELLE DUPLESSIS was standing on a needlepoint stool in her boudoir while Madame Elmyre on her knees snipped and pinned a bouffant cloud of *mousseline de soie*. Madame herself possessed neither youth nor beauty but she was inflamed with the dedication of a high priestess by all that pertained to her *couture*. The fabrics she handled so tenderly were as much part of her service as was the sacred fire to the Vestals. What matter if most of her clients had none of Mademoiselle's beauty? Madame could at least lend them the semblance of loveliness. It was exhilarating joy to her, however, whenever she was called upon to confect for Mademoiselle Duplessis who not only set off the artistry of her creations, but also made them the fashionable imperative.

This time she had found her client strangely subdued. Ordinarily during their sessions they would review the chronicle of the *beau monde,* a world Madame Elmyre had the privilege of observing from the most intimate of vantage points, the bedroom and the boudoir. The latest liaisons passed before her scrutiny long before they reached the inquisition of the salon, and had she cared to profit by her observations she would have earned as much by her knowledge as by her needle. But she was a discreet woman who knew that one false step would have deprived her of the one thing she lived for, the work to which she gave her entire devotion.

Still, she delighted in gossip, which made the time pass agreeably. Perhaps out of discretion she had acquired the habit of using nicknames for the subjects of her *chronique scandaleuse*. Walls have ears, and so did her flock of apprentices who accompanied her in a separate carriage and, whenever they went on foot, followed in her wake in the precise formation of ducklings after their parent.

Time had dragged for her, however, these past few days, for Mademoiselle Duplessis said very little, and only about her new clothes. "As *magnifique* as the trousseau of a princess," Madame Elmyre commented tentatively, receiving only a sigh for answer.

She had sighed pretty frequently, now Madame Elmyre thought of it. Another odd thing, she received no visits, certainly not from the gentlemen who sometimes came to advise at the fittings, as indeed they might, since they paid for the finery. In the depressing silence Madame Elmyre almost wished herself with her girls whose voices came through the door in gay chatter and trills of laughter.

"If it weren't for the lace and the décolletage I'd almost think Mademoiselle is thinking of becoming a nun. All this white, white, white! You must promise to let me choose the color of your next gown, something rich and glowing."

Her forced enthusiasm trailed away at the silence of the young woman who was standing as still as the lay figure, an exact duplicate of Mademoiselle, shrouded in layers of fabrics in a corner.

"Can anybody become a nun?" asked Mademoiselle Duplessis after so long an interval that Madame Elmyre was startled by the question.

"A nun? Oh, a nun! Why, I think so, after instructions, a novitiate and that sort of preparation. I really don't know for certain. We've never had any nuns in the family. There's too much to do in the world, God knows. Mademoiselle isn't really thinking of taking the veil?" She had a way of neatly spacing her words as if they were stitches.

Since no answer came she resumed her thoughts and her work. Something was going on which she knew nothing about and she was dying to know. Was Mademoiselle weary of her kind of life? But how could anyone ever get tired of plays and the ball and all the luxuries and caprices one's heart desired?

The question flared and died of its own enormity in the mind of the virtuous woman who had belonged to only one man, but a pleasurable afterglow of speculation remained. She glanced at the lusters, the inlaid woods, the paintings, the gold door knobs. Why, not even the Elephant (her name for the stately Princess de B——) had anything to compare with them in her palace, though she boasted of her period pieces. Bah! Period pieces! The Sylph (her name for the Duplessis), would have given all such rubbish to the junk man! That diamond necklace alone, lying as carelessly as a tape measure on the night stand was worth ten times the

Elephant's period pieces—and it was only one of the Sylph's jewels.

What was the Sylph's particular attraction? Perhaps that she was tall and straight and slender, a candle to lure lovesick moths. (Madame Elmyre, said the naughty apprentices, was like a sadiron, getting broader toward the bottom.) Perhaps it was her skin, smoother than satin all over, elbows and knees too, where even the finest ladies were often as rough as a cat's tongue. (Madame Elmyre, giggled her girls, had her profession cut out for her with that face pocked like a thimble.) Or maybe—the blessed saints forgive the thought—it was the sweet look she had, that innocence of a bride of Christ going to her communion.

However, Madame Elmyre had always been shocked by the *prie-dieu* in Mademoiselle's bedroom. Of course there had always been a *prie-dieu* in her own chamber throughout those dutiful years with her good husband, rest his soul. But that was different. And she still had the holy pictures hanging over the bed, although as a young bride she hoped the saints miraculously closed their eyes whenever her good man felt the temptations of the flesh. However, the priest to whom she confessed her scruples had assured her that the sacrament of matrimony sanctified what happened in the alcove. Mademoiselle had never had such sanctification. Therefore, to Madame Elmyre's scrupulous mind, the *prie-dieu*, out of respect to the saints in heaven, had no place where it was. She had often meant to speak tactfully to Mademoiselle about it, and the subject of the nuns gave her an opening, but before she could say a word she heard a scratching at the door and Delphine's voice announcing Dash.

The dog trotted in head high carrying in its mouth an elaborate package done up in floral paper and ribbons. "The coachman brought it," said Delphine. "There's a card in it from the giver, he says, and he'll be waiting outside if you want him."

"You open it," said Mademoiselle indifferently.

"The coachman says the giver said to open it yourself, Mademoiselle."

"Oh, well," sighed the young woman stepping down from the stool. "Good Dash," she patted the proud head. "Give it to me, now."

When the women saw the jewel tree and the bird they clasped their hands in ecstasy and were young girls again, thrilled with their first love and their first awareness of spring. But suddenly Mademoiselle turned pale and clutched the back of a chair.

"I—I guess I've been on my feet too long," she said, sinking down into the seat.

"It's the way you've been starving yourself to death these past few days," said Delphine. "Why, even this pretty little colibri couldn't survive on what you've eaten.—Oh, look, there's a key back here. Maybe it sings, our little bird!"

"*Mes enfants,* come in! Look! Listen to the marvel!" exclaimed Madame Delphine flinging the doors wide for her apprentices.

The girls tripped in like well-behaved pensionnaires in their gray uniforms and starched caps, their lids chastely lowered before the meretricious splendors they were ordinarily not permitted to behold. "Form a line now, and file by one at a time. And don't loiter too long—there's work to be done."

Dutifully each girl paused for a few seconds before the lovely toy and on every one the same rapture glowed as she walked away. It was as if Biennais had hidden some charm in his singing bird which communicated happiness, like some creature in a fairy tale.

Mademoiselle Duplessis looked transfigured. She was leaning forward, her whole being drawn toward that vision of innocent joy. The bird's trilling filled her heart with peace as if at last she had been forgiven the careless cruelty of the child long ago. But the light in her eyes had its source in the card which she had secretly read: "I have come in vain to the door of paradise. One smile, I beg, O you [here followed a musical phrase] who fill my dream! Franz Liszt."

"Who's the nabob who sent you such a treasure, Mademoiselle?" asked Madame Elmyre. "There's a fortune in precious stones hidden in those blossoms."

"And that's the truth," agreed Delphine. "In all my days I never had anything like it, not even from the king."

Their words reached Alphonsine Duplessis only as a rush of sound in the privacy of her own thoughts. He had come to see her! The great Liszt had come to her door and had been turned away. Surely that's what he meant by the door of paradise. But why hadn't anyone told her? "Delphine, what friends came to call this past week?" she asked.

"Only the usual ones," said Delphine, flushing. "Why, Mademoiselle?"

"I was merely wondering."

"You know the porter, Mademoiselle. If he drinks a glass

too much he loses his memory," she said. "There might have been others. Who knows?"

"Who knows?" echoed the young woman, a smile quivering about her lips as she clutched the card in her palm. "Who knows?"

Delphine gave her a sidelong glance. Could it be that she knew Monsieur Leets had come calling? Several times these last few days Delphine had been on the verge of telling her what the Burgundy had bubbled clear out of her mind, but decided in the end to abide by her trouble-saving device of leaving well enough alone. As it was, she had played into the hands of fate eternally engaged in puppeteering with human lives. Delphine's forgetfulness had spurred Liszt's desire, making a pursuer of the pursued.

Suddenly Madame Elmyre let out a shriek as Dash decided to settle down in comfort on a heap of precious samples. The girls echoed her agony, a chorus of priestesses before the desecrated altar.

"Here, Dash," called Mademoiselle, taking a bonbonnière from the powder stand. The dog jumped up, making havoc of the fabrics which the girls, on their knees, hastily put away in a hamper. After giving Dash his reward his mistress sent him out with Delphine. "Tell the coachman there is no answer," she said.

The girls also retired at a sign from Madame Elmyre. For a few minutes she worked in silence broken only by the twitter of the little bird which Mademoiselle had wound up again. Madame Elmyre was hoping that Mademoiselle would confide in her as she had often done. But Mademoiselle only listened, her elbow on the arm of the chair and her closed hand against her cheek with the expression of Saint Catherine hearing the music from heaven.

"I have heard the Shah of Marrakech is visiting in Paris," remarked Madame Elmyre when the birdsong faded away. "My little *nègres* met some of his blacks at a Montmartre ball. They say, if you're to believe them—they say his utensils, even the commonest, are all of solid gold."

"It's not the Shah of whatever the name is, if that's what you're implying, Madame Elmyre." Alphonsine laughed. "Besides, I'd not be to the Shah's taste. Perhaps you had better introduce him to Madame the Elephant."

"Well, then, if it's not the Shah it's some nabob, I insist. Only a man with the wealth of the Indies could make such a gift."

"That's who he is, the Nabob!" Alphonsine clapped her hands. "An Eastern prince right out of the *Thousand and One Nights*. Do you want to know what he looks like? I'll tell you, Madame Elmyre. He's as slim as a palm tree and his eyes are like stars and when he looks at you your heart flutters and sings like this little bird. That's why he sent it, I think. And he's a powerful magician. When he waves his hands he carries you away to another world and you forget who you are and you become a princess in a fairy garden where the roses have no thorns and nothing dies, and the birds sing day and night."

"If I didn't know you were making fun of me I'd almost believe you," said Madame Elmyre, "even though it's the kind of nonsense you read out of a book."

Alphonsine turned to her gravely. "And yet it's all true," she said.

Madame Elmyre shook her head diffidently and put down the flounce on which she had been basting an edge of lace. "Shall we go on with the fitting, Mademoiselle?"

"No more today," said Alphonsine, rising. "Just finish pinning up the hem, Madame Elmyre. There's not much more to do on this gown, is there?" she asked, getting up again on the stool.

While Madame Elmyre snipped and pinned she was perishing with curiosity to know what was so tightly clasped in that hand, just a few inches from her face.

"I hear you have been sewing for Madame d'Agoult," said Alphonsine. "Is she a new client?"

"Who, the White Blackbird? Goodness, no! I made her trousseau and her children's christening robes. Why, the very month she came back to Paris she sent for Madame Elmyre."

"The White Blackbird! What an odd name! What makes you call her that?"

"I don't know. It just came to me. Something about her, I can't say myself what it is. A sort of freak of nature—that hair so very pale, her face so thin you'd think it had been caught and squeezed in a door. And then that drooping way she has. You'd expect all that to go with a gentle character, but she's iron, that woman. You'll sooner break her than bend her."

"Yes, but why the White Blackbird?"

"Can't you see? She should be black and yet she's white. There should be something about her to give warning as with those snakes they have in America that ring a little bell on their tails."

"Are there really such creatures?" exclaimed Alphonsine, delighted. "How did they get those little bells? Do people tie them there?"

"They're as real as this hand, those snakes." Madame Elmyre held up her heavy paw which yet did such delicate work. "They go about their own affairs like you and me, but if anybody comes to bother them they ring their bell as if to say, watch out! *Le bon Dieu* did not give them a voice, so He had to think of something. They say the bell sounds like a child's rattle."

"You believe all that, Madame Elmyre?"

"Why shouldn't I? Everybody else does."

"Yet you don't believe in my wonderful Nabob. But tell me more about your White Blackbird. Is she still young?"

"Ah, no, Mademoiselle. Her spring is far behind her." Alphonsine beamed. "But it doesn't mean she knows it."

"Her mirror must certainly tell her."

"No, Mademoiselle. Her mirror would deceive her. She's still a beautiful woman. At any rate she knows how to make herself attractive. What arts and what airs! Those books she's always sticking her nose in, and that drawling way of speaking as if she were dropping pearls. Half the time I don't know what she's talking about, but the gentlemen go into ecstasies."

"But she's—hasn't her family taken her back?"

"Oh, her family is proud of her friends. They're all famous men and as far as I can see there's nothing in it but a kind of

lovemaking with words. Such words as you couldn't even remember if you tried to find out what they meant."

"It was more than words that made her leave home," said
Alphonsine with a hardness that made Madame Elmyre
look up.

"They say the chaste Susanna herself couldn't have resisted
the young Monsieur Leets, Mademoiselle. But who are the
countess' admirers now? Monsieur Sainte-Beuve who looks
like an old man at thirty, Monsieur de Girardin— I wish you
could have heard Madame de Girardin the other day, Mademoiselle. 'Your Madame d'Agoult,' she flung at me the moment
I came in. 'They say my husband is *en coquetterie* with the
lady, but it doesn't trouble me in the least, I assure you.
There's nothing to worry about with brainy women. It's only
with the stupid ones that men go too far—there's so little to
*say!* '"

"Does she ever speak of the great romance?" asked Alphonsine. "I imagine a grand passion like that would leave
its mark forever like, well, like an earthquake. One would
try to hide the damage with words, with things, but the
chasm would still be there, maybe more dangerous for being
hidden."

Madame Elmyre slowly shook her head. "I'm no judge of
affairs of the heart, Mademoiselle," she said. "I've known only
two men in my life, my father and my husband, and I can't
say I understood either of them. As for women, they're another mystery. I can only tell you if I were Saint Peter I'd
sooner open the door to you than to the White Blackbird. At
least you're an honest woman."

Mademoiselle Duplessis got down from the stool and wound up her new toy. "You had better take the figure, Madame Elmyre," she said. "I won't be having any more time for fittings."

# 9. The Love Theme

L ISZT dismissed the carriage and glanced up at the windows of Mademoiselle Duplessis's house. A streak of light shone between the curtains of the balcony. With a troubling sense of unreality, as if he were doing what he had often done before in a dream, he stood with pounding heart in the street for fully a minute before he rang. The door opened instantly. But what a difference in the obsequious porter from the surly guardian of last time.

"Monsieur Leets? Come in, come in! Mademoiselle is expecting you."

As the porter lighted him to the vestibule where he left his cloak, hat and gloves, he felt himself enveloped by a gust of fragrance, a mingling of the scent of flowers and of opulence. Up the short flight of deeply carpeted steps he bounded as if on clouds, with the eagerness, and something of the terror, of a youth on his first tryst. Always the analyst of his emotions— he had not been a public performer for so many years without developing a duality of character—he questioned his nervousness. He had no time to explore it, however, for Delphine, in sumptuous mauve velvet, met him at the landing.

"Monsieur Leets, I am Delphine Prade, Mademoiselle Duplessis's companion. She will be happy to receive you." Her voice, as much put on for the occasion as her gown, borrowed from it some of its smoothness.

Liszt gave her the curt nod reserved for the retainer in his infinitesimally graded protocol. He was too much the man of the world to be ignorant of the real place Delphine Prade occupied as agent, or procuress, in Mademoiselle Duplessis' life. As he passed through the exotically trellised antechamber into the salon, he looked for the flowers he had sent, not camellias but red roses.

He marveled at the glimpses of splendor he caught as he went through the intervening rooms, but what he had not expected was the tasteful arrangement of rosewood and ormolu pieces, of the paintings on the walls, the statuettes and the bibelots which, more than anything else, reveal their owner's essential self. He had sought in vain in many a palace the indefinable rightness he found in this house of a courtesan.

Delphine, preceding him, kept up an obligato of chatter which he scarcely heeded till the words "in the boudoir" startled him to attention. He had expected more subtlety. Where were his roses? Had they not been delivered?

"Mademoiselle?" called Delphine, tapping at the door of the boudoir. "Your guest has arrived. Monsieur Leets."

He resented the addition of his name but before he could ask himself why he heard a muted voice say, "Do come in." Delphine pushed open the door and discreetly took her leave.

Liszt stepped forward, obeying the summons, but stopped short, catching his breath. It was not because of the living roses that carpeted the floor. It was not because of the quivering of a score of wax lights, caught and thrown back by the mirrors. He stood there, staring at the blindingly fair body under its vaporous shift twinkling as with stars. A semicircle of diamonds clasped her head which was reclining against the cushions of the chaise longue. Her feet were bare but for thin gold ribbons that caught and crossed the large toe and wound about the instep and ankle to form a sandal.

Nervously he reached for the door knob and made as if to back away, an intruder in a temple of the mysteries where a virgin was awaiting the dread descent of the god who would lie upon the altar of her body.

"Please come in and shut the door."

The voice called from a distance of centuries. He obeyed, the snap of the lock rousing him to reality. Beneath his tread he felt the roses exhaling their crushed life in fragrance.

Hardly knowing what impulse moved him, he fell upon his knees and kissed the hands she held out to him. The book she had been reading fell soundless to the floor. Bound in white satin and clasped with gold, it looked like a casket for something as fragile as a butterfly. Liszt picked it up quickly and restored it to her. *"Manon Lescaut,"* she said. "I have just left her dying."

"Shall I read you the end, then? I should like to."

"No, let her live, at least until tomorrow."

He expected to answer the smile upon her face but found instead that her eyes were moist. "You'll discover I'm a very simple girl," she said, apologetic. "Sad stories always make me cry. This one has nearly broken my heart."

"Out of pity for the faithless Manon?"

"Out of pity for myself," she said. In the moment of silence her mood swiftly changed and she asked archly: "Are you aware we have not been introduced, Monsieur Leets? You don't even know who I *really* am." She stressed the word like a child.

"Mademoiselle Alphonsine Duplessis, the most beautiful woman in Paris."

As he stood above her beside the couch, his heavy-lidded gaze swept over her. From the flawlessly modeled feet, along the veiled body it wandered, lingering on the throat and face which, as he looked, turned from ivory to rose while her hands in unconscious pudicity leaped to shield her. He turned away, stirred by her blush even more than by her beauty. Such modesty was hardly to be expected from one of her calling. Indeed, he had never met it in his extensive wandering through elegant boudoirs. What grace in that compliment to him, her returning his roses as a carpet for his feet! It brought poetry into what would have been mere eroticism. The desire which had tormented his nights and risen unbearably at the sight of her gave way to a feeling of tenderness.

"I was wrong," he said, turning again to her. "That is only your name. You are the woman I have looked for and never found, or found only in a painting, in a phrase of music, sometimes in a dream. This too may be a dream. But I did not dream that." He pointed to the jewel tree on the stand beside her. "I remember I had it made for you on another day, before we were born into this life."

She had drawn a cashmere coverlet over her. With her

elbow propped on the cushions and her head resting on her hand, she was a figure on a stele, looking forth ruefully on the world she had lost. "I am Alphonsine Plessis," she said in a soft, even tone. "My father was a brute, my mother was a saint. God gave me beauty and I sell it for a price."

The words lashed like whips, but it was herself she was flagellating. Something of proud defiance was in them too, the rebelliousness of a humiliated spirit. "Those who come here—all but one—want only my body. I give it and that is all. Is it not what you came for, Monsieur Leets? I have been more generous with you than with the others. I have shown you the —the merchandise before you bought . . . and you do not desire it."

With that she buried her face in the pillows.

Liszt's nerves shook like violently plucked strings. "My dear," he said, kneeling beside her, "you do not understand. Oh, how can I tell you?"

He tried to reach her hands so that his touch would communicate his emotion but she shrank away, tossing her head from side to side in mute refusal. "My dear, my dear," he murmured helplessly, his desire flaming at the excitation of her self-humiliation and her affront to him. That terrible word "merchandise"! What had he done? What spring had he inadvertently touched to set off such a convulsion?

He stroked her hair gently. When her sobbing ceased he rose and paced about the room waiting for her to come to herself. Somehow he pitied those roses underfoot. Her beautiful gesture had become one of scorn. You send me a fortune in flowers. You think you can buy my soul with gifts. See, this is what I think of your gifts. Alphonsine Plessis, *not* an aristocratic Duplessis, the daughter of a scoundrel and of a long-suffering mother stamps upon your flowers. Men buy the pleasure of my body, Monsieur Leets. They do not buy my soul.

He stood by the window and parted the hangings. Below, the street was dim and silent as Paris lay in an untroubled sleep in this almost pastoral part of town. He looked back at the girl who was sitting up now. She was turned from him but he could see her in the forward-tilted mirror of her dressing table, which was so long that the flying cupids holding aloft their circlets of light on either side had a distance of six feet dividing them.

He caught her face beyond the splendid carelessness of the luxury on the table. She was calm now but for her moist cheeks shadowed by the longest lashes he had ever seen. So intent was she on untying her sandals of ribbon that she was unconscious of her naked breasts whose reflection in the mirror dazzled his gaze. As he stood watching her she opened a drawer and put the ribbons away.

"A dressing table with seven drawers," Ronceval's voice hissed in his ear. "The gift of seven admirers . . ."

Liszt found himself counting. The table had only five drawers, two on each side and one in the middle. The discovery filled him with unreasonable joy. Crossing to her, and taking her bare shoulders between his hands, he stood behind her and addressed her reflection in the mirror. "My dear, come dress and let us go out together. Let us forget you are Alphonsine, forget I am Liszt, forget there are other people in the world. Come, my princess! Let us live our fairy tale."

The look she fixed on him began in somberness but at his words a light filled her pupils and spread over her face. She held him for a long time, saying nothing, her insistent witchery going through him. "What did you call me?" she asked softly, lingering on the words.

"My princess. My fairy princess."

"Princess?"

"Yes, yes!" he whispered, lifting her up and pressing her to him.

She did not resist, neither did she respond. Yet though her arms hung limp the quickening of her breath and the quivering of her lashes against his cheek in an involuntary caress betrayed her. She struggled away from his kiss, however, so that his lips seeking hers slaked themselves on the hollow of her throat. He felt the artery pulsing to his mouth. That symbolic draining of her blood as in some arcane rite excited him even more than her erotic magnetism. "My lovely one! My princess!" he whispered as she slid down through his arms into her chair.

"Must it *always* be a princess?" she asked reproachfully.

"It is my name for you," he said, "till I find another no one else has used. I am not like the others—forgive me!—who want only your body. I am insatiable and demanding. I want all of you."

A thrill went through her, mingling delight and fear. This man dominated her. He had authority. His tall, slim body concealed the strength and elasticity of a bow. Those hands, as light as moths in the shudderings of desire, could also crush her. He was a male, potent, exacting, accustomed to getting what he wanted, indeed, of having it thrown at his feet before speaking his wish. How different from the dandies of the Jockey Club with their curling young beards, their azure pantaloons and their tight-fitting redingotes! Some of them—poor Édouard!—some of them looked like girls dressed up as men. She could do with them as she pleased, and she did, not from hardness but from boredom. Except for Édouard she had never loved. Even then it had been pity more than love that she had returned for his almost desperate passion.

"What if I don't choose to give all of me?" she asked.

She did not look at him but pretended to be engrossed in the fit of the lace stockings that sheathed her legs halfway up the thigh.

"You'll not be able to help it," he said, "because you love me."

"You presume too much, Monsieur Leets," she said with unconvincing calm. "I gave you no reason to think so. Indeed, my behavior should convince you of quite the contrary. I refused to see you—"

"Because you wanted too much to see me. Am I blunt? But then I know about you through myself. I know now why you left while I was playing your encore. Because I did not give you any outward sign. Why not? you ask. Because you were too much in my thoughts and I rebelled against the tyranny. You see, I've suffered too much from women—"

"And I too much from men."

"Then let us heal each other's wounds."

"You talk as if I were one of your good women. I'm not a good woman. I don't even know what that kind of goodness is. Yet I believe in it, Monsieur Leets. I believe in it as I believe in God, without knowing what God is, or even understanding."

Her words came from behind the screen which she had unfolded about her to dress. Liszt was so touched by her simplicity that he could find no answer.

What a development for an assignation! First a fit of hysterics and now a homily. Idly he picked up a gold handmirror from the dressing table. It was in the shape of a heart surrounded by forget-me-nots in high relief. The unimaginative gift, no doubt, of E. de P. whose initials it bore. Probably his lovemaking had been as uninspired, but he had been grateful.

Liszt examined a powder box and a hairpin holder, also in gold. Their lavish givers had had their names set in diamonds. Everything he examined, or almost everything, bore different ciphers, and there were many more than the seven drawers of Ronceval's anecdote. E. de P.'s initials recurred most often. Édouard de Perrégaux's? Of course, of course! Poor boy, he sighed.

Distracted by the rustle of intimate silks, he tried to identify the other names. It was easy to recognize those who had engraved their crest as well as their monogram. Most remained merely letters. A sudden revulsion made him set down the *étui* he was holding. What the devil was he doing here? He, Liszt, Herr Doktor Liszt, *Hofkapellmeister* at the Grand Ducal court of Weimar? Liszt, the favorite musician of the Pope? Liszt, the composer of church music? Liszt, the honored guest of the most exalted houses, the romantic Harold who, except for that humiliating episode with Lola Montez, had slept only with crowns and coronets?

He had an impulse to steal away and never come back when a wisp of birdsong, floating in as if from some yet innocent Eden, held him there. "Haven't you wondered why I have not thanked you for your gift?" asked Mademoiselle Duplessis, emerging from behind the screen with the jewel tree in her hand.

Liszt gasped. Spring and hope and beauty had come back with her. The innocence of girlhood floated about her in the flounces of white muslin, looped and caught by clusters of wild rose and forget-me-nots. On her left shoulder a posy of them held an intoxicated butterfly. The puffed sleeves covered only her upper arm. Her breast and shoulders were revealed in their gracile beauty yet with a suggestion of voluptuousness more alluring than full-blown charms.

She walked past him and into the salon toward the piano on which she set the tree. Immediately the bird stopped singing.

"Out of deference to the master," she laughed.

Liszt followed her in a chaos of emotions. Whereas a moment earlier he had been on the point of escaping, he now longed to crush her in his arms but for the virginal fragility warding him off. Who could have guessed that the serenity of that face had been disturbed but a few moments since by such violent passions?

"How sweet and good you are," he said, taking her hands. "I want no thanks, dear child—only to make you happy."

"You have done more than that," she said. "You have made me suffer."

The words thrilled him by their subtlety. "You love me, then?" he asked.

"Love means suffering," she said. "I am ready for the pain."

She freed her hands and placed them upon his shoulders, lifting her head and rising on her toes to reach him. Softly her lips touched his, but lingeringly also, in a caress that was the soul of a kiss. In a surge of passion he crushed her till she moaned.

They did not go out.

"*Mon amour,* Camille," he whispered as, leaning against the piano, they clung heart to heart in the semidarkness. "That will be my name for you, Camille."

He sought no consummation but she was as spent by his caresses as from a night of orgies. "Enough, ah, enough!" she sighed after each lifetaking kiss. "Enough or I die!"

At last he released her and as she sank into a chair he sat down at the Pleyel. "Listen," he said. "My theme for you . . ."

Caressing each wistful note he played a haunting motif, the theme he had written on the card he sent her. There were only eight notes but they held all aspiration and all yearning. "Listen," he said, as he played a companion melody and fused it with the first in an expression of desire soaring to fulfillment, "Listen. It is you and I and our love."

# 10. Winged Souls

DELPHINE could have sworn the old days of glory had
come again. Mademoiselle Duplessis had had generous
admirers, but none to compare with Monsieur Leets. Never
had Mademoiselle been so showered with jewels, and not just
gold. Monsieur Leets gave her a pendant with a diamond as
big as a pigeon's egg which shone at her throat like a piece of
the sun. Because one evening she complained of the cold, he
bought her an ermine wrap bordered with little black tails,
exactly like a king's mantle in Monsieur Perrault's storybooks.
He also bought her a new bed, and that made Delphine
wonder. It was much more beautiful than the old one, but so
far as Delphine could discover he had not once slept in it nor
fought what one of her ancient lovers used to call the battle of
love. That puzzled her—his lavishing all that money and
those gifts just for Mademoiselle's company. It couldn't be
on account of Mademoiselle's conversation because she was a
quiet kind of girl who usually had more to say to Dash than to
any human being. Delphine tried to penetrate the mystery and
even asked Mademoiselle some direct questions. But she was

more quiet than ever, the deep one, and answered only with a faraway smile.

Maybe Monsieur Leets was some sort of priest, as the porter said. He was certainly different from Perrégaux. "Mark my words, he'll die like the Dauphin of France, that young cockerel," the porter used to say at the height of the love affair, "and kill the mistress, too." It was true history, the porter said, about the dauphin who pleasured his way to death for love of his bride—at sixteen, too.

She wished she knew about Monsieur Leets, however, and why he didn't go to bed like the others instead of spending the night playing the piano and thundering like a hurricane so that nobody could get a wink of sleep. It was all right for Mademoiselle. She could sleep through the morning, but the servants had work to do. They were all getting so cross from their ruined nights that the porter was even talking of cutting a few of the piano strings. Just now they were enjoying a little peace because Monsieur Leets was off playing somewhere and he'd be away for maybe a week. Still, Delphine wished the mistress would take up with Perrégaux again. She had been seeing him prowling about like a shadow, and a shadow he had become these past few weeks from heartbreak and jealousy or whatever takes men when they cannot have the woman they want.

In any case it wasn't Laure Jeanne who was sapping his strength, and Delphine had it from Laure Jeanne herself. "He comes to me like a son, and I treat him like a son," said Laure. "You see, Delphine, he never had a mother. She died when she gave him birth and the aunt who brought him up never married. So he comes and cries his heart out on my breast and pays me as if I'd given him all the pleasures. Isn't it odd, Delphine, how many come to us just to pour out their pain!"

It was certainly true in the old days too. Once the king himself shed a few tears. She still had that chemise. What a relic it would have been, something like the *baignoire* of Marat, if the king had died that time they tried to assassinate him. Too bad one couldn't see the mark of his crying, since tears don't leave a stain, like blood. However, the kingly eyes had wept and her generous bosom had received his tears.

She had been looking more delicate than ever, the Duplessis. Her eyes were so large that they almost ate up her face and excitement burned her cheeks like fire. No wonder, with her going out to the *spectacle* and to concerts and balls and whatever else Monsieur Leets desired, and then getting drowned in all that music when she should have been sleeping the sweet sleep of a woman who has given her lover pleasure.

Well, it was all confusing to Delphine for whom the spectrum of the emotions did not exist. Things were either black or white with nothing in between. Except for the large-handedness that she always admired in a patron, she was somewhat in dread of this Monsieur Leets and, strangely enough, for that very quality. He was like the character in the crazy Balzac novel who had a piece of magic leather that gave him all his wishes but got smaller and smaller each time he used it. There was something against nature in the whole thing. Probably Monsieur Leets had no such talisman, but he gave Delphine that feeling. His kind of looks, too, made her uneasy, as if he had walked out of one of those paintings where men wear gold chains on their velvet coats. Anyway, whatever his power might be, he was certainly using it on Mademoiselle, who went about like a sleepwalker. If she'd only be sensible enough to know how to send him about his business, before that magic leather disappeared!

"Julie! Julie!" she called. "Is Mademoiselle's breakfast ready?"

The girl tripped in as fresh as a wild rose in her cap and frilly apron which seemed almost too elaborate for her simple prettiness. Paris had not taken the bloom from her cheeks nor the blue of the young morning from her eyes. She was seventeen but looked younger, perhaps for the pertness of her nose and her fresh mouth, red and dewy as a cherry. "I was waiting for you to call, Madame Delphine," she said.

"Well, take it to her, then. It's almost noon. But go in softly and if she's asleep come right back. I can't say anybody's had much rest these nights with all that racket."

"What racket, Madame Delphine?"

"You don't mean to say you don't hear all that piano playing?"

"Oh, yes, Madame Delphine, I listen to it. It's so beautiful it puts me to sleep."

"Ah, for the nerves of youth! Well, get along, child."

Mademoiselle was still in bed but she was not asleep. She was lying with her elbows propped on the pillows and her chin in her hands. Julie wished her good morning and set the lacquered tray with Mademoiselle's coffee and *croissant* on the table beside her.

"Good morning, Julie. Is it very late?"

"The church just rang noon, Mademoiselle."

"Strange, I did not hear it."

"That's such a pretty picture, Mademoiselle," said Julie. "So much prettier than the wooden angels on the old bed. I like something in color myself."

"It is very pretty," said Alphonsine, still gazing up at the headboard where the naked infant Eros had overtaken a fleeing maiden and imprisoned her in chains of roses while a woman with uplifted arms pleaded with him for mercy.

"That boy can't be an angel, Mademoiselle," remarked Julie, blushing, "even though he's got wings. What's he doing to that girl in the white dress?"

"Can't you see, Julie? He's caught her in a rope of roses. She's a virgin and she doesn't want Love to catch her."

"She can't be such a virgin, Mademoiselle, going about in that thin dress and one breast all bare, though maybe it slipped out because she was in such a hurry to get away from that boy. He's got a wicked look in his eye. He'd probably be the kind to tie the women's shawls together in church and set off firecrackers under the old folks' benches."

"He can do worse than that, Julie," said Alphonsine, sitting up. "He can break people's hearts. He has even been known to kill."

Julie's eyes widened in candid horror as she set the tray before her mistress. "And you're going to keep that scamp on your bed, Mademoiselle? Me, I'd get back those angels right away. It's true they looked more like devils, but *le bon Dieu* would always have been around to keep them in order. As for that one—" She threw up her hands.

"Tell me, Julie, do you love your young man?" asked Alphonsine as she sipped her coffee.

"I love him with all my heart," said Julie.

"How do you know you love him?" She broke off the tip of her roll but put it back on her plate.

"Because, oh, because I love him. If it weren't a sin I'd say it's because Michel is like *le bon Dieu*. When I go to bed, there he is. I don't actually see him but he's there. When I wake up, there he is again, as big as life. For he's a big lad, my Michel, as tall as that screen, and the hair on his head is straight and yellow like straw. When his smock is open and you can see his chest, there are hairs on it too. But these hairs are curled like little wires and they shine when he's out in the sun. He'll be getting his father's farm someday, that's why he'll be needing a wife with a good dowry. We're going to have lots of children."

The girl's words carried Alphonsine back to her own girlhood, when she too had glanced with shy wonder at the half-naked boys in the fields of Normandy and felt strange stirrings that drew her to them yet made her want to run away. There had been one with just such little golden wires on his arms. His eyes were as blue as the flax flowers and his lips as red as the poppies that waved over them in the field where he had caught and taken her, at fourteen. She remembered only the terror and pain and the youth's eager lips sealing her mouth. Later, the boy planned to run away with her, but he was called to military training. And then she had been so sick that they had to send for the midwife. They said it was a baby, three months along. It was after this that her father took her to Paris and washed his hands of her. The only good thing was that her mother had died; it would have broken her heart.

"Have you always been a good girl, Julie?" asked Alphonsine.

"Oh, yes! Mademoiselle has seen all my references. Do you think I would have come to take the position if I hadn't been an honest girl?" Her ingenuous eyes grew large at such an implication. "Besides, Mademoiselle—"

"Yes, Julie?"

"We *had* to be good, I mean, Michel and me, and I can tell you it wasn't easy out there in the country. Mademoiselle is a real Parisian. You wouldn't know the temptations for young people in love, especially in the spring. Everywhere you turn the birds are singing and making love, the stallions prancing after the mares, their manes flying so you'd almost think they had wings. Even the butterflies, Mademoiselle! You'd imagine they're too pure to know about such things. But there you'd find them as if they were sewed together, their little wings trembling, trembling and so drunk they didn't even know they were in danger. I once saw a pair of them gobbled up by a bird, just like that. Michel said, Well, they died happy. Do you think so, Mademoiselle? I don't."

"At least they died quickly. That's also a mercy. Why don't you think they died happy, Julie?"

"They had no children. Oh, I know it's different with *petits riens* like butterflies. I was really thinking of me and Michel. I can tell you this, Mademoiselle, because I know you'd understand. But it's not easy for a girl like me, so much in love, to keep her flower, as they say, in my part of the country. Not with a healthy lad like Michel who's never been one to go with bad women. Everything starts up the devil in him, as you can imagine, and so he begins with a little this, and no more than that. Before you know it, it might be too late. Not with me, though. I have that wedding sheet waving like a flag in front of my eyes all the time."

"What are you talking about, Julie?" laughed Alphonsine. "You haven't dipped into your hope chest already?"

"Oh, no, Mademoiselle! That's as sacred as the treasure in the church."

"Then what's this about the wedding sheet?"

"Well, you see, it's the sheet we'll sleep on the first night, when I do my duty as a wife. We keep the old ways in our part of the country, Mademoiselle, so I'd think of that sheet every time Michel wanted to go too far. It's a blessing Madame Delphine got me to work for you. Now, when we get married and Michel's mother comes for that sheet in the morning, she can show the neighbors that I had my flower."

"What, Julie? She shows it to the neighbors?"

"Not really. She hangs it out where they can see it if they want to."

"And if there is no flower?"

"God forbid! Why, then she'd take me straight back to my parents and I'd probably be braiding Saint Catherine's hair for the rest of my days. Unless I want to become a bad woman. A girl in our village did just that and now she goes about in a hat and feathers. But they don't always turn out so well.—

I'm sorry I've chattered too much," she said, misinterpreting her mistress' silence. "My mother always said if words were money I'd not have to work for my dowry." She smoothed her apron self-consciously. "Does Mademoiselle wish anything else?"

"Just my bath, Julie." The girl still waited. "And yes, would you wind up the little bird to wish us good morning?"

"I was hoping you'd ask me!" cried Julie joyfully.

When she was alone Alphonsine drew out a letter from under her pillow. The very touch of it went through her like fire and her lids drooped in languor. "If reading could wear it out there would be nothing left of it," she thought. But she must read it again even though she knew every phrase by heart.

"I left you twenty-four hours ago but I am full of you still. I am lost in you. It is an ache yet it is sweet, this yearning that brings you as close to me as if you were standing behind me, your cool hands over my eyes, as on that evening when for the first time you responded to me in a gesture of tenderness.

"You chided me at the Luxembourg for not admiring the beauty about us. How could I? Were you not, are you not always, like an aura about me? What can I admire, love, adore, if not you?

"Your heart is awaking to love, my Camille, the heart which you told me has never loved. Do you know what the name Camille means? The pure and stainless virgin. To me that is what you are. That is why I would not have you give yourself to me as you gave yourself to other men. 'Because they desired me,' you said. You must come to me because *you* desire me. I shall wait. When the time comes your heart will burst through its chrysalis and fly to my heart in that final liberation of self after which our souls, like our bodies, will merge. Your Franz."

She pressed her lips on the name.

*Seigneur,* what did he want of her? What days and nights they had spent together in the unreality of a dream, except that the dream lingered through her waking hours, making her feel a stranger in the world she knew. Was that love? With Franz gone, it was as if he had taken her with him, leaving only her shell, like those lifelike cases the cicadas left clinging to the trees after the winged creature had emerged. Your heart will burst through its chrysalis. . . . That must be the meaning of the struggle within her which made her break out in sobs and sudden tears, in moods of gaiety and again in causeless despair.

Franz! Franz! The name thrilled her and made her go weak, like the passion of his kisses. Was that love? When she was with him she felt herself glowing like a lighted lamp. When he had gone life itself was snuffed out and she went about, a thing without a soul, longing for that soul to return.

Perhaps there was truth to the wonderful things Franz would tell her, about wandering winged souls that soared to the highest heavens to bask in the light of perfect beauty. But sometimes they lost their way and fell earthward, perhaps because they had bruised their wings, or for the lure of some glimpse of loveliness here below which they mistook for the lost beauty of heaven. The bruised wings grew again and the soul in love struggled to unite with the beauty lost and now found. That, said Franz, was love.

Then what of desire? What of those kisses that left her quivering? Was that how souls loved? What did Franz want of her? *O Seigneur!* Why did he not understand there was nothing she would not give? Soul, wings, body, everything!

# 11.  Hashish Dreams

PRINCE STACKLYN went up the stairs step by step like a child, his valet following close behind. The hand on the banister shook as it glided along. His head too had a slight tremor. Delphine at the landing almost fell on her knees like one of his own serfs as she took his extended right hand and kissed it.

"Welcome, welcome, Your Highness," she said. "Mademoiselle is most anxious."

Indeed, Alphonsine was already at the door of the salon, reaching out her hands which he clasped as he kissed her on both cheeks. He had to raise his head and straighten up to do it, age had so shrunk his frame.

"*Ça va bien, ma petite?*" he asked after she had helped him into an armchair and sat down on a hassock at his feet.

"*Assez bien, merci, cher* Alexei. But tell me about you. . . . Oh, I'm so glad to see you," she said, reaching up to embrace him. He kissed her hands before he let them go.

"*Assez bien?* Only pretty well, dear?" he asked with concern.

"Oh, the east wind, the change of seasons. Everything has its effect upon me, as you know. But let me look at you."

She saw the lean, enfeebled body in clothes too large for the shoulders, too wide for the wrists. The tightly drawn skin over the prince's head and face had a pearly sheen through which she could see the veins, as distinct as those of a leaf which winter had eaten away. The sunken eyes still held fire like those of a hawk over the thin, beaklike nose. The whole head, it seemed to Alphonsine, was like a lamp whose flame was dying out. How old was Prince Stacklyn? Eighty-four? Eighty-five?

"*Vous avez bonne mine,* Alexei," she said, thinking, however, that he had aged many years during the four months that she had not seen him.

"I manage to keep well," he said. "But you, dear. I am concerned about you. Sometimes I think you do not take your condition seriously enough. Your eyes . . . there's something in them I don't remember seeing before—"

"It's because you've been away. You have forgotten, Alexei."

"No, I tell you, it's something different in your eyes. It is the sweetness and the fire I have been waiting to find. Don't move. Don't turn away. Just sit there quietly. Fold your hands in the old way and look at me with those burning eyes. You are not wearing the white dress? No, don't change, it does not matter. Annette, my beloved, look into my eyes."

"Alexei!"

"That new thrill in your voice! Oh, my Annette!"

He leaned forward, joining his cupped hands which quivered like a heart as he peered nearsightedly into the young woman's upturned face. His head shook more violently. "It is so long since I have seen you, Annette."

"Yes, long, very long. The nights seemed like months and the months like years."

"It has been years, my love. But you have not changed, unless you are more beautiful. But no! No one could be more beautiful than my Annette." The old man gave a violent jerk of anger. "Stop! You have made me spoil it."

Alphonsine started. "I am sorry," she said. "What have I done that's wrong?"

"Everything! Your face, your voice, your dress." He covered his eyes with his hands. "You have ruined the illusion."

"I'll go and change my dress."

"It's no use. I've been away too long. I'm no longer Alexei. You're no longer my Annette. You've made me lose her." Something like a sob broke in his voice.

The young woman twisted her fingers. She felt sorry for Prince Stacklyn, but there was nothing she could do. Sometimes his fits of grieving lasted for hours. Once he stayed through the night, sunk in his chair with her head resting on his knees, while he stroked her hair and called her by the name of his first love who had been dead for more than sixty years.

"Alexei," she called softly. He did not answer.

Uneasily she waited for him to come out of his mood. The clock on the mantel ticked like the heart of the room. Just then it hummed and a hidden bell told the hours. Eleven o'clock.

The blood coursed like lighting to her heart. Where was

Franz now? Like children they had agreed to look at a particular star at this hour so that their eyes and their thoughts might meet in space.

It was the hour they had found their star one night just before his departure when they escaped into the air to let their hearts catch breath from their annihilating kisses. They had not walked far, only to the churchyard of the Madeleine. It was a moonless night and they, alone on their stone seat, shared the silence and the peace with the dead. Franz twined his fingers through hers and the contact of their linked hands made the marble burn. They were too full of their love for speech, but they could hear their rhythmic breathing. Now and again they sought each other's eyes in the darkness. Then, by a shared impulse, they glanced up into the sky and in one breath whispered: "Our star." For there, in the empty sky, a single point of light took on the wonder of all the heavenly galaxies.

Alphonsine wanted to rise and go to the window but she was held by the fear of disturbing the old man. A glance told her that nothing at that moment could have reached him in the region where his mind had lost itself. Pity overwhelmed her at the sight of those shaking hands covering eyes absorbed in the shadow of a love to which she was sometimes called to give a momentary reality.

Crushing her skirts to her so that they would not rustle she tiptoed to the window. As she peered through the glass she could see no star nor, for that matter, anything but a vaporous curtain between herself and the sky. Noiselessly she opened the casement and stepped out upon the balcony, the air enfolding her in a chill caress that thrilled through her body.

No, their star that had been all the heavens was not shining for them in that low-hanging fog which blotted out everything but the black outlines of the trees and Prince Stacklyn's carriage, below, like a quiescent beetle, its lantern eyes sending out beams in which the fog motes whirled. She hugged herself against the night air, as the blood washed in hot and cold waves over her, bringing a moisture to her forehead and oppression to her breast. Pressing her handkerchief to her lips she hurried back into the room and shut the window.

"Annette! Annette!" the old man called from his revery. "Sit as you were, my love, but come closer so that I may touch you. The coughing is worse. What! After those long months at the spa? After the quantities of goat's milk, all that jelly of ivory dust? Nothing, nothing helps!"

He took her face in his hands and leaned forward. A faint smell of eau de cologne mingled with another, a sickly sweet, weedlike exhalation that seemed to come from his skin and his clothes. "I never told you what the doctor said, Annette."

Alphonsine waited but his eyes closed and his lips tightened in a grimace of pain. What had the doctor said? The answer somehow became very important to her, Alphonsine. She had met Prince Stacklyn at the spa where his Annette had died of the same phthisis that affected her own lungs. It was her illness that had brought them together and something else about her, perhaps only her youth, which reminded him of his Annette. She knew little about her disease because doctors like to keep their secrets. She was therefore only vaguely aware of its gravity. Since Korff assured her that he could make her well she tried not to brood and would fool herself into blaming the east wind, overexcitement, everything but the true cause of her crises.

Again she became Annette. "What did the doctor say, Alexei?" she asked him in the trancelike voice of the role she had been enacting for the prince for the past five years.

Her question was a stone falling into still depths, so profound was the old man's absorption in the past. The clock ticked on. Her heart echoed with passing life the passing time. Against her cheeks, not quite touching them yet close enough for her to feel the agitated air, those restless hands fluttered with a life of their own.

The prince was leaning back now, his head inert against the back of the chair. Was he dead? She had often been in dread that he might die, and then the horror, the scandal! But no, those hands. She felt like screaming but terror tightened her throat. Now she found herself staring at the light of the lamp reflected on his shining skull.

"Alexei! Alexei!" she cried, falling on her knees and shaking him by the shoulders. "Alexei!"

"What is it? Ah, Annette . . ." He started up in a daze. "You woke me from such a beautiful dream."

"Alexei! What did the doctor tell you?"

"That was so long ago, my love."

"I must know, Alexei."

"So long ago! What need have you to know, Annette?"

The lids drooped. Again his mind was sinking into the well of the past.

"Alexei!" Alphonsine continued shaking him in desperation, fearful that he might die and carry with him a secret that meant her own life or death. The head nodded in puppetlike inertia but the old man did not awaken from that stupor far deeper than sleep.

For a while she remained kneeling, not knowing what to do. Should she call Delphine? No. She had no need to do anything. This visit was no different from the others. The valet would be let in after the proper interval to lead his master away. If the prince was asleep the porter would help to carry him down into the carriage. She flicked away a few brownish-green particles, like bits of dried leaves, from the lapels of his coat. She never knew where they came from but she found herself always brushing them off.

"What did the doctor say?" she urged him in a tense whisper. "Alexei, tell Annette! What did the doctor say?"

She might have been addressing a corpse but for the spasmodic start of his whole body and a jerking of his hands and feet. The face too changed with his emotions as when things glide under still water, suggesting pale, mysterious shapes. What shadows moved in the depths of his mind? Now and then the lips twitched and vague sounds rumbled in his throat. "What did the doctor say, Alexei? Tell Annette—what did the doctor say?" she repeated in hypnotic rhythm.

"Doom . . . terrible . . . at any age . . ."

She caught the words and held her breath to miss nothing of what might follow. He merely said them over and over like a child's doggerel except for their dread implication. Ah, that was it! Doomed. In spite of Korff and the other doctors at the spas who had promised miraculous cures she had known it deep within. She had seen too much, even though she blinded herself to what she saw, saying that such things could never happen to her: beautiful eyes sinking deeper into the skull, cheeks burning till the flame of the disease ate up the flesh and left the face of a wraith. The cold sweats and the fevers and the coughing, and the terrible restlessness, the frenzy of the doomed to capture all of life within a few years, a few months.

"At any age . . . terrible. At twenty-one . . . it kills. . . ."

She got up from her knees, trembling. Ah, that was it. Doomed! At twenty-one . . . it kills. And she was twenty-one. It was Annette's age when she died and that old man had lived four of her lifetimes! What remained of Annette's beauty under the ground? A few frail bones and her long hair and horror, horror, horror!

"It kills . . . it kills. . . ."

"Stop, Alexei!" she screamed, clutching her pounding temples. "Delphine! Delphine!" She staggered to the door and threw it open. "Delphine!" she shrieked.

Prince Stacklyn's valet required the help of the porter to carry his master to the carriage. They arranged the limp body on the seat and bolstered it up with cushions. The valet sat down facing him. "One of these days, old man," he said in disgust, "one of these days you won't wake up from your hashish dreams."

The church bell struck midnight, spreading the reverberations in a cloud of sound over the quiet neighborhood and entering, muffled, into the Duplessis house. Alphonsine set down the cup of hot *tilleul*. "What good is a tisane, Delphine, when there's a tiger of restlessness in me?" she cried.

Indeed, she looked like some lithe wild thing as she got up and paced the room. "Sometimes this life is too much for me," she said, "and yet what other can I live? I am spoiled now for anything else. All this," she swept her arm to include the Henry II pieces, the tapestries and glittering *objets d'art*. "How can I leave them and find happiness in a garret with some young fool who would feed me verses?"

"Forgive my bluntness, Mademoiselle," interrupted Delphine, "but you have your fortune and you let it slip through your fingers. Right now, this very minute, there's a faithful heart that would throw itself at your feet."

"Édouard again? Really, Delphine, I'm beginning to think your concern is not entirely disinterested. Ever since Monsieur Leets went away you've done nothing but talk Édouard. What is he paying you for this special pleading?"

"I swear by all the saints, not a sou. It's only that I can't bear to see you living like a nun and neglecting your friends simply because you think you're in love with this piano player. In my day he would have had to come in by the servants' entrance, instead of which it's the Vicomte de Perrégaux who slips in that way, just to be near you. He's there this very minute—"

"Édouard here? Now?"

"And has been every night since Monsieur Leets went away."

"What does the mad boy want?" Alphonsine's tone held

more vexation than curiosity. But there was also a note of pity which did not escape Delphine.

"Just a glimpse of you as you come and go. Just a breath of the air you breathe after you've breathed it, the poor young count!" She gave the title a significant stress to differentiate Perrégaux from a mere piano player.

A wave of loneliness swept over Alphonsine. The empty days since Liszt's departure, the long solitary nights dedicated to him out of a sense of fidelity wholly new to her, and now this sudden and terrible premonition of doom reawakened her hunger for pleasure and excitement. After all, Franz would not be living the life of a monk. At this moment no doubt he was being tempted by some princess—it was always a princess—in whose arms he would forget Camille whose body he had not yet possessed. A longing to be loved swept over her again, lingering in her eyes as a slow, heavy-lidded look that touched off her lovers like a powerful aphrodisiac.

"Poor Édouard!" she said. "I have been so cruel to him."

"It is always sweet to ask forgiveness, though if I know the young count it'll be he who'll be falling on his knees." Delphine waited for her mistress to speak, but Alphonsine's thoughts were far away. "Well, Mademoiselle?" she asked.

"Order my carriage," she said impulsively. "Tell Édouard to give me time to dress. The night is his."

When Perrégaux saw her he staggered as from a blow. "*Mon ange, mon amour!* How ravishing you are!"

He would have got down on his knees to her as usual but that she held out her arms. With a cry he clasped her, growing instantly dizzy at the contact and that subtle emanation of sensuality which roused his every nerve to desire. Crushing her head against his shoulder he clung to her mouth sating upon it the hunger and jealousy of the past wretched weeks.

"Édouard! Please!" she gasped, turning away.

"You love me, *mon âme!*" he cried, kissing her again in an ardor of possession. Her yielding, her unprecedented response turned his blood to fire. "Let us not go—go out," he stammered.

His stumbling speech brought back the cruelty of her taunt that night in the carriage. It also materialized Franz before her.

"We must go out, Édouard." She panted from the passion which had awakened her own. "I am stifling in this house. I need air. I need life."

"Dear angel, I've wanted you so—so long! It's heaven and hell to—to hold you and to have to let you go."

"Later, Édouard," she said, freeing herself.

"You promise?"

"I said the night is yours."

"But you promise?" he insisted.

She gave him a light kiss for answer and walked quickly to the waiting carriage. He followed, between delirium and despair. As they drove off he held her as if at any moment he might lose her as he lost her to his intoxicated sight whenever they passed from the lighted to the darkened sections of the city. They said little. For Édouard it was sufficient that he had regained paradise. What could a grateful Adam give but the silence of his adoration and the passionate proof of his happiness? He demanded from Alphonsine neither explanation nor apology. She offered none. It was enough to Édouard that she returned his kisses, rather, enough that she did not repel them.

Her head against the soft velvet, Alphonsine allowed herself to sink into a voluptuous swoon. What matter that it was Édouard and not Franz? The kisses—if one closed one's eyes—were the same. She kept her lids tight shut. The alternating lights, however, struck through and shattered the illusion. She ordered the coachman to drive through the park. There, in the unlighted alleys, she gave herself up to the devouring mouth and questing hands, echoing his passion with sighs that came from the heart because that heart was filled with Franz.

"*Chère âme,* now I know that you—you really love me," sighed the enraptured youth.

From the park they returned to the lively haunts of Montmartre and to the Boulevard des Italiens that never slept. Their nerves were strained to breaking by their aroused but unappeased desire. At the Italiens they left the carriage and made the rounds of their favorite places, Édouard striding beside her, hoping the Jockey Club would see him with Mademoiselle Duplessis on his arm, in spite of the much talked about tenure of Monsieur Leets.

They wound up their rounds at the Café de Paris. Only the habitués were left and the waiters were beginning to toy with the glasses on the tables of the too long lingering guests. Ronceval, deep in a magazine, raised his head at the popping of a champagne cork and immediately joined the new arrivals, taking the review with him.

"Well, good old Ron-Ronceval!" Perrégaux welcomed him. Ronceval had seen him with the Duplessis! His happiness was complete.

The journalist kissed Alphonsine's hand and took the chair Perrégaux offered him. "You writing men," he said. "You're like—like drunkards with a bottle—never, or hardly ever, without a piece of reading in your hands."

"This happens to be remarkably interesting reading," said Ronceval, laying the open *Revue Indépendante* on the table.

"*Nélida,* by Daniel Stern," read Perrégaux. "Do—do I know the gentleman?"

"The gentleman happens to be a lady," said Ronceval. "Madame d'Agoult."

Alphonsine who had been playing abstractedly with a knife suddenly dropped it. "Madame d'Agoult?" she repeated. "Why does she use a man's name?"

"The better to tell the truth about—her friends," said Ronceval with meaningful hesitation. "Especially a most intimate friend. Ah, *le cher maître!* She calls him Régnier, but even a simpleton could recognize the portrait. "I've read only a couple of installments. What fury, what hate in the novel!"

"Hate, Monsieur Ronceval?" asked Alphonsine.

"The woman scorned, Mademoiselle. No doubt she owes him a few reproaches, but his worst fault, really, was the very human one of being no longer in love." He did not miss the flash of pleasure in her pupils. "Her fury only betrays that she is hurt and probably still in love. . . ."

"A woman in love would never turn against the man she loves," said Mademoiselle Duplessis, so softly that she might have been talking to herself. "She would do anything to try to keep him, but she would never turn against him."

"Perhaps you are right, Mademoiselle," said Ronceval. "But who can read the depths of the human heart?"

"Let's rather get to the depths of—of another bottle," said the young man.

"Thanks, no, Perrégaux. I've an article to finish before morning. I've got to keep a clear head."

Alphonsine who had only sipped the wine, drank it all after the journalist had gone. "To Monsieur Leets!" said Édouard. "May he be well roasted."

"Yes, to Monsieur Leets!" cried Alphonsine.

"May he be well roasted. Come, say it."

"May he be well roasted," she said after him in a bubbling of laughter. Yes, yes! The more Madame d'Agoult hurt him, the better for her, Alphonsine. Then Franz would turn to her for love and comfort. Then he would know how much she loved him. With her whole heart—and if it were a goblet full of her life's blood, she would give it all to him, to drain as she drained this glass. "May he be well roasted!" she cried again, crashing the empty goblet against the wall.

On the way to the carriage she ran ahead of Edouard along the boulevard, holding up her skirts like a girl romping on a high meadow. "Come, catch me!" she shouted, tossing her head.

Her plumed hat slipped off and hung by its ribbons down her back. The night echoed her laughter. With his coat flapping about his knees, Édouard staggered dazedly after her.

Toward the middle of the boulevard Alphonsine changed
her run to a waltz step.

*Tra* la *la* la,
*Tra* la *la* la,
*Tra* la *la*
*Tra* la-*la* la-*la* la-*la* la-*la*-lah . . .

She sang Weber's "Invitation" to tones that thrilled the silence, as she danced and whirled and waved her arms in a
solo down the street. The few late stragglers stopped to watch
the airy vision appearing and disappearing in the light cast
by the rare lanterns high up in the air.

At the turn of the boulevard where they had left the
carriage she beckoned to Édouard. "Give me some money,"
she said softly.

He handed her his purse. She drew out a banknote.
"Thanks," she said, returning the case.

Without glancing at the note she walked to the arcade
and stopped in front of what looked like a bundle of rags
except that two heads could be distinguished on it. One was
a child's. It was asleep. The mother too was sleeping. Alphonsine rolled up the money into a tube and tied it to the
end of a ribbon which fastened the baby's cap. With her
finger on her lips she then joined Édouard.

"To the Vicomte de Perrégaux," she directed the coachman.

"But—but you promised," interposed Édouard.

"That the night would be yours. Look!" She pointed to
the east where the dark was parting for the faint green haze
that would blossom into day.

# 12.  Threat of Doom

ALPHONSINE had barely awakened when Julie announced Edouard. It was past noon and he had been waiting for over an hour. She drank her coffee, got up and dressed quickly. She was not going to let Édouard find her in her nightgown and in bed. To avoid any emotional complication she asked Julie to admit him into the dressing room.

"*Chère âme!*" he greeted her, taking her in his arms.

Why did men call one "dear soul" when it was the body they wanted? Alphonsine took warning and let his kisses fall on her cheek. "I was such a beast last night, drinking all—all that champagne," he apologized. "Did I say foolish—foolish things? Or do anything dis—disgraceful? I was so drunk just being with you that—that everything went to my head."

"You were a dear boy, Édouard. Good and gentle and obedient. But what brings you here when we parted just a few hours ago?"

"*Chère âme*, you—you said—"

"Here, sit down beside me." She slid sinuously out of his arms onto the sofa. "I must have said things I've forgotten, too."

He remained standing peering down into her face to discover what it was in her that enslaved him. How clear and childlike were his eyes, thought Alphonsine, and how ingenuous. He had never had a woman before her, he confessed the first night, and she had known the truth of it by his insatiable importunity. He had never had another woman after her. "Can't you see I love you?" he flung out desperately when in a moment of impatience she had told him to go elsewhere. "Can't you see you have ruined me for anyone else?"

"You have often said things—things you later forgot," he said with a new earnestness. "You've also made me forget many things. Last night didn't I tell you—tell you something very important?"

"That you love me? But I've always known that, *cher enfant.*"

He gripped her shoulders and said with a defiant laugh: "Well, you can't call me *cher enfant* any more. Last week I reached my majority and—and I am now my own master."

"And I forgot! Oh, you must forgive me, Édouard. I'll give you a party at the Maison Dorée. We'll celebrate—it's not too late?"

"How could you remember my birthday? You had so many things on—on your mind. Besides, you had shut your door to me. Last night I wanted to ask you for—for my birthday gift."

"I'll give it gladly, *mon ami*—I mean, Your Excellency, or whatever they call you now." She got up and laughingly made a curtsy. He remained grave and his childlike eyes gathered depth as he looked at her squarely. "You will—you will give me yourself?" he asked. "In marriage?"

"Édouard! I've told you—"

"It's different now. I am asking you as—as a man. I need no one's permission now, according to the will."

"But Édouard, my dear, I don't—"

"Don't love me? But I—I love you. Enough to make up for both of us."

"No, that's not it, Édouard. I've always had a great tenderness for you, you know that. But—"

"You love someone else?"

She was silent.

"Monsieur Leets?"

She turned away as a wave of blood mounted to her cheeks.

"Monsieur Leets is not a—a man whose heart you can hold for long, *cher amour*. Artists are like that. Let Korff tell you. He—he knows. Did Monsieur Leets ever think of—of marrying the Comtesse d'Agoult?"

"How could he when she was already married?"

"His good friend the Pope could have granted—what is it they call it?—a dispensation. Another thing. Even—even though she had a title she couldn't keep him. How long do you think you—you could hold him?"

"That, Édouard, is my affair," she said sharply.

"Darling!" He took her gently by the shoulders. "It—it is also mine because—because I love you." She stared in wonder at this new Édouard, so suddenly matured. "I don't want you to be hurt. Korff told me—"

"Ah, so it's Korff who's advising you? Is he worried he'll

make no more money out of you now that you don't have to borrow from him?"

"Korff told me Monsieur Leets has to—to be very careful now he has this new post at the Grand Duke's. So proper, he said. So aristocratic."

"Really, Édouard, you sound exactly like that old charlatan. Did he also advise you to marry me? Perhaps he's afraid I may not always have the money to meet my bills?"

"That's not fair, darling. As if I hadn't asked you six—six times before this. I remember each one. But now it's different."

"Different! No, Édouard! Because the answer is still the same. No!" She turned to pull the bell cord. "Now please go, Your Excellency le Vicomte de Perrégaux!"

"I knew it would end like this," he said. "Oh, yes, I was prepared for it. You see I'm not falling on—on my knees and begging you as before. I love you. Remember that. I love you. Whenever you want me I shall—I shall be there."

He made a profound bow and left before the servant could come to escort him.

Alphonsine could scarcely believe the change in him. Was this the adolescent with his passions of kisses and tears? It was as if with his independence he had become a man. She was astonished, pleased and at the same time dismayed. Had she lost her power over him? No, because he still trembled at her least touch. Had he been speaking through the promptings of Korff? Perhaps. But he was also voicing his own imperative desire to have her for himself, entirely for himself. La Vicomtesse de Perrégaux. She smiled at the thought as she walked across the room to the Venetian mirror and studied herself in the antique glass that had the rainbow surface of filmed water. La Vicomtesse de Perrégaux . . . Would the title sound aristocratic enough at the court of the Grand Duke of Weimar? What was Franz doing at this moment? Where was he? He should soon be coming back.

She was not looking well. Or was it the mirror? It might account for her color but not for the fever in her eyes nor for that shadow under them. What wonder after the nightmare of Prince Stacklyn? Even the champagne—she had drunk more with Delphine before going to bed—had not brought her oblivion. For hours, despite the drawn blinds and the closed bed curtains she could not blot out the head of the old man, glowing like a phosphorescent thing in the dark, as it moved its lips and repeated over and over: "At twenty-one . . . it kills. . . ."

At twenty-one. Before long she would be twenty-two. Would the curse then be lifted? Korff assured her that her condition was not yet alarming. Not yet, but did it not mean that it might become critical? How foolish of her even to doubt it! Had she not seen at Baden-Baden the beautiful youths and girls of one season cut down the next? Oh, they had taken delightful walks together over the flowering valley to the Black Forest. They had gone on gay excursions to the Old Castle and sketched that other castle of rocks, the Felsen, which nature had built there. They had drunk the mineral waters at the Trinkhalle and goat's milk on the terrace, and they had played and waltzed and flirted in the Konversations-haus. Yet all the while Death had been playing and waltzing and flirting with them as in those frescoes Franz described to her one night when he told her she looked like someone he had fallen in love with in the paintings. She must resemble a great many women: the prince's Annette, Franz's Italian lady, and a princess in a fairy tale whom the Duc de Guiche had rediscovered in her. Édouard alone had seen only herself, perhaps because he had no imagination. Or was it because he alone of them all loved her for herself? No, no, it was Franz who loved her!

The piano was open. She went to it and struck the keys. "Oh Franz! Franz!" she sighed.

Softly she played the notes of their love theme. The poignant melody filled her with him as on those nights when, as she sank to sleep at last, he came to her in dreams and possessed her as he had never done in reality. What must the full flood of him be when just a wave in her fancy so transported her?

It was madness to love and to love a man like Franz who had to be free, or at least not encumbered with a Mademoiselle Duplessis to whom honest women gave a gross name. Perhaps Delphine was right. How long would her youth and beauty last? How long her marred health? With Édouard she would have an honorable name as well as the prestige of being a wife. She would have his devotion. She could still have Franz in whose eyes she would be more attractive for being the Vicomtesse de Perrégaux. At Weimar the Grand Duke's court would welcome the Vicomtesse where it would snub Mademoiselle Duplessis.

But it was all idle speculation. She could no more belong to Franz, really belong to him, than to Édouard. She had been spoiled by her life of luxury. She needed beauty and lovers and public admiration to make up for the squalor of her childhood. She needed constant excitement and change in a hunger for life which she knew she would never appease. How much time, how little time would be hers before the blight did away with her forever? At twenty-one it kills. . . .

The tears were constantly on the brink these days, perhaps because her nerves, keyed up to breaking point by Franz, had not been given release. For many weeks now she had been chaste. It was this continence which Delphine blamed for her malaise. "A woman is like a flower, Mademoiselle. Without the rain of love she withers away."

Just then Delphine entered with the tray containing the *cartes de visite* and the mail. There was only one letter but it was all Alphonsine wanted. At the sight of the handwriting she involuntarily clutched at her heart. Delphine noticed and shook her head.

"I tell you he's killing you, that man!" she said. "I don't know what his power is over you but I don't like it. By the way, what did you do to that poor young man, Mademoiselle? He tore out of the house like the wind—"

"That's strange! He seemed extraordinarily composed when he left me. What exactly is back of all this, Delphine? You weren't always his advocate."

"People can change. Besides, he's rich now and his own master."

"He hasn't changed so far as I'm concerned. Anyway, *I* haven't changed. Please go now, Delphine. I don't want to be disturbed."

"Not even by Dr. Korff? It's his day, Mademoiselle."

"That's different. He comes on a professional visit."

"He should be here any moment."

"Show him in as usual. But go now."

Alphonsine held the letter without daring to break the seal. What if Franz told her he no longer loved her and was never coming back? She had had the same fears when his first letter arrived and had kept it for an hour before she opened it. How vain her anxiety had proved before the certainty of his passion! Men had told her many things in their voluptuous moments, but never had anyone written her in such adoration. How she had envied Manon her Des Grieux who loved her through all her infidelities! But Franz was greater than Des Grieux. Franz was desired by all women as she, Alphonsine, was desired by all men.

What if he were writing that he loved another? The thought made her set down the letter in terror. There would be time for that news tomorrow, next week. No, she would never read the letter. She would wait, wait till Franz returned, and then he could tell her what the letter contained. She would tear it up. But how could she destroy anything that came from Franz?

When Dr. Korff arrived he found her so unsettled that he pretended difficulty in opening his bag to give her time to compose herself.

"Wonderful weather for December, is it not, Mademoiselle Duplessis?" he began. "Ah, but I forgot. You haven't yet been out. How is the sleep?" he asked, though the shadows under her eyes told him. "How is the pulse?" He also saw how her hands were shaking.

"Never mind the weather, Korff," she answered with unaccustomed firmness. "I want you to tell me the truth today. The truth, do you understand? No more pretty pretenses about highly unusual constitutions and temperaments like aeolian harps. I'm a creature of flesh and blood. Also, I'm no longer a child. I can take the worst."

"Now, now, now, what sort of talk is that, dear and beautiful lady?" he said. "When have I ever lied to you? Today you're all agitated for some reason and your pulse is galloping like one of the Duc de Guiche's race horses—I beg pardon, I shouldn't have mentioned—"

"To the point, Korff," she said stamping her foot, "and never mind apologies. What if you do mention the Duc de Guiche? Very well, he was one of my lovers. I've had others since, so let's not stress the obvious. About my condition, now?"

Korff, who had been studying her closely, maintained his unruffled exterior. "Your condition, Mademoiselle?" he inquired. "If it's the state of your nerves, it has never been worse. Too much excitement, too little rest. Too many late hours, not enough sleep. Have you ever gone to bed before midnight, Mademoiselle?"

"Not since I was fifteen."

"Observe the birds and be wise. They tuck their heads under their wings the moment the sun sets. That's when nature begins to lose her forces and so do all her creatures who have with her the subtle affinity of the child to the mother.

Man is not a nocturnal animal like the cat that likes to sleep by day and prowl by night—"

"Korff," said Mademoiselle Duplessis with a calm she did not feel, "what are you trying to keep from me?"

"Keep from you? Have I ever kept anything from you, Mademoiselle?" he asked with the blankest of china doll stares, meanwhile missing not the least fluctuation of her wrist under his fingers while he studied what was really more important, the rise and fall of that lovely but corroded breast. "As I was saying, man is not a nocturnal animal. He needs the fortifying hours of sleep before midnight when the atmosphere is still vibrant from the sun's rays, though we do not see them, and—"

"Korff! Korff! You're driving me to hysterics," she cried, pulling away. "Tell me the worst and be done with it!"

The doctor walked over to the window, took a deep breath and rubbed his hands as if he were washing them in the sunlight. "Yes, beautiful weather for December," he said. "But how long will it last? The first week of the month has always more of autumn than of winter. Then the snow begins to fall, the air grows chill and cuts like a knife. It is not good for weak lungs."

"If it's my going away you're hinting at, I've no intention of obeying," she said. "How I hate those resorts with their coughing guests and their eternal goat's and ass's milk, and the mild exercise and the afternoon nap, and ten hours' sleep at night. No, thank you! I'm staying here. The Paris winter is life to me, not your cures that don't cure. I am worse, then?" she asked abruptly.

"You couldn't expect to be better, Mademoiselle, defying all my orders," he said reproachfully. "I cannot lie to you. Your condition is aggravated and you insist on committing suicide by remaining in Paris."

"I tell you I need this life. It's all the difference between living and dying."

"It will be dying, I'm afraid, unless—"

"Yes, Korff?"

"Unless you modify the pace of your living. I know a way you can do it and still have your pleasures."

"I can stay here, then?"

"There's the Vicomte de Perrégaux who has just come into his fortune. He's more than ever in love with you. He would give his life—"

"Oh, so that's back of it all! I should have known! No, thank you, Korff. I prefer the pace of my living, as you call it."

"Believe me, Mademoiselle, it can only lead to disaster. I'm speaking to you like a father." She gave a bitter laugh. "With Perrégaux you could have all the joys of marriage, the luxuries, the trips abroad, and none of the uncertainties— forgive my frankness—none of the uncertainties of your mode of life. Your youth can't last forever. Your beauty is not eternal, and patrons, alas, vanish with the vanishing of these attractions."

"I shall never lose my youth and beauty," she said with sibylline gravity. "It is not in my star. No, thank you, Korff."

"I warn you it is suicide to go on this way."

"Who said a short life and a merry one?" she asked ironically.

"I'm powerless to do anything for you when you're in this rebellious mood, Mademoiselle," said Korff, shutting his bag.

"I'm afraid my mood is chronic like my disease," she said. "I am sorry if I hurt your professional feelings. You haven't any other kind, have you, Korff?"

When the door closed behind the doctor Alphonsine's defiance crumbled. She was worse, then. But she hadn't needed the doctor's confirmation for that knowledge. At twenty-one it kills. . . . You insist on committing suicide. At twenty-one . . . Suicide. The phrases played their counterpoint in her brain.

Since she knew so much, why not learn the very worst? She took up Franz's letter and snapped the seal.

"My love," she read. "Camille! Camille! Camille! Oh let me repeat the name over and over, a hundred, a thousand times! For the weeks I have been away it has possessed my heart, my mind, all of me. I have always before my eyes your exquisite mournful beauty beneath which, as under a silent sea, you hide the glow of a passionate sensuality the thought of which sets me on fire. Ah, for the ultimate bliss, eternity in your arms! All rapture, all torment, all, all of you, Camille, beloved!"

In joy and despair she burst into tears.

# 13. The Return

IF LOVE wasn't witchcraft then it must be insanity. What else could this fixation be on the one face, the one voice? Or was it a fanaticism of worship like that of the fakir who fixes his gaze upon the sun until its image is seared upon his eyeballs to the exclusion of all other objects?

Liszt desired yet rebelled against the tyranny of his obsession, which interposed itself between him and everything he did. At night, exhausted from the sapping concentration of the day, he found himself praying for respite from the thing he loved, only to be haunted by it in dreams of terrible reality wherein Camille and the lady of the Campo Santo whirled with him in a frenzied dance on a field of pianos whose keyboards became grinning deaths' jaws champing at their fleeing bodies.

His whole generation had been overshadowed by death, he reflected, as he glanced at the fields covered by a light shroud of snow on either side of the carriage that was taking him to Paris. Were they not all the offspring of a Europe which war of empire had turned to a graveyard? Eighteen eleven. That was his year, also the year of Napoleon's heir, engendered be-

tween wars and the innocent cause of greater wars to come.
The King of Rome had been born in Paris and he, the Emperor of the Piano, in an obscure Hungarian Village. Yet
both had seen hovering over their cradles the shadow of the
wings of Death, godmother to them and to their fellows.

What wonder then that they should all be more than half
in love with Death and with her handmaids, violence and
suffering? How else account for the general unrest, for the
outbreaks of bloody lust, the assassinations and the frantic
love of pleasure, to make them forget one day what they had
done the day before? How explain those novels of perverse
loves, the plays full of unholy desires wherein nature suffered earthquake and the mind lost its sovereignty? What
were these works of the imagination but the recurrent night-
mares of a generation conceived in darkness and terror on
the cold slabs of a tomb? Romanticism was the name they gave
to their spiritual rebellion and he, Liszt, was one of its leaders.

But the soul of the Romantics, like the soul of the damned,
also aspired to God. A hunger for the infinite, for love and
for brotherhood, kept it in constant torment. The hunger, Liszt
admitted, was more urgent than ever in him, yes, stronger even
than in those days when, a practicing Saint-Simonist, he had
struggled into the "fraternal" waistcoat of the society—a *gilet*
so made that it had to be buttoned in back by someone else as
a sign of the dependence of man upon his fellows. He had
worn other more or less symbolic hairshirts since then. They
had not mortified the desires of the flesh. Indeed, they had
pricked not only the body but the soul which, impatient of
the bones and sinews that encased it, sought through the

ecstasy of union to break through fleshly barriers and, in the ultimate embrace, arrive from the imperfect to perfection. Had he ever attained that perfection? In his youthful, almost virginal desire, he thought he had done so through Marie d'Agoult who, from the eminence of her greater experience, assured him that he need never seek elsewhere.

"Illusion! Illusion!" He contradicted the memory with such an impulse of the body that the copy of the *Revue Indépendante* which he had been reading, fell from his knees.

Marcel, from the seat opposite, leaned over to pick it up.

"Leave it there," said Liszt. "She has trampled on my soul with both feet. What worse could happen to me?"

"I told you not to read it, *cher maître*," said Marcel.

"That's only the beginning," said Liszt, not heeding. "How far will she go in her spite and hate? Hate, Marcel. That's what I can't understand. Hate from the woman to whom I gave the flower of my manhood, my very soul. My Beatrice, she used to call herself. Bah! It is the Dantes who make the Beatrices!"

Marcel said nothing but studied that face whose serenity was shattered by the internal storm. No wonder women lost their heads! It was the face of the century, expressing in its duality the spiritual and physical struggle that tormented them all. Marcel had been with Liszt for ten years and had seen life altering and refining the youthful sketch. The masterpiece was now achieved. With almost feminine interest Marcel lingered on the richly curved mouth and on the deep ridge which gave the upper lip a voluptuousness that had an overpowering effect when combined with the clear

blue pupils as darkly compelling as the hypnotic eyes of an
Italian. But the fire in them found its source in the creative
soul.

The brow reflected the soul's lambency as an alp will capture the glow of the sun consuming itself far below on the
horizon's edge. On the mind's altitude Liszt was an angel,
but below, at the subtle demarcation of personality, indicated
where the powerful, fierce-breathing nostrils could not take
in enough of life for his sensation-hungry being—what was
he? Neither demon nor monster but one of that extraordinary
order of men who made of their beings the battleground of
the Romantic conflict. He was a precursor of modern man,
living on that dangerous ledge between a world that had not
yet died and one that was being born.

Marcel wished that he could express his many thoughts to
Liszt. But what genius was ever helped on his headlong
course by the signposts in his way? It was remarkable how
blind Liszt could be about himself, and how helpless that
conqueror of a continent in the hands of the weakest of
women. This latest romance of his—how would it end? The
great artist and the great courtesan. As far as Marcel could
see Liszt was in love with Mademoiselle Duplessis. Passionately, though from all he could gather Liszt's love had not
come to fulfillment. Perhaps this very lack was the reason for
his being at such fever pitch that the Weimar women, coming
in contact with him, caught the erotic contagion and spent
their days reclining on sofas like so many languorous cats, or,
losing control, fell into swoons and hysteria. They blamed
everything on the master's music, but Marcel knew better.

His sense of order offended by the magazine at his feet, Marcel picked it up and laid it beside him.

"I think," said Liszt, "that I shall cut out the front page of *Nélida* and hang it over my bed as a *memento mori*. We die, everything dies, even the love we think eternal. Oh, I believed in that immortality, Marcel, and so did she in that first year."

"The old biological illusion, *cher maître*. The world would die of depopulation, if not for that."

"It is easy for you to say that. You have no interest in women. But a woman can be the sublimest influence in a man's life, the guiding genius—"

"But you've had so many of them, *cher maître*—the guiding geniuses, I mean. The trouble this time is that the genius has turned tables, and it hurts."

"Hurts! It's like being dissected while I'm still alive, with every quivering organ exposed on the marble slab. All the gamins of Paris will know my secrets now. Ah, these intellectual women! George and Chopin, Marie d'Agoult and Liszt! I sometimes wonder whether Goethe didn't show the supremest wisdom when he married ignorant little Christine, the girl of the people. How his Weimar mistresses must have chafed in their patrician spite!"

Liszt's introspective eyes wandered across the shrouded fields and returned to their brooding. "Tonight we shall be in Paris," he said. "I want you to buy everything in Madame Barjon's shop and fill the Duplessis house with flowers. I wish it to be spring there and in my heart."

The two men lapsed into silence. The master had been

deeply hurt, both as a man and in his love where he was most
vulnerable. So ended the brave romance of the century! In
the soiled pages of a magazine that would kindle the sticks
under the *pot-au-feu* of the Faubourg Saint-Antoine—the only
fire of an effulgence that Liszt once believed would enlighten
the world.

Alphonsine waited in an agony of suspense. How would
Franz find her after all these weeks? Did he still love her?
Would he now want her or had the princesses of Weimar
drained him of all desire? Would he still find her beautiful?
Would she see again in his smoldering gaze the passion for her
which he would not satisfy? Oh, he must not keep her in
torment. Not now that for the only time in her life she wanted
to be possessed, hurt, made to moan and cry out. If only she
could have come to him a virgin! She would have begged him
to rend and tear and do her violence that by the pain she could
pay for the intensity of her bliss and heaven would not be
jealous. But would not Franz be taking her virginity, the first
voluntary offering of her womanhood? The thought made her
head swim. She tottered toward the balcony and flung the
window wide.

The air sent a shudder through her but she remained in the
opening, enjoying the temporary relief from the fever that had
been boiling in her blood from the moment the flowers had
announced Franz's return. There they were, massed all over
her rooms, making May of December. But outside it was
winter. The death of the year lay gently, a feathering of white
on the black branches across the street. The flakes, like

drenched petals, were still falling, their candor glowing in the rosy halo of the lanterns. Apple and hawthorn drifting down, softening the wrought iron of the balcony and spreading a carpet on the street for the steps of her beloved.

If only she were that snow to be crushed under his tread! Body and soul, she longed to throw herself before him in an abasement of adoration and surrender. But would he want her tonight? Or would it be again a struggle between desire and denial, until their martyred bodies lay in a coma of frustration? She could not go through such hours of torment again. "Franz, you must take me tonight," she murmured, joining her hands unconsciously in pleading. "Tonight I want you, Franz."

The flakes caught on her lashes and melted on her lips. She took the moisture with her tongue and quivered as from a kiss. Oh, she was sick, sick with lovesickness, and only Franz could relieve her.

The cold on her lightly clad body brought on her cough. She crossed her hands over her bare breast to still its spasm but the fit grew more violent. Pushing the window closed with her shoulder she went to the bed and lay there till the racked body came to rest.

Franz's bed. From the day it came she had slept in it alone, pleading illness or putting off her admirers with other excuses, to the despair of Delphine, who saw the money drawer getting low. Alphonsine never worried about such matters. She would order whatever pleased her fancy and charge it with the charmed faith of a fairytale character that somehow it would be paid for.

The church clock struck twelve, the strokes muffled as if they too were smothered in snow. Twelve, the hour of magic when all wonderful things happened. Franz would soon be coming. Those might be his carriage wheels she heard. "Franz, dear Franz, I love you!" she said aloud. "Come! Don't torture me with waiting. I've waited so long, so long for you, Franz!"

As she spoke she was aware of a pain at her throat and realized that she had been tugging at the emerald locket that held her little cross. "Oh God, dear God," she prayed, clasping it tight. "Let this be my wedding night, dear God!" Her prayer had the ingenuousness of a child. "Dear God," she added, "don't let me die yet. Give me just one little year of Your eternity."

The clang of the bell brought her to her feet. She ran to the mirror, smoothed back the few stray wisps from her forehead and started at the look which met her from her own eyes, burning with desire in a countenance that might have decked an altar. Her gown, which hung from the shoulders, leaving bare the arms, back and bosom, fell to her feet in voluminous fine pleats of blue-green gauze that covered her like the ripples of the sea and revealed her body at every move as through a watery transparency. A band of rose coral clasped her beneath the breasts. Another band of coral and small iridescent shells weighted down the hem so that even in repose every curve came through in subtle sculpture.

Liszt burst like a tempest into the room. The door clattered and slammed in the sudden wind which also whirled her about toward him. He took a few hurried steps and stopped short, his traveling mantle furling to rest about him. She saw above the folds and the wide black collar a disembodied pale, pale face whose luminous eyes spread over it a bluish glow. She could not move, fixed to the spot by that gaze which drew the very soul out of her body.

How long did they stand there draining each other with their eyes? It might have been a moment, it might have been an hour until a simultaneous impulse hurled them together in a vehemence too great for even a cry. They clung to each other with their mouths, their bodies, their arms, their hands which curled and clawed and dug as if to pierce through the barrier of clothes and flesh. They swayed, impelled by their passion, and their souls, excruciated by their longing and now by their contact, exhaled themselves in sighs.

At length their mouths parted and he held her face between his hands, contemplating it like some treasure which after years of searching he had wrested out of the ground. But he could not sustain the look, not when her eyes, closed in desire, lifted their lids and from their depths flashed the imperativeness of her need.

The unspoken avowal thrilled him. She wanted him as he knew she had never wanted any other man. He crushed his lips fiercely against hers in a kiss that almost took her life with her breath. "At last, my love," he gasped. "It has happened at last! Oh, my Camille! Mine! Mine!"

She could not answer, she could not breathe for the grip of his arms about her, for that mouth like a burning thing fluttering on her brow, her throat, her breasts and the hollow between them where it came to quiescence as he released his embrace and sank on his knees before her.

"Come, my love," he murmured, sliding his hands in a slow caress along her body to her feet, bare and perfect in their gold ribbon sandals. She stroked his hair gently, then with a lingering look withdrew to her dressing room.

The sound of drawers being pulled, of crystal bottles clinking, the breath of perfume floating out to him like a promise brought him to his feet. He flung off his mantle, unwound his black silk stock and began to undress. One of his cuff links slipped out of his fingers and fell upon the carpet. At first he could not find it, but the lamp caught the gold and made it glint. He picked it up and the muscles of his cheeks began to throb. Marie d'Agoult had given him those cuff links long ago. To the careless observer they were two triangular baubles of gold, but they represented a mountain peak, with around them the posy, *"In alta solitudine."* He smiled bitterly at the irony of that lofty solitude now, thanks to *Nélida*, shared by a mocking Europe.

The unhappiness he thought he had dispelled descended upon him. Blankly he stared about him. What was he doing in this room, one of the countless bedrooms wherein, just as he was doing now, he had undressed for the human warmth of a lovely body, to forget—forget what? The disillusionment of the love he thought would last forever? But alas, even at the height of that love he had longed for some fulfillment he had never found. Or was it love itself he had sought in vain? All those women, Marie more than the rest, had given themselves because of the glamour of the public figure. How often, at the sexual ecstasy he aroused in some *grande dame,* he had bitterly asked himself: "What if I had been merely Ferencz Liszt, son of the manager of the Esterhazy estates?"

But he had sinned in the same fashion. Marie's position, as much as her beauty, had seduced him. Most of all, however, he had seduced himself by making her the source of his inspiration. Another delusion! How often had he fixed his imagination on some object, fancying he loved it, when he was really serving his art? Might he not be doing the same thing now with that lovely girl? She was coming to him for the love he had set out to arouse with the deliberateness of a general mapping out a campaign. Would he give her love in return, or would he be listening in the beat of their passion for the rhythms of the "Dance of Death?" Was it Camille he would be possessing or the lady of the Campo Santo?

Whichever of the two it was, tonight he wanted to be loved as a man. Marie's perfidy had wounded more than his heart and his pride. Her rejection had lessened him as a human being. He felt chilled and alone and in need of the comfort of a woman's breast. A courtesan's? The cynical query flashed. A virgin's, he answered it. There are greater virginities than that of the hymeneal veil. In all else Camille was untouched.

He threw off the rest of his clothes in a resurgence of desire and, parting the curtains, lay down upon the bed.

That was the way she saw him when she came into the room, and the sight first halted her step then rushed her to his side so that the flame whirred in the urn in her hand. She stood for a moment surveying his nakedness with ingenuous wonder. "How beautiful you are!" she cried. (So, thought

Liszt, must Psyche have gazed on Cupid—and a theme began pulsing in his brain. No! No! He must not think of his music tonight!)

Slowly she walked away and began blowing out the lamps one by one. As each flame died a curtain of intimacy enfolded the lovers, shutting out the world. Liszt watched her through half-closed lids as she glided about the room, her transparent gown first a nimbus then a shadow about the flame of her body. When she returned to the bed her urn, now the only light, left all in darkness but for her face and throat, where the green fire of a cluster of emeralds smoldered.

She laid the urn on her night table.

"Come, my love," he said tensely, reaching out to embrace her.

She stood hesitant between the curtains. "I—have to—I never sleep naked," she said.

"Come, my bride."

The huskiness of his voice roused her flesh like a hot breath as he undid the ribbons that held her gown at the shoulders. It rippled like water to her feet.

"Camille!" he breathed against her lips. "You are mine."

For a moment her hands struggled to unclasp her locket but she left it there as, with her lover's arms strongly about her, she sank, one with him, upon the bed. The urn flickered, flickered, then spurted into flame.

"Franz! My Franz!" she sighed in rapture.

# 14. Charitas—Love

WITH the pruriency of a spinster prying behind curtains, the Jockey Club had been following every move of Liszt's since his return, in expectation of the affair with the Duplessis which its senior members had been predicting. They were not prepared, however, for the flamboyance of its culmination, raised to the public view like a crimson banner. Everywhere the Duplessis and the master appeared together, their heads leaning toward each other in magnetic attraction, their lithe thighs touching and moving to the same rhythm. Whether at the theater or on the boulevards they had eyes only for each other. That absorption which enfolded them as in a cloud, and their extraordinary beauty, gave Paris the exaltation of a city miraculously visited by two immortals.

Korff went about rubbing his hands as from a personal triumph. "Genius and Beauty have returned to the earth," he would say to everyone he met. "What wonderful things will come of their conjunction! Marcel says the master has never been so productive. What fire! What music! At last the Duplessis has found one worthy of her."

Smiling his wry smile Ronceval listened and at first said nothing; he had his own opinion of the affair. One day he gave it in his column. "Is genius, too, subject to human failings? Is Duplessis the answer to *Nélida?*"

Édouard de Perrégaux wore his anguish on his face. His friends, pitying him, talked to him of everything but the cause of his torment. Like an outcast he prowled along the fringe of groups, hoping for some chance word which masculine loyalty would not have uttered in his presence. Like the rest, he, too, had seen the lovers in their entranced obliviousness, and once, in the lobby of the Comédie, he had sustained the long look of Alphonsine. But he knew that she had not seen him nor, for that matter, anyone or anything but the image of the man beside her.

Delphine alone unsealed her lips to the old key of bribery and told him everything from her vantage point. Her explicit accounts of Liszt's visits, of the time passed in the bedchamber, of the sights and sounds and other indices impressed on a vulgar mind pricked Édouard to jealousy while keeping him in a rage of lust. That was the ferment of his twenty-one years. But he also loved, and it was the force of his love that agonized him. Édouard was inexperienced, he was not brilliant nor even intelligent, and he had little imagination. But in his love of Alphonsine he had the inspired vision of the untaught shepherd who suddenly sees God and learns to sing in the voice of angels. Not that Édouard could utter anything but a stammer at the height of feeling, but his love had the exaltation of the inspired even though at its peak, as at this time of anguish, it remained mute.

What if Alphonsine had forgotten him? Had she not forgotten everyone else in her infatuation with the Hungarian
musician? She would grow tired of him too, or perhaps he
would grow tired of her—his fickleness was notorious—and
then she would awaken from her trance. and return to the
gay world of which she was the queen.

Meanwhile he, Édouard, would wait. He was young. They
were both young. In his moments of hope he imagined her
repentant and unhappy, leaning her head upon his shoulder
while he kissed away her tears. He saw her worn out from the
excesses of love and from her illness, that blessed illness which
had so often thrown her upon his comfort, and he would bring
her back to health and to himself. For he would be there, as
he had always been, from the first day when she had made
him the captive of her beauty.

But he would have loved her, he often told himself, if she
had had the face of some ugly wooden martyr in the cathedral.
Ah, but Alphonsine could never have been other than she was,
and everything that she was he adored, even the things about
her which made him suffer. Yet had not the others suffered
too? The Duc de Guiche, even Prince Stacklyn, whose
carriage only the other night he had seen turned away at
her door? She had always come back to him, Édouard, perhaps
because his love was greater than the pride which had weaned
away the others.

How sweet the reconciliations had been—the reunions,
rather, for though driven away by her he had never quarreled
with her. Always, except for this last time, she had atoned to
him with a thousand caresses in that old bed with the carved

angels. Why had she got rid of it? But he had bought it back, at twice the price, from the dealer to whom Delphine had sent it. He and Alphonsine would be happy in it again when she became his wife, for she must be his wife. Their children would be born in it and then, full of years, they would both die in it—he first, for he could not bear the thought of death for the loveliness of Alphonsine. Reality, however, differed from the dream and then Édouard would voice his misery to Korff.

"I did my best for you, dear boy, as you know," Korff consoled him, "and she seemed to listen to reason. But what can reason do against a force of nature like Monsieur Leets? The Duplessis is only human, though. She'll come out of it, and then I'll begin my campaign for you again, I promise. One has to tread lightly with a woman who thinks she's in love."

It was a tenuous hope but Édouard clung to it.

As for Alphonsine, she was like one no longer master of body or soul. She was wholly Franz's creature, possessed by him, motivated by the thought of him, living and breathing through him since the night when, in an unending embrace, he had welded her to him forever. Oh, she knew that *forever* was a fairytale word which wisdom smiled at, but she also knew that in the limited *forever* of her life Franz would be like the star they had seen together. "The star that never dies," he called it.

For the first time in her life that night she had been fulfilled as a woman. She had not even known that such ecstasy was possible, least of all for herself who had given but never experienced it in her own flesh. But the rapture had gone beyond blood and nerves, beyond the awakened flesh, beyond sense. It was her soul itself which Franz had taken and joined to his.

Perhaps it was all true then, what he had once said about the winged souls seeking each other. He told her so many wonderful things. Some of them she understood. Others left her in a dream through which she wandered after he had gone, making it impossible for her to go back to the ordinary things of life or to the people in it. One of his fancies, about the lady who looked like her in the old painting, frightened her. It was not good for anybody to look like someone else who had died. In fact it was even considered a bad omen to have one's portrait painted, since the soul might decide to leave the body to live in its likeness. That's why she had never wanted to be painted in spite of the artists who were always asking her to sit to them. But Franz insisted on having her portrait. "What shall I do when I have to leave you again? It will be for many months this time. Half a year, perhaps longer. At least I'll have your image, my Camille."

"You'll have me in your heart as I have you in mine, Franz."

"But my eyes will not have you. Would you cheat my eyes?" He had given her such an appealing look that she felt as if he had drawn her into himself.

"Before you leave I'll have my portrait painted," she said.

"You swear it?"

"By these eyes." She kissed him on both lids.

That had been a week ago and she was sorry she had promised. She hoped he would forget, but only last night he had reminded her. "I've asked Vidal," he said.

"Vidal? What for?"

"To paint you. Have you forgotten?"

"I was hoping *you* had."

"You're a strange girl! Other women would do anything . . . What are you afraid of?"

"They say it's bad luck," she faltered. "They say your soul might go into the picture. I don't want to die, Franz. Not now that I've found you."

At first he tried to laugh away her fears, but then he looked grave. "It's only a foolish superstition," he said. "There's even a belief that if you meet yourself in a dream it's a premonition of death. I've had that dream repeatedly. There are hundreds of portraits of me and I'm still alive. But if you don't wish to be painted—"

"Why don't you take me with you instead?" she broke in eagerly.

"With me? To Weimar?"

His shocked amazement did not escape her and she lowered her lids not to be hurt by what she might read in his expression.

"That's impossible, Camille," he added quickly. "You would hate it. You'd die of boredom among those stiff old ladies with their eternal coffee drinking, and the court etiquette—"

"Besides, I haven't a title," she said, her eyes still averted. She did not want to see that face in embarrassment, nor in humiliation, nor in any aspect that would make her remember him unworthily. "I am not a lady," she added. "Isn't that it, Franz?"

He was forced to meet her simple directness. "You would be

made most unhappy, dearest, and that I could not bear. There are conventions. I did not make them; I cannot violate them. There's too much at stake. My music—"

"And what about our love?"

"*Mon amour!*" He stood in front of her and took her face between his hands. "Look at me. Can't you see that our love is the thing I live for? What are those old duchesses to me? What is Weimar? What is even my music against our love which is music and life and—death if you should cease to love me?"

"Still, you would prefer it if I were a countess," she persisted. "I would be good enough then to go with Monsieur Leets to Weimar, wouldn't I?"

"Camille, dearest! I would be proud to take you just as you are, before Almighty God."

"Yes, but Almighty God is not so exclusive as the Grand Duke of Weimar. *He* admits into his kingdom the beggar and the courtesan."

"Camille!" He pressed her to him. "Don't cut me to the heart with your words! Would I willingly part with my life? Without you, dearest, I am nothing but a ghost. I live only through you, Camille. I love you."

His breath against her lips, his kisses coursing along her throat cast her into a wordless languor in which her senses floated, helpless. He could do anything with her then. Like the lapping of waves his words sent rippling thrills along her flesh.

"Oh, you don't know what you have done to me, Camille!" he went on. "You possess me body and soul. I sometimes wonder, are these not her eyes through which I gaze? Are these not her hands? The nights when you're not with me and I feel that I shall die I say, is it not Camille who winds the life spring of my being? Love me, *mon amour*! I am weary, weary from the storms of life. Let me find peace with you. I need it. My music needs it after the eruptions of my heart. They say our most beautiful mountains are extinct volcanos. Appease my heart to beauty, my Camille!"

Instead they appeased the turbulence of their senses, after which Franz sat for a long time at the piano improvising variations on their love theme which drowned her in another sensuous sea. For the moment Weimar was forgotten.

On leaving Camille's house that night Liszt met Korff just stepping out of his carriage. The doctor had only caught glimpses of the master on his rounds with the Duplessis, so he grasped his hand in effusive greeting. "Eros agrees with genius," he said, peering up at Liszt in the light. "What fire in that glance! What radiance!"

"It's only the street lamp," said Liszt, annoyed.

"Ungrateful!" retorted the other. "You would not minimize the virtues of our Venus? Though perhaps virtues is not the right word?"

"On the contrary it is exactly right," said Liszt with a crackle of anger in his voice, "although I would use it in the singular."

"A charming lesson in style, Monsieur Leets. Ah, so the *cher maître* has made that discovery! Then you must indeed be in love. She is an adorable creature—forgive my use of the word of the moment! adorable!" He kissed his fingers toward the balcony. "It is quite extraordinary that her, what shall I call it? her *métier* has not corrupted her heart, I might almost say, her innocence."

Innocence was the very quality which Liszt had discovered in Camille from the first. But somehow he did not wish to hear it mentioned, not at this moment when he was full of the exaltation of her embrace, nor by this man who looked like the embodiment of all the corruptions of the world. He was about to leave when he stopped short at the words that followed. "Be good to the poor girl, *cher maître*. You'll have your reward in heaven."

"What melodramas have you been seeing, Korff?" inquired Liszt, though he felt a sudden pang.

After a cautious glance upward at the balcony the little man came so close that his polished head, grotesquely magnified by the nearness, looked almost disembodied. "Our rose, I should say our camellia, has a fatal canker, *cher maître*. She does not know it, at least I have not told her the whole truth, but she is not long for this world."

Neither the artificiality of the words nor Korff's Hoffmann-like weirdness could turn the scene into nightmare. This was nothing, thought Liszt, from which reality could awaken him. He stared, fascinated, into the two greenish moons which the street lanterns made of Korff's dilated eyes, as the doctor went into detail in the technical jargon of medicine, tracing for him the history of that beautiful girl who was as much doomed as the victim of a judicial sentence awaiting the axe of the executioner. "How long? How long?" repeated Liszt in desperation.

"That's recorded in a book no human eyes can behold," said Korff. "Mercifully, perhaps," he added.

Liszt would have returned to Alphonsine but the doctor dissuaded him. "Your alarm would betray too much," he said. "Be good to the poor girl," he repeated. "Make her happy. It is the best medicine though, alas, no cure. Sometimes I wish our art were indeed a branch of sorcery as it was once believed to be. So much is still beyond us!"

In a havoc of emotions Liszt walked home, trying not to hear the sounds which, at the stress of strong feeling, made his head a tower jangling to a thousand bells. Camille under sentence of death! "Death," breathed the wind about him. "Death," whispered the folds of his mantle. "Death, Death," thudded his footsteps.

The square in front of the Madeleine was deserted but, as he passed by, he saw the shadows of lovers embracing in the dimness of the columned portico. Love, at least, was deathless. Like beauty. Like music. Lovers die, love lives on. But what solace was that to the desolated heart? Those shadows clinging together in such rapt oblivion cared as little for the future as for the past. They sought their joy in the living moment so soon to die, die, die!

With a groan he halted in his walk to change the insistent rhythm. Oh, how he cursed his music at such moments when he was possessed by a power stronger than his will! He took out a cigar and was about to light it when, as if solidified out of the darkness, a shape tugged at his cloak. In the flare of the light he saw the face of one of those women grown old in the city's depravity, who sought in alms what they had once obtained by their beauty.

"For God's sake, charity!" came a croak from that ruined mouth.

*Charitas*—love! The word and its association rose to the surface of Liszt's mind. "Charity, Monsieur!" implored the woman.

*Charitas.* Was love what she wanted? As a Christian could he have given it? The thought sent a chill through him. Fortunately what she wanted was easier to bestow.

At the feel of the banknote, not the coins she had expected, the woman's eyes glittered. *"Merci, merci, Monsieur!"* she mumbled, hurrying away as if afraid he would repent of his generosity. Something of the ethics of her old trade, perhaps a code of honesty among streetwalkers, made her turn back and ask: "Perhaps I could do something for Monsieur?"

He shook his head and fled, but no matter how he hurried his thoughts kept pace. *Charitas*-love. *Charitas*-love. The new rhythm now supplanted the dull beat of "Death. Death. Death."

"Liar! Hypocrite," he accused himself. If he had really believed in his ideals he would have picked up this crone and redeemed her through love. No, not redeemed her, for who was he to arrogate so much virtue to himself? "As long as you hope for my amendment you do not love the real me." Was not that another of the tenets of Romantic love? He would have taken her as she was, and by loving that unseen spark of the divine which is in every human being, he would have redeemed himself. That, perhaps, was the true meaning of *charitas.*

Instead, he had fallen in love with a woman whom every man desired. When he learned that the Duplessis's favors were for sale the little Christian in him had rejoiced. Ah, *charitas*—

love! In his self-deception he tried not to see how everything in him, sense and imagination, responded to the effect of Camille. Deep in his soul he delved for other motives for this love. Ah yes, it was to wound the *grande dame* Marie d'Agoult that he had taken up with a *femme entretenue*. But that reason had not seriously counted as he was not vengeful by nature; nor had his other motive, that the cupidity of the professional courtesan would disenchant him and harden him against the lure of women.

How different was reality! The sinner turned out to be an ingenuous girl with a fierce pride of self-respect. He had gone to her for moments of forgetfulness and she had given him love and such exaltation as he had never known. Most of all she gave him beauty which his thirsty soul absorbed like rain and sent forth again in the fruits of his genius. From the moment they had looked at each other in the Allée des Acacias she had come to live in his imagination side by side with the phantom he had loved and who inspired the music he was composing. Now Camille dispelled the woman of the Campo Santo. She was herself the marked prey of Death, and he loved her with passion and despair.

# 15. Julie and Alphonsine

HE LOVED her also for his music, and there, perhaps, she had the strongest hold over him. For the creative artist is only a transient in the world of men. He comes to it for the diurnal needs of the flesh, but his soul has its fixed abode in the realm of the imagination. It was to this realm that Liszt had admitted Alphonsine before he thought of her as a creature of flesh and blood, and because she lived in his creativeness she was never out of his thoughts.

Her presence was sun and rain to his music. Embryonic themes, long sleeping in the dark, sprang into living sound. Under her influence he finished his three "Sonnets from Petrarch," so long frustrated that he thought they would never come to life. The "Dance of Death" was taking final shape. But there was another, more personal, composition in a form he had not so far attempted and whose germination promised the flowering of his genius and his love.

It had its genesis in the love theme inspired by Camille. From those first eight notes other motifs were daily springing forth with the prodigality of a tropical growth. He heard them for the piano alone—it was to be his first piano concerto—

he listened to them in the tender plaintiveness of the strings. He imagined them in the sensuous woodwinds and in the foreboding clash of the brasses. One theme, light and elusive, like the flitting of the will-o'-the-wisp of illusion, he heard accented by the tinkle of the triangle.

That night, after his encounter with Korff, Liszt had wandered from room to room, wishing Marcel had not chosen this particular time for staying out. He needed someone to talk to. Yet what could he have expressed of that jangling within him? Ah, music, accursed gift! *"Du holde Kunst,"* another Franz had called it, but for him, Liszt, it was closer to demonic possession.

He would sit down at the piano, his hands would wander over the keys, but the musical phrases in his head warred in a contradictoriness that made him feel he was losing his mind. Then he would bolt up again and whirl about on the impulse of his obsession. "Camille! Camille!" he called through the silent rooms, and the music in his brain echoed the name in a thousand weird effects. Alphonsine was the restless spirit in his music, waiting for the incarnation of sound.

At one point that night he was tempted to return to her. He even put on his cloak and went out into the street. The paling sky told him it was nearly dawn. He must let the poor girl rest. He was destroying her, first by his torturing incitement and now by the exigence of his passion. But she became a flame whenever he touched her and there was no appeasement for their burning but the fusing of their fire till they lay as spent and as pale as ashes.

He flung his mantle on a chair and began to undress. He

too must have rest. Rest, sleep. Sleep the sister of Death. Death. Death. Again the thud of the rhythm that had pursued him through the streets. Again the clang and jangle in his head where all the tones he had ever heard clamored to be resolved to music. "God! God! Shall I never find peace?" Peace. Rest. Sleep. Sleep the sister of Death . . . Be good to the poor girl. Our camellia has a fatal canker. Death. Death. Death.

Half dressed as he was, he crashed out on the piano the opening chords of the *Dies Irae* which he had used with apocalyptic power in his "Dance of Death." The room became a bell reverberating to the tremendous sounds. They surged about him in waves, submerging him. He reeled back as if he were about to lose consciousness, then sat up rigid, his fingers still and stiff on the keys.

The overtones died down. In the hush his breath came in quick gasps. When it, too, had quieted down his fingers relaxed and, softly, scarcely touching the keys, played the motif of Camille and their love. Over and over, like her name which he would murmur, breath to breath, in all the accents of tenderness during their embraces, he played the theme of their love. But it was altered now. At the close, a single added note told of the sorrow of parting and loss.

He played the theme in an inertia of resignation. Then suddenly the piano thundered to a new and terrible motif: seven mocking chords, like a parody of the *Dies Irae*, a pause, and a final chord like a peal of satanic laughter.

Dawn, piercing through Alphonsine's bed curtains, startled her from a dream that drenched her in a cold sweat. Something, a vague shape of horror, was pursuing her through a gloomy forest through which she was running naked. Her hair tangled in the shrubs. Her body bled from the thorns that reached out to hold her in her flight from that dread shape which she heard only as a flurry of wings, growing louder and louder like an approaching wind. She dared not stop, she dared not look back, fearing the sight would kill her, but staggered on and on, knowing the thing was gaining upon her with every faltering step. Then suddenly she could not move as a chill breath turned her into ice.

The hands she held before her to blot out the dream were still numb with dread. Her brow was moist. When she sank back and pressed her cheek against the pillow she started up at the clammy contact.

"Julie! Julie!" she screamed.

On the snowy silk, drops of arterial blood, still moist, were scattered like the vivid petals of a poppy. There was no mistaking that brilliant red, life itself which was draining from her.

Julie stumbled in, still blinking from sleep. "Mademoiselle called?"

"Julie! Julie!" was all that she could say.

The girl ran to the bedside and saw the blood. "Oh, Mademoiselle, you've had a nosebleed," she said without alarm. "They say it's a sign of a good constitution. Too much sap and it has to find a way out. You'll feel all the better for it, Mademoiselle."

As she chatted she took the pillow and slipped off its case. The blood had seeped through to the satin beneath. "I'll get you a fresh pillow right away. They say if you put an iron key at the back of your neck it'll stop the blood. But you're not bleeding any more. Shall I bring you some coffee? A little cordial, maybe?"

Alphonsine caught at the girl's words with eager hope. Perhaps it had been a nosebleed. Undoubtedly that's what it was and her dream had made her think the worst. "Yes," she said, "yes, bring some rose cordial—and a glass for you, too, Julie."

"Ah, Mademoiselle is so kind! That'll be so nice!"

Deftly Julie slid a new pillow into a fresh case and patted it in place beside the one on which her mistress was lying. Mademoiselle was looking very pale, thought Julie, but kept the observation to herself. Maybe that's what love did to one. Certainly Mademoiselle was as much in love as any human being could be with that handsome Monsieur Leets who played the piano, and anyone could see that he was as greedy of her as a man after a ten days' hunger. But she mustn't let her mind wander off on such matters. They set her to thinking of Michel, and Michel made her long for things she would have to confess to the priest.

She returned with a decanter and two stemmed glasses on a tray which also held a dish of cookies. Alphonsine looked at Julie's firm, shapely feet under the folds of the heavy linen which shrouded every curve of that healthy young body, and then at the fresh face lighted up with excitement at the treat.

"Come, Julie, give me the tray and sit here," said Alphonsine patting the tufted coverlet.

"Oh, Mademoiselle, I can't," protested the girl, eager yet embarrassed.

"Very well, get in with me, then," said Alphonsine. "Come on, now, I'll hold the tray." Julie scrambled in like an awkward colt, her solid flesh making the bed sag.

"Watch out!" cried Alphonsine as the tray listed perilously, clinking the glasses together. Their laughter tinkled with the crystal sounds.

"Oh, it's *so* wonderful!" sighed Julie, passing her hands over the satin sheets. "I always wondered whenever I made the bed what it would feel like to lie on such shining sheets. Like solid water," she said.

"B-r-r-r! That would be ice," shuddered Alphonsine.

"Well, then, like sunny water," said Julie. "Shall I pour the liqueur, Mademoiselle?"

"No, I will, because I'm the hostess," said Alphonsine, like a little girl at a party. The nightmare was forgotten in the innocent intimacy that warmed her spirit as well as her body.

"Oh, how pretty!" exclaimed Julie as the pink cordial flowed in a thin stream into the glasses, filling their transparency like a rose opening into bloom before their eyes. "It smells just like roses, too. Do they make it from real flowers?"

"From the deep red ones. The petals," said Alphonsine.

"Oh!"

"Well? Aren't you going to drink?"

"It's so pretty! Your health, Mademoiselle!"

The conventional toast summoned a momentary shadow to Alphonsine's face. "Your happiness, Julie," she said with a wistful smile.

"And yours, Mademoiselle," replied Julie, touching to her lips the liqueur which was of the same color. "It tastes just like real roses," she marveled. Then, turning grave, "I have a sin to confess, Mademoiselle," she said.

"Just one, Julie? I have so many."

"Oh, no, Mademoiselle! You're as good—as good as bread," she said earnestly.

The words instantly evoked Alphonsine's childhood and the poverty and the vision of the yellow wheat in the fields, other people's fields, and the good smell of fresh bread on baking days in the village oven. She had had so little, even of bread! She tasted again the goodness of that slice, so eagerly awaited. She felt its warmth in her hands and smelled the thread of olive oil poured on it, the only luxury in the hard winters.

"Did I say something wrong, Mademoiselle?" asked Julie. "You look so sad! You're not worried about my sin? It's not a big sin, really, but I'll feel better after I confess. Do you remember the sugared violets one of the gentlemen sent you the first week I was here, and how quickly they disappeared and nobody knew how, because you didn't touch them? Well, I ate them. Little by little, like a mouse with a piece of cheese."

"I knew you ate them, Julie."

"You knew? And you didn't say anything? Well, you see I'm right. You're as good as bread. Oh, I was so terribly homesick, Mademoiselle! You can't imagine! That's why I ate them."

"I know, Julie. I was homesick, too, when I came to Paris,

even though I had nothing but misery to remember. But when the cobbles hurt my feet I was homesick for the grass, and when I was cold I thought of the summer fields."

Julie stared at her in wonder. Then Mademoiselle was not a grand lady? She knew about grass and fields. "Did you miss the violets too?" she asked. "They're the first flowers down our way, and I came to you in the spring—do you remember, Mademoiselle? Maybe if I had come in the summer those violets wouldn't have tempted me. Oh, you don't know what good they did me, even though I cried when I ate them. Of course, it was really because of Michel."

Alphonsine nodded. (As it was because of Franz that she searched the heavens for a particular star and was unhappy when she did not find it. Because of Franz that she cared for none of the pleasures which had meant so much to her. Because of Franz that she wore what she wore and drank a particular wine and used a special perfume. He had only to express a liking for something for her to love it and make it part of herself, so that he would turn that liking toward her. Did he love her in the same way? Do men ever love women the way women love them? Yes, yes! Franz loved her. During "those moments" he called her his soul, his music. He whispered beautiful, exalted things that she only half understood, or understood with her feelings rather than with her mind. "The fount of art is eternal. You will last in me as long as my music, and my music is immortal because it springs from the eternal fount." The words thrilled her and frightened her. The loveliest music died in the air. If he were a painter, no, a sculptor, that he might leave his art in marble!)

"They say some statues in the Louvre are thousands of years old," she mused aloud.

Julie threw back her head in ingenuous laughter. "Madame Delphine did say Mademoiselle has no head for wine!" she cried. "And you've hardly drunk any. Perhaps you had better eat some sweets?" She looked longingly at the cookies.

Alphonsine laughed with her and refilled the glasses. "Funny, the things that pass through one's head," she said. "I don't care for any," she indicated the cookies. "Help yourself."

Julie drank the sirupy liqueur and ate the cookies with the *gourmandise* of her healthy youth, while Alphonsine watched her, smiling. The girl's nearness soothed her. She felt like drawing closer to her and pressing her shivering self against that modestly shrouded body, so full of warmth, even through that voluminous linen. Julie, setting down the empty glass, leaned back with something like a purr and the lazy stretch of a satisfied kitten.

The clock struck six. "I feel so awfully drowsy," she sighed.

"It's much too early to get up," said Alphonsine. "There, just put the tray on the night stand. Good. Pull the bed curtains so that the sun won't shine through. Sleep, dear child. I'll wake you up when it's time."

"Aren't you going to sleep, too?" asked Julie.

"I'll try."

She lay back, rigid, gathering herself together against the very nearness that would have comforted her. Julie, out of politeness, tried to stay awake though her eyes refused to obey.

"Rosy dreams," she said softly.

When Alphonsine did not answer, "Are you asleep, Mademoiselle?" she whispered. She was conscious of a slight vibration from the other side of the bed and reached out to touch her companion. "Why, you're as cold as ice," she said, wide awake. "You're shivering."

With the naturalness of a mother toward an ailing child, she thrust one arm under Alphonsine's shoulders and enfolded her with the other. "Come, rest your head on my breast," she said, "and close your eyes tight. You'll soon be warm and sleeping like a baby."

It was Julie, however, who fell asleep.

Wide-eyed in the gentle dusk Alphonsine was lulled by the soft breathing of Julie, whose young breasts thrust hard yet yielding against her cheek. Some day they would suckle Michel's children and Julie would know all the joys of a wife, without ever questioning in her innocence what sort of woman Mademoiselle had been in whose house she had earned her dowry.

What sort of woman? At that moment Alphonsine knew only that she loved and that her future would never be like Julie's because she was Camille and Franz was Franz Liszt.

# 16. New Year's Day

SINCE early morning the bell had scarcely stopped ringing at Mademoiselle Duplessis's house. With her hair draped in a turban Delphine went bustling from room to room directing the messengers with their succession of *étrennes*. Never had she known such a New Year's Day as this of 1846, nor seen so many gifts. "You'd think everybody's a Rothschild the way they spend money," she said, feeling through the wrapping to guess at the contents.

"That looks like another *bonbonnière*," said Julie with delight.

"Yes, the hard, lasting kind, from the jeweler's," said Delphine. "In my day gentlemen were not so generous." She embraced with a sweep of her arm the packages on the tables, the chairs, on the floor and on top of the piano.

"Not even your friend the king, Madame Delphine?" asked Julie.

"He was as bad as the rest of them. On New Year's Day they all got tender consciences and thought of their families. Get along with you now, Julie, and see whether she's stirring yet. God knows how she manages to keep her strength with that man keeping her up till all hours of the morning."

"But Madame Delphine, are you sure I should go—?"

"Oh, I forgot. Well, they'll get up when they feel like it. I notice *he* didn't forget it was New Year's Day. Four gifts, from four different places—though I think he could have saved his money on that camellia plant. How does he expect it to live through the winter?"

"It's so beautiful, all full of blossoms! Look, I can almost stand under it," said Julie. "If I know the mistress, I think she will like it best of all."

"Yes, she's that impractical," snorted Delphine. "Thank God he has also sent her what's more substantial. Three boxes, from the best jewelers of Paris. Things that can be sold."

"But Mademoiselle would never sell the gifts from her intended!"

"Get along with you now, child. We're wasting time. Have the breakfast tray ready. Remember, two cups. Monsieur Leets likes his coffee black and bitter. There goes that bell again!"

In the bedroom Alphonsine heard it and started awake. Only a few inches away Franz's eyes were looking down into her face with a grave tenderness that moved her even more than his ardor. "How beautiful you are, my love," he murmured.

Her head was lying against his shoulder and his left arm still encircled her as when she had drifted quietly into sleep. She could hear his heart beating and thrilled at her closeness to the source of his life and strength and genius and love.

"You fill it all," he said, reading her thoughts.

To his endearments she had but one answer, a whispered

"Franz!"—the name that encompassed her whole existence. He felt her quivering under his look. At the slow fall of her lids, which in moments of love veiled with inciting modesty a fire that would have been too bold, he pressed her to him fiercely.

Outside a group of begging children had begun to shrill their demands for New Year's alms. They had the freedom of the streets on this one day and they clamored loud and long. Their singing and the drone of a hurdy-gurdy penetrated the bedroom as the sounds of the terrestrial world reach the depths of the sea. Vaguely the lovers, lulled in the languor of their appeased senses, listened for a long time to the noise before rousing themselves to its meaning.

Suddenly Alphonsine sat up. "Why, it's New Year's Day!" she cried with laughing excitement. "It's New Year's Day! I had completely forgotten!"

"Happy New Year, dearest," he said, kissing her on both cheeks. He was fond of using the English endearment, which strangely thrilled her. "The happiest year of your life." He held her face tenderly between his hands.

"Happy New Year, Franz," she echoed. "The happiest year of your life."

They gazed at each other mutely, as lovers will, in the trance and wonder of renewed discovery. "Could any day be happier than this day, Camille," he said at last, "waking up beside you, knowing you are mine, all mine?"

"And you, Franz? Are you all mine?" she asked, searching his eyes.

"Heart and soul, forever."

The dust of all lovers of bygone ages rose in an uneasy sigh which came through the shutters in the whisper of the January wind.

"That is not enough," said Camille.

"Not forever?"

"No, heart and soul."

"And body? But you have that, Camille. You possess it like a lasting hunger. You're in my blood."

She shook her head slowly. "That is not enough."

He was silent, uncomprehending.

"How can you leave me if you love me?" she inquired. "One little month together and then all of January you'll be away on another tour. Another month, perhaps two, and you'll be leaving me again."

"But, dearest, it's my career."

"I know, and it means more to you than our love, than Camille. I am jealous of your music, Franz. Franz! Why don't you take me with you?"

"You know I cannot, dearest. It is no life for you, the fatiguing journeys, the cold, the discomfort, the constant nervous activity—"

"And the titled ladies who would snub Mademoiselle Duplessis, your mistress, no, your kept woman!" The last words broke on a sob.

Liszt was helpless before her tears. "Camille, my love, my dearest!" he said, holding her close though she tried to struggle free. "I cannot bear to see you cry. Listen! It is impossible to take you with me next month, and the summer in Weimar would kill you with ennui. In the autumn, Camille—are you listening—in the autumn I shall plan a wonderful tour, the Mediterranean and then—it has been a dream of mine for years—Athens and Constantinople. You will come with me then, my love. Ah, you're smiling again. The black cloud is gone?"

"In the autumn, Franz?" she said wistfully.

"In October, when everything is dying here, we'll go where it is still spring."

She calculated on her fingers. "It will be ten months. Everything will be dying. Camille will be dying, too—without you," she added quickly. "Franz! Franz! Take me with you now! Let it be your New Year's gift to me, now that our love is young and we're young. Ten months is a long, long time when one is doomed to an early death. Oh, Franz! Why do we deceive each other? No, let me speak. Listen to me, Franz. I know I'll not last long. This life will kill me, if nothing else will. And yet I can't live in any other way. Take me with you, Franz!"

"Camille, dearest, calm yourself! We'll see. Perhaps it will be possible."

"Take me with you, I don't care where. I'll not show myself in public if it will embarrass you. I'll hide, I'll sleep during the day. In the evening I'll go to the theater, I'll come to your concerts in disguise, and at night I'll be yours to do with as you please. Franz! Franz! Don't leave me."

He whispered against her ear something that sounded like a promise. It was a faint ray of hope but it was enough to fill her with joy. When Delphine came in with the tray, for Julie was not allowed to bring it except when her mistress slept alone, she found them at the casement window, enjoying the antics of the singing boys to whom Franz had been throwing handfuls of coins.

"Happy New Year, Mademoiselle! Happy New Year, Monsieur!" she greeted them.

"Happy New Year! Happy New Year!" they responded.

"Happy New Year!" shouted the whole frenzied city.

In Liszt's carriage, loaded with candy boxes, dolls and toys, and with Dash in a holiday collar sitting proudly before them, the lovers started out for the neighborhood of Les Halles. Everybody was in the streets. Along the boulevards the late morning sun caught at the bright new finery of the little girls, escorted by trim governesses, on their dutiful visits to grandpapa and grandmama. Many of them carried posies with long streamers and gifts wrapped up in shining foil. Young beaux, uneasy in the handling of their first cane, walked with self-conscious dignity, their valets two steps behind carrying the packages to be left at the houses of attractive young ladies. The confectioners, jewelers and toymakers did a thriving business that day as the population of Paris, like files of ants come upon a grain bounty, scurried to and fro with their *étrennes*.

Bundled up in a sable cape and carrying a muff made festive by a bunch of red camellias, Alphonsine could not restrain her excitement. "Hurry! Hurry!" she cried to the coachman at each halt, unmindful that every coupé, hack and buggy in the city was whirling about the streets in a feverish haste that sometimes caused wheels to tangle and coachmen to swear. The words caught at Liszt's heart. "Hurry! Hurry!" as if she could not move fast enough to catch the fleeting pleasures. Her eager joy which communicated to her cheeks the vividness of this day's camellias cast a gloom over him. As if to steady her headlong pace he passed his arm about her shoulders.

The people were pouring out of the church of Saint Eustache. Some were carrying garlands of immortelles and paper flowers to place on the graves of those who had not lived to see the new year. Liszt followed Alphonsine's gaze to a small child from whose arm hung a wreath of ivy and fresh roses. Her yellow hair floating down her back from under her fur bonnet glistened in the sun. The wind had twined one curl round the rosette of black ribbon on her shoulder. The young man who held her by the hand wore a mourning band, but the still rebellious sorrow of his countenance told more than any symbol the greatness of his loss.

"She must have been very young," said Alphonsine.

Liszt pretended not to understand. "Who?"

"The child's mother."

They drove on in silence for a while, when suddenly Alphonsine flung her arms about his neck and covered his face with kisses, as she cried: "Franz! Franz!"

Soon they came to Les Halles. The noise and bustles of the hours after sunrise that turned the markets to a giant beehive had lasted well into this holiday morning. The stalls with every bounty had been replenished and still the white-capped *bonnes* and the *petite bourgeoise* came to fill basket and reticule from what the wholesale buyers had left. Near the poulterers' section Liszt ordered the coachman to halt.

"I'll be only a few minutes, dearest," he said to Alphonsine, but she insisted on accompanying him.

"You wouldn't know a tough old hen from a pullet," she laughed. "You can tell by their feet."

The coachman looked after them, shaking his head as he saw Mademoiselle's satin slippers picking their way through the litter of squashed fruit and greens dropped by the farm carts. Dash, even more excited than his mistress, strained at the leash. It needed Liszt's firm hand to tear him away from the smells that magnetized his nose at every inch of those wonderful paths. Everyone turned to look at such unusual visitants.

"Some crazy English milord," said one.

"Bless her sweet face, what a beautiful lady!"

"I'd carry her in my arms like a saint if she was mine," remarked a farm youth whose head was a cluster of reddish ringlets. He clasped his hands in frank admiration and the men who were with him nodded gravely.

Alphonsine flushed with pleasure and was glad Franz had heard. If only she could be a thousand times more beautiful that he might love her a thousand times more! Then perhaps he would find it a thousand times harder to leave her. The thought that gave her no peace cast a gloom over the moment.

They stood in a small cleared space surrounded by the reed and wicker cages whose occupants joined in such a symphony of clucking, quacking, crowing and honking that their own voices could scarcely be heard. As it was, they had already attracted the horde of poor children who had been prowling about the markets since daybreak for whatever charity the

New Year spirit threw their way. At first they had stared in awe, especially at the dog whose collar was shining with colored stones, but once the boldest let out the first yell the rest joined in with glee.

Alphonsine, on Franz's arm, walked appraisingly past the cages, taking her hand out of the muff to point at what she wanted. The dealer then loaded the cages onto a cart. "To the Fountain of the Innocents!" Liszt shouted when the cart groaned under its noisy freight. "To the Innocents!" he called to the coachman.

Led by the cart which several of the market men helped to pull and with the "milord" holding by the feet a brace of protesting capons for which there had been no cage room, the procession trooped joyfully toward Goujon's fountain. The carriage was already there and so was a welcoming crowd of the poor of the neighborhood who, with the uncanny sense of the needy, had learned of the unexpected blessing that was in store.

Never had Goujon's nymphs witnessed such a sight in the long years since the sculptor had surprised them in their magical grace and captured it for eternity. But who could heed their beauty now as scrawny arms reached for the bounty which the beautiful lady handed out from inside the carriage with a smile so sweet that even if she had given them nothing they would have gone away rewarded.

"Blessings on your sweet face," said the women, wiping their hands before touching the package which they then held at arm's length as too precious to touch their persons. Little girls snatched for their dolls but were so overwhelmed that they turned away speechless, not heeding the promptings to "Say thanks to the lovely lady."

From the steps of the fountain Liszt and the coachmen were distributing the fowls whose squawking roused Dash to competitive outcries. Liszt's gloves split. He ripped them off and threw them on the steps which a light snow of feathers had begun to cover. To his amazement nobody bothered to pick them up. Was it possible no one had recognized him? Once when he had dropped his handkerchief after a concert a group of women had torn it to shreds and disputed the pieces. But his vanity had no chance to brood as he went on, handling the live New Year's gifts with bare hands. Alphonsine saw and melted with love at those hands, those famous hands, those wonderful hands, so humbly employed.

As the carriage and the cages emptied the crowd thinned, the lucky hurrying off to their houses to make sure of their luck in a world where nothing is ever certain. The market men went back to Les Halles, Liszt and Dash joined Alphonsine in the carriage and the coachman jumped onto his seat. The bells of the church towers tolled noon, but as the strokes were not together they lent their own magic to the New Year by giving the mid-day seventeen hours.

The lovers exchanged happy glances, interpreting the phenomenon as something especially arranged for them. "What an auspicious omen!" cried Liszt. Unquestioning, Alphonsine agreed. From a special compartment built into the side of the carriage Liszt took out a bottle of *eau de cologne* and sprinkled a few drops on his hands. He then drew on a new pair of gloves from a supply in another drawer.

"To the Boulevard de la Madeleine," he told the coachman.

"Oh, not yet," said Alphonsine. "Let's go across the river to the *étudiants!*"

Down the Rue du Pont Neuf and onto the bridge galloped the horses. As they caught sight of the equestrian statue Liszt doffed his hat and with a flourish called out: "Happy New Year, Napoleon."

"But that's Henri Quatre!" laughed Alphonsine.

"Louis Philippe calls it Henri Quatre, but it's made from bronze statues of Napoleon."

"Why did they do that?" she inquired.

But before he could answer Alphonsine's interest was attracted by a *friturier's* stand farther up the bridge: "Stop! Stop!" she said eagerly. In the huge frying pan the bubbling fat was singing, making the golden potatoes whirl in a mad dance. "Franz," she said half abashed, "would it shock you if I had some? I'm so hungry suddenly."

The coachman got down, bought a *cornet* and handed it to Mademoiselle Duplessis. The curling slices sent up a tempting aroma from the paper horn mottled with grease. "Will you hold it a minute, Franz?"

While she was slipping off her gloves Liszt, staring at the paper bag, heard Ronceval's voice as on that day at the Jockey Club. "You should have seen the yearning in her eyes . . . for those sizzling potatoes. They were the impossible dream." Was Ronceval's story true, then? For a moment he had the impulse to throw the horn and its contents out of the window. The next he asked himself why. He was ashamed of the answer.

No, he was not a snob, he answered himself. This girl was a thousand times more a princess than those billowy matrons whose fat, beringed hands he had to kiss. She had more exquisite instincts, more pride than many a duchess. Violently he rejected Ronceval's picture of the miserable, ragged girl at the Pont Neuf.

"Thanks!"

Alphonsine took the *cornet* from him and began to nibble on one of the pieces. She took another, brought it to her lips, but threw it out of the window, together with the rest. "To think there was a time I thought them the most wonderful delicacies in the world," she said.

They drove on in silence, Liszt wishing she had not said that. It confirmed Ronceval's story and with it all the other stories. That girl with her tatters and her hungry look dispelled the woman of the Campo Santo and it was with the woman of the fresco that he was in love, the woman he had found after so many lifetimes.

"Why do you look at me like that, Franz?" she asked.

He started. "How was I looking at you?"

"As if you . . . Oh, I don't know. I was imagining it, I guess."

"Imagining what, dearest?"

"Ah, you call me dearest! Then I *was* imagining. For a moment I thought . . . I had a feeling you did not love me."

He had no chance to protest. At that instant the carriage was caught between two seething, roaring streams of students converging at Saint-Michel from the School of Medicine and the Sorbonne. They met and swirled about the carriage like contrary currents round a rock, bubbling, shouting, singing, dancing, at times carrying on a mock battle ending in grotesque embraces and resounding kisses on both cheeks. In vain the coachman snapped his whip. In vain he shouted his rich vocabulary at the horses. Even if they had had wings like Pegasus, they could not have flown past that crowd.

Meanwhile from the little halls along the boulevard happy couples still entwined in their dancing came out into the street, followed by the fiddlers scraping their bows with elbows high. The noise brought to the windows other students in the garrets of the tall, old narrow houses. They too joined in the singing and showered the dancers with flowers, bits of colored paper and even with the corks of the bottles they had early begun to empty.

All of a sudden the surge round the carriage stilled as at the wave of a wand. "La Duplessis!" someone shouted.

"La Duplessis! La Duplessis!"

Liszt, fearful for her, placed himself at the door.

"Monsieur Leets! It's Monsieur Leets!"

At first the two names came antiphonally. Then, "La Duplessis! La Duplessis!" sang the solid enthusiastic chorus.

Out of nowhere, it seemed, but really from a float of the École des Beaux Arts appeared a giant shell on the shoulders of four stalwart mermen in thick green tights. "La Duplessis! La Duplessis! La Duplessis!" sang the crowd with the rush of an ocean. "To the crowning! To the crowning! La Duplessis to the crowning!"

There was no denying that joyful invitation. After reassuring Liszt, Alphonsine stepped to the door of the carriage and flung it open. In an instant she was lifted onto the shell and carried amid cheers toward the fountain of Saint Michel, Liszt following in the carriage, and the students in a frenzied procession, still chanting the one name. It was a novel role for Liszt to be a spectator at another's triumph. "But then," he said to himself, "love is greater than art. Perhaps."

On the square before the fountain a throne had been set up under an arch of leaves and flowers. The living stream rushed to it, surrounded it, as Mademoiselle Duplessis was carried to it on the shell of the goddess of love and beauty. She had taken off her bonnet and her dark hair framed her face, aglow with excitement and joy.

A dozen arms lifted her from the shell and carried her to the throne where she flung off her wrap and appeared in her thin dress of frothy white. Liszt, at the carriage door, frowned with concern. It was so cold that his breath formed a mist in the air. He watched a youth in the mantle of Zeus sprinkle her with drops from a shallow antique cylix and then place a wreath of white roses on her head.

"Anadyomene is crowned!" chanted the classics school. "Rejoice! Rejoice! The Goddess of Love is crowned!"

"Anadyomene! Anadyomene! The Goddess of Love is crowned!" echoed the rest.

When they carried Mademoiselle Duplessis back to the carriage some minutes later, her face was as white as the roses in her hair but her eyes were burning.

"Happy New Year!" shouted the students through the carriage window as the coachman cracked his whip. "The happiest year of your life!"

# 17.  Command Performance

HOW SWIFTLY time flies when one is happy. Another fortnight, fourteen enchanted days and nights and then life would lose all wonder. During Franz's German tour in February she would be alone. How could she endure the month? She could see it crawling leadenly, stretching out longer than a year while she devoured her heart with jealousy. For she was jealous. For the first time in her life the Duplessis who could magnetize any man from the very couch of Venus tormented herself with visions of Franz in the arms of another woman. If only he would take her with him! She had even suggested the fantastic idea of cutting her hair and going with him as his page. "No one would know me in that disguise," she tried to convince him. "I am so slight, and I am growing thinner and thinner."

"A page? Am I Lord Byron?"

How lightly Franz had dismissed the plan for which she had even consulted Madame Elmyre! Instead of the page's costume about which Madame Elmyre had voiced voluble misgivings, Alphonsine had ordered a new gown, all Alençon lace, to receive Franz on his return—a romantic, billowing, beautiful dress trimmed with white satin rosebuds, an immaculate, fragile thing, almost like a wedding gown. Madame Elmyre had very nearly completed it but was waiting to put in the intricate finishing touches until she had given the last fitting to the Comtesse d'Agoult.

Alphonsine had not yet relinquished the hope that Franz might change his mind and take her with him after all. Was he not constantly telling her that he could not live without her? That he needed her not only for his happiness but for his art? What wonderful things he was composing! Several times he had taken her to his studio. Out of the shallow drawers of the music cabinet he had taken sheets and sheets of paper covered with clusters of notes, like black grapes on a trellis.

"That's exactly what they look like," she had said and, smiling, he answered: "Yes, Camille, for the wine of the soul. You and I, my love, are the grapes. We are here and here and here." And then he had gone to the piano and played the new things he had added to his compositions. But each time she had been distracted by the crest inlaid in gold in each of the twelve drawers of the cabinet. She had counted them and each repetition of the motif had given her a jealous pang. Whose gift was the cabinet? She did not ask him so that she would not be hurt by the answer. Would he be seeing that duchess or countess or Fürstin, whatever they called titled ladies in German? Ah, to have been born Mademoiselle la Comtesse du Plessis! Then Franz would not have hesitated to show her anywhere.

She looked for the tenth time at the clock. Twice within

the past week Franz had been late, only a half hour but it was half an eternity to her impatience. She had sat waiting as she was waiting now, listening for the bell, but whenever it rang it had been someone she did not want to receive.

"You will ruin yourself, Mademoiselle," Delphine had warned the third time Alphonsine had refused to see Prince Stacklyn. "Do you think your funds are inexhaustible? The poor prince! If you don't take pity on your pocketbook you should at least have some feeling for the poor old man, sending him away like a beggar. No, not like a beggar—you've always had a soft heart. Like a leper, that's it. Well, the only kind of leprosy he's got is money and God knows I don't care if it's catching."

The doorbell! Franz was here at last! Dash, dozing at her feet, shook himself in anticipation. Jumping up from her chair Alphonsine stood in front of the long mirror. She was glad she had on the gown he liked most, the sea-green with the border of corals—"*il velo greco*," he called it in Italian, because of that lady in the Pisa painting, she had no doubt.

Again the bell. Ah, no! No one must trouble her last few meetings with Franz. "Send them away! Send everyone away!" she called to Delphine.

It was not Franz but Marcel Arnaud whom Delphine admitted.

"Monsieur Leets sends his regrets, Mademoiselle Duplessis," he said, bowing.

"Oh? Do sit down, Monsieur Arnaud." Her voice was trembling.

"I cannot, Mademoiselle, forgive me! I've only time to tell

you the news and then I must be off at once to arrange the
master's effects. He's leaving immediately—"

"He's leaving?" she gasped.

"A command performance for His Majesty the King of
Prussia. The inauguration of the new concert hall, Mademoiselle, the end of this month."

"Ah, then I shall not be seeing him? Not even to say
good-by?"

"How thoughtless of me, Mademoiselle, forgive me! I
should have told you in the first place—Monsieur Leets begs
that you will receive him, but it cannot be till after midnight."

"It is now seven. Five long hours!"

He knew she was not talking to him. When he left she
scarcely acknowledged his farewell. She was still deep in her
brooding when Delphine rushed into the room.

"Mademoiselle! Monsieur le Vicomte de Perrégaux with
great news! He can't wait to tell you, he's so excited. You've
simply got to see the poor lad. Why, he's down to skin and
bones!"

Alphonsine stared at her without saying a word. Delphine
interpreted the silence as consent and opened the door for
Édouard. Annoyance at seeing him roused Alphonsine and a
frown gathered on her forehead. Then she smiled a bitter
little smile. Always Édouard. She longed for word from Franz
and she got a note from Édouard. She opened an unexpected
gift and it was from Édouard. Her heart would leap when she
heard the bell. It was not Franz who came but Édouard.
Exasperation brought angry words to her lips. But at the pleading in those pale, lost eyes and his dumb adoration as he

kissed her hands she said instead: "So it's you, Édouard. You must have quite a hold on Delphine to—ah, well, I'm glad to see you, anyway."

It was hardly a warm greeting but to the youth it was boon enough that he had not been turned away. "Are you, dearest? Really glad?" he said. "It's been so—so long this time, so very long!"

She drew her hands away and motioned him to a chair. "Don't call me *dearest*," she said. It was Franz's word. Édouard had no right to it.

"But you are my dearest," he protested. "Yet perhaps it's —it's really not the right word since you are my *only* one."

Alphonsine started. She had never thought of that implication. Did Franz perhaps call her *dearest* with reference to others who were less dear? "Your English seems to be improving," she said.

"I've been working hard at it," he said, unmindful of the irony. "I've had plenty of time for it, Lord knows! But—but I nearly forgot, you so turn my head. I've my London appointment at—at last!"

"At the Embassy? Well! Felicitations!"

"You—you don't seem to understand. Don't you know what it means? You can go with me to—to London. We can be— we can be married quietly there and without any trouble. I've looked up the laws—"

"You're insane!" She flung out her hand impatiently and struck the jewel tree on the table beside her. Franz's jewel tree with the singing bird. No, she must not be cruel again to Édouard. "Please forgive me," she said. "I've been so irritable these days! My health, that bad cold that's been hanging on since New Year's."

"I know. I've seen the light at—at your window burning all night, night after night."

Then he must have seen Franz and Franz's carriage. "And you still want to marry me, Édouard?"

He was grateful for the restored gentleness in her tone. "It's—it's the one goal in my—my life, *chère âme!*"

Though his broken speech betrayed his emotion she saw what she had detected once before, a mastery over himself which kept him in his chair instead of flinging him at her feet in adolescent abandon. And she—what did she want? Toward what goal had she set her life? At this moment what she longed for most was to hear Édouard's words from the lips of Franz. The impossible goal. Why was not Édouard Franz, and Franz Édouard?

"We could be so happy!" he was saying. "No one would know—know anything about it. But what does it all matter? People wouldn't d-dare ask questions. Not about the Comtesse de Perrégaux, wife—how beautiful it sounds!—wife of the new envoy. Besides, they say the English are different."

"You are so good, Édouard, and so generous," she said. "I'm sorry it's impossible."

He was about to leap out of his chair but gripped its arms and said with extraordinary control: "You have time to consider, dearest—I mean—my love. I do not go to London till the end of this month. I—I've waited so long, I can wait a few days longer. Only re-remember, I—I want you more than anything in my life."

He left quietly without any of the old "scenes" and simply kissed her hand. But he kissed it so fervently that a mark, like a red petal, remained on the back of it. She herself was completely shaken.

That evening she left untouched the dinner from the Maison Dorée which she had ordered for herself and Franz, and munched only some biscuits dipped in wine which Delphine pressed her to eat. How the moments dragged! She wandered aimlessly through the apartment, picking up some object only to set it down, sinking into a chair only to start up a moment later. At the embrasure of the dining-room window she stood for a while plucking the curling leaves from Franz's New Year's camellia. Many new blossoms had burst into bloom in the almost tropical heat which she maintained to keep the plant alive, and it cheered her to count them. Then listlessly she began to pick them and scatter their petals on the carpet.

Delphine, watching her, lifted her brows and shrugged. For her part she would be glad to see the last of Monsieur Leets. "That man is killing her, as sure as if he did it with a knife like an apache," she muttered to Julie, who widened her eyes and crossed herself.

At eleven Alphonsine bathed and began to dress herself again. She had spilled some wine on the gown Franz liked, but she had others, so many others. She must make herself beautiful. Carefully she selected what she was going to wear: the long, transparent silk stockings, the garters with the ruby clusters, and then the flounced petticoats, three of them for fulness. No stays—she needed none—and only the flimsiest of camisoles which did not succeed in veiling the rosy centers of her breasts. Ordinarily she did not wear as much as that, but Franz loved to help her undress. "Like coming to the heart of the rose, petal by petal," he said. Oh, she would give him such rapture tonight that he would never want to leave her!

The church clock struck, remote and melancholy. It always made her sad, like the tolling for a death. In that neighborhood of genteel houses the rhythm of life was so different from her own! Behind those carved doorways everyone went early to sleep and the noise of wheels that roused the quiet street was almost always for her. She listened in vain for wheels now. But she remembered that Franz was to come after midnight.

*Mon Dieu,* that might mean another hour of waiting, two hours! The thought set her moving about again feverishly. Ah, Franz did not love her as she loved him. It was impossible, a thousand times impossible. How often had she said those words to him in perverse self-torturing, for the thrill of his instant reassurance: "It is ten thousand times possible, my Camille. I love you, love you, love you, my life, my music."

How jealous she was of that word! It was because of his music that he was leaving her now. It was his music that was stealing from them two weeks of happiness, two weeks of life. She knew it was because of his music too that he was not taking her with him. His Majesty the King might be scandalized. The fine ladies of the court might be shocked. Édouard didn't care a fig for what the world thought, and he had a name a thousand years old. If only Franz had been Édouard! Or if only she loved Édouard as she loved Franz! But that was impossible, ten thousand times impossible, and for that assertion she needed no denial.

It was past one o'clock when Franz arrived. He found her so listless that instead of clasping her he took her hands to kiss. She pulled them away. "What is it, Camille? Are you ill?" he asked, startled. "You shouldn't have waited up for me, dearest. It's all my fault . . . you've had so little sleep!"

"Don't call me *dearest*!" She caught at the word to release upon it the turbulence that had been gathering in her mind. "I hate that name!"

"Camille, my love! What has come over you? I do not know you. Is it because I am late? I could not come sooner, there was so much to do. We leave at two—"

"We, Franz? Franz! Then you're taking me with you?" She wound her arms about his neck and began covering his face with frantic little kisses like a child who had been punished and now was forgiven. "I knew you would!" she said. "I knew you could not leave me! Franz! Franz!"

He waited for her excitement to spend itself, not daring to contradict her, and tried to soothe her with the small words of love. But how could he take her with him? From the first the papers had hastened to spread the particulars of his new liaison all over Germany, which had not yet recovered from the staggering Bonn scandal. Camille, certainly, was not Lola Montez. She would never have used his name to force herself into a solemn banquet commemorating Beethoven, and dance a fandango on the table. Even now he shuddered at the memory. Camille was an angel of goodness. Had she also been angelically sexless he might have taken her with him. But she was a woman, and too well known, and so much was at stake for his music!

"Camille, my adorable Camille," he murmured, pressing her face against his so that he would not see her tears. "Listen to me! Try to understand. I cannot take you with me this time. It's impossible."

"Oh, but you said—" Her voice caught and she could not go on.

"I meant Marcel and myself, *mon amour*. He's coming with me. Please don't, Camille! I can't bear it! It destroys me to hear you sob! I beg you, dear, dear child! I'll soon be back. Before you'll have a chance to miss me I'll be here. February is such a short month."

"It's a long, long month. Six weeks long with these two you're stealing from us. Oh, Franz! How can you leave . . . now . . . when we so need our love! You called me your life. Franz, Franz! You *are* my life and you're leaving me."

"Only for a little while. Look, Camille—come with me." Half supporting her he led her to the window. "Those trees out there, dearest—yes, I will call you dearest. They're cold and barren, as I shall be, away from you. But they're only waiting, as I shall be waiting, to come to life again. Before you see the first leaves I shall be by your side."

She looked obediently at the branches, turned to meet his eyes and nodded sadly.

"The spring will be ours, Camille, and then our wonderful autumn."

"After Weimar. If you ever come back from Weimar," she said tonelessly.

"Camille! Camille!" He took her by the shoulders and held her firmly. "How can I have any peace if I leave you in this mood? You make me feel as if we were parting forever."

"Oh! Then you're leaving me now? At once?" she asked in a wisp of a voice. "Oh, Franz, I thought—"

"Didn't Marcel tell you? We have a change of horses waiting at the border in three hours. One makes better time at night."

"Better time! And I'd give a year to keep you a minute longer!"

The huskiness in her voice excited him. Crushing her to him he carried her to the bed and kissed her till she cried for mercy. Suddenly he tore himself away and rose, running his fingers through his hair and tossing his head as if to free it of its storm. He then bent to her again and kissed her gently on the brow and eyes. "Good-by, Camille, good-by, my dearest," he said. "Love me as I love you, till we meet again."

He strode rapidly to the door and went out. She listened to the clatter of the horses' hoofs till it died down in the night. She did not trouble to wipe away her tears.

# 18.  Appointment in London

FOR over a week the Jockey Club had been speculating on the sudden departure of Liszt, refusing to accept the simple explanation of Korff.

"I tell you I got it from the Duplessis herself—a command performance for the opening of the new concert hall. You can't refuse a king, you know."

"I would refuse the emperor of the universe for just one night with the Duplessis!" cried a youth who had been sighing in vain.

"You would because you've been adoring the goddess from afar," said Ronceval. "But after you enter the temple, my boy, the wonder and the mystery are gone—and the *cher maître* has worshiped at many shrines. You could tell us much on the subject, Korff. The sacred fire is going out and the *cher maître* must keep the lamp of his genius burning."

"How wrong you are, Ronceval!" said Korff, pausing dramatically to be coaxed.

"Well? Isn't it true that his fervor is waning?"

"Bah! If you want the truth, gentlemen . . ." He became the great Talma in one of the actor's eloquent suspensions.

"If you want the truth, I'm glad Monsieur Leets is going away. What was it Lord Byron said? The sword outwears the sheath and the heart wears out the breast. . . . Yes, I'm glad he's giving my fair client a rest. He was consuming her with his fire."

"Aha!" mocked Ronceval. "The fiery Zeus and the unfortunate Semele. Then you expect to be sweeping up her ashes? I must say the Duplessis is burning her candle at both ends. The Opéra one night, the Ambigu the next—"

"But by herself, Ronceval. Her bed remains as chaste as any faithful wife's. . . . She loves him, the foolish girl, and that's always unfortunate."

"By herself, you said? Are you so sure, Korff?" inquired Ronceval. "Where's Perrégaux?" He looked about with a triumphant smile. "Has anyone seen our young chevalier? No? How extraordinary that the most faithful member of the Jockey Club shouldn't put in an appearance for days! Well, gentlemen, I've seen him in the blue coupé and he was not alone."

The effect of Ronceval's words sent a tint of verdigris over Korff's face. "That's impossible!" he sputtered. "I'd be the first to know it. In fact I'd encourage the Duplessis's friendship with the young vicomte. I've been trying to bring them together again for weeks. But after the absinthe of the *cher maître* Perrégaux is like *eau sucrée*. There are a dozen blue coupés in Paris, Ronceval."

"But only one with an English greyhound."

"Oh, it was Dash you saw with Perrégaux, then. Probably the count was taking him to the dog stylist for grooming."

Ronceval smiled ambiguously.

Korff wasted no time. His reputation as the chief purveyor of news of the *beau monde* was at stake. Besides, if the Perrégaux-Duplessis friendship was on again, there might be something to be gained from one side or the other. Hailing a fiacre he hastened to Perrégaux's rooms. The young master, said the valet, had gone to the British Embassy. Astounded at this development which somehow had eluded him, Korff directed the hack thither, but the Embassy, alas, had just closed for the midday respite. Off he went to the Boulevard de la Madeleine.

In front of the door he found Madame Elmyre's carriage from which her assistants were taking out a *corbeille* heaped high with feminine luxury. Agile as a cat, Korff leaped past and ahead of them into the house. In the dining room he was amazed to find Perrégaux at luncheon with the Duplessis. She was dressed as if she had just returned from a drive, and Perrégaux was in the fashionable young gentleman's morning attire. Obviously, therefore, he had not spent the night there.

"I had no—no difficulty whatsoever," Perrégaux was saying, "and they assured me we—we wouldn't have any either when we go there." His voice had an unaccustomed ring. "A few days in the capital and then—then we'll—"

Alphonsine, seeing the doctor, touched Perrégaux's hand lightly and said: "Why, if it isn't our Korff! What brings you here? This is not your day, is it? I've been in such a whirl I hardly know. *Mon Dieu!* Here's Madame Elmyre too! Édouard, you'll be an angel and excuse me, won't you? The doctor will drink a glass with you? I'll see you tonight, then, for the theater."

Édouard got up, kissed her hand and opened the door to the inner rooms. Madame Elmyre went in, followed by her handmaidens. "I'm sorry I can't see you today, Korff," called Alphonsine from behind the door. "I'm feeling well, very well. In fact I've never felt better." She sounded almost defiant.

Korff looked as if the stable world were teetering about him. Perrégaux beaming and almost manly, the usually docile Duplessis sending him packing without ceremony. And that strange levity in her manner!

"What's been happening behind my back, Perrégaux?" he asked, waving away the wine. "No thanks. Give your old friend a little elucidation instead. What capital were you talking about? And what were you doing at the British Embassy? As your adviser I have a right—"

"The British Embassy?" repeated Perrégaux innocently.

"Your valet told me I'd find you there."

"Oh, that! I'd forgotten. It's that—that old post for which I was being considered. I have it now."

"Well! Well! The capital is London, then? And you're taking the Duplessis with you? You said *we*, if I'm not mistaken."

"Oh, yes—I meant—I meant myself and my valet. A few days in the capital and we—we shouldn't have any trouble— with our English. I did very well at the Embassy. No trouble —no—no trouble whatsoever." Korff's puppet stare dismayed him. "No trouble whatsoever," he repeated lamely.

"Any news of the *cher maître*? I didn't have a chance to ask Mademoiselle."

"She hears from him almost every—every day," said Perré-gaux.

"Letters?"

"I guess so."

"You don't see them?"

"I don't—I don't read other people's correspondence," he said. "I know only what I'm told."

"Ah, well, forgive me. I must be off. The sick like the poor are always with us. Let's see—who's next in my little book? Ah, la Comtesse de L——. A slight case of non-conjugal pregnancy. I've a fiacre waiting. Perhaps I can take you some-where?"

They left together.

In the dressing room Madame Elmyre was kneeling before Alphonsine. "Ah, Mademoiselle! You'd bring down the very saints from heaven!" she gasped. "It's beautiful enough to be a wedding dress. So simple, and such workmanship! Every rosebud is a work of art, but I must say that you set it off to perfection. There's just one thing, Mademoiselle, if I may say so—a trifle. I would suggest a touch of color here and there. A few pink rosebuds?"

"No, Madame Elmyre. Leave it all in white."

"It's only a feeling I have, I'm sure a foolish one. I always think unrelieved white is either for a wedding or for a burial —that is, if the girl is a virgin. Otherwise, a touch of color. But as Mademoiselle desires. Does it meet your pleasure?"

"You are an artist, Madame Elmyre."

"That's just what the White Blackbird said, only yesterday."

"You were at Madame d'Agoult's yesterday, too?" Alphonsine asked quickly.

"She's not like you, Mademoiselle. With her it's always change this and do that. But then she no longer has her youth, nor her figure—not that she ever had anything to comfort a man. Saint Joseph certainly went over her chest with his plane, though you'd never know it to see her in one of my gowns."

"Were there any interesting people?" Alphonsine sounded casual. "Like that lady from Germany?"

"Oh, that one's staying with her, I found, for yesterday there she was in a dressing gown and her hair done up in papers. She'd had a letter from her husband, a Graf or Grave or something like that. You know those German titles—and there was more in it about Monsieur Leets. *Mon Dieu!* What's this?" she cried aghast, inspecting nearsightedly a tiny imperfection. "A double thread in the weave, oh, dear, and we didn't see it! Look, Mademoiselle. Oh, these weavers nowadays! They'd do much better to stick to their looms instead of striking. Thank goodness we can hide it by bringing that flower down a little."

"Yes?" said Alphonsine weakly. "What did it say?"

"Oh, the letter, Mademoiselle? The same thing I told you the other day about Monsieur Leets and the Forestine, only more detailed. It almost made the White Blackbird turn black, especially the part where it said this Forestine is very beautiful. She's some sort of kin to the king, at least that's what I gather Forestine means."

"It's Fürstin, Madame Elmyre, Fürstin. I've got to sit down. I can't breathe, this bodice is so tight!"

"Well, Fürstin or Forestine, it's all the same to me. Tight, Mademoiselle? Impossible! There, see!" She thrust several plump fingers down the front opening. "I can almost put my whole hand in. *Mon Dieu,* how you're panting! If you're tired, Mademoiselle, I can come back tomorrow."

"No, no, I'll be all right in a minute. Besides, I must have that dress at once. I'm sorry I interrupted. You were saying —?"

"Oh, yes, about the Forestine. She goes with Monsieur Leets everywhere so that it's a great scandal. The worst of it is she has a husband, and everybody's afraid, the king's afraid, she may desert the nest and fly off with her lovebird. But this isn't what infuriated our lady. Is she a Forestine? A real Forestine? she kept on asking. As if that was the most important thing about it!"

"Madame Elmyre, you must forgive me," said Alphonsine. "I—I feel so faint. It's this bodice, I tell you. It's like a straitjacket. I've got to lie down."

While Madame Elmyre was adding the final touches to the gown, Alphonsine, in the bedroom, was possessed by the nervous unrest which made her as helpless as a leaf in the wind. In her petticoat and with only a light fichu over her shoulders, she was flung by that inner compulsion from the chair to the bed, from the bed to the dressing table, from the dressing table upon her knees at the *prie-dieu.*

"*Aidez-moi, O Seigneur!* God, O God help me," she prayed in an urgent undertone. Then again she rose and moved about, a caged bird beating against her invisible cage. "*Aidez-moi, O Seigneur! Aidez-moi!*"

Suddenly she opened a drawer of her escritoire, took out a crumpled paper and smoothed it out with shaking hands. The writing was large and spaced; the few sentences filled the page. She read them aloud word for word. "Camille, my dearest, do my thoughts reach you? Do you feel my longing? When, oh when shall our breath mingle in those kisses which alone give me life? Do you look for our star? I saw it just now over the spire of the great cathedral, and the house of God became the monument to our love. Love me, Camille, as your Franz loves you."

It was the only note she had received. It had come that morning, after days of doubt and anguish. She could not make out any date, but the frank mark showed it was from Germany. Where was the great cathedral? In what city? Was he alone, or had he stolen a moment from the beautiful Fürstin to look at their star?

"Franz! Franz! *Aidez-moi, Seigneur!*"

How could God help her up there in His heaven amid the noise of the prayers of the world? "Franz! Hear me, Franz! I love you. No one has ever loved you as I love you. I know you love me. But she is beautiful and she is with you, so she is stronger than your Camille. Oh, if you could only hear me, Franz! I would tell you that even now, even now I would say *no* to Édouard though it broke his heart. I think some hearts are made to be broken. His and mine, Franz!"

For a long time she remained kneeling at the *prie-dieu* unaware that it was Franz whom she had been addressing.

"Mademoiselle, it is finished!" fluted Madame Elmyre at the door. Alphonsine rose and went to open.

Madame Elmyre strode in majestically, followed by her girls and her turbaned Blackamoor who was wheeling in the lay figure vested in the new gown. Madame motioned him toward the window. Obediently he set it against the background of the hangings and the girls arranged themselves on either side in adoration of this new marvel of Madame Elmyre's.

"See, Mademoiselle, the ugly thread is concealed. It is a genuine work of art and I challenge all the Forestines in Germany to wear it with the grace of the Duplessis!"

"Thank you, Madame Elmyre." Alphonsine's eyes had a fleeting sparkle. "It is indeed very beautiful."

"You hear that, girls?" Madame Elmyre surveyed her worshipful handmaidens. "This comes from the queen of fashion of our *belle France!*"

All that was needed was a fanfare. The Blackamoor provided it with hoots of delight that revealed the even ivory of his teeth.

Alone again Alphonsine sat down at the piano but she did not play. It was enough for her to touch what Franz had touched to conjure him up. *"Seigneur! Seigneur!"* She twisted her fingers nervously.

What was she doing to all their lives? What if Franz should never return? Ah, but Franz would come back. He could not leave her because he loved her. With all her experience in the ways of men she knew he loved her. The Fürstin? Only another of those women who threw themselves at him and the flattery of whose title he could not resist. But perhaps he had known the Fürstin was waiting for him. Perhaps he had even arranged their reunion. He had behaved so strangely the night he left, tearing himself away with his, "I mustn't! I mustn't!" Was it because of the eager Fürstin?

She let her hands fall on the keys in a rumbling discord and left the piano. She would keep her promise to Édouard no matter what happened. "*Seigneur! Seigneur!* Let the days pass quickly!" It was this dragging weariness of time that was killing her.

That night at the Comedie-Française every glass was focused on the Duplessis loge where, for the fourth consecutive night, Camille had been in the company of the Vicomte de Perrégaux. "Monsieur Leets is gone! Long live the vicomte!" commented Ronceval. "But how long will he reign?"

Édouard himself, however, was not yet too certain of his ascendancy. But he had never been happier. At the Club his euphoria after the long dejection manifested itself in his insistent invitation for everyone to drink a toast with him.

"To your London appointment?"

"To—to my new life!"

That the new life was connected with the Duplessis everybody surmised, especially the shopkeepers of the Rue de la Paix. Mayer sold him ladies' gloves by the dozen. Gagelin turned over to him his two most precious cashmere shawls. At Mottet's Édouard bought a fan of amber and lace and—in midwinter!—a parasol with a carved ivory handle from Canton. "Is Monsieur taking the lady on a Mediterranean cruise?" asked Mottet.

"No, we're crossing the Channel," he answered. Mottet, with an indulgent smile sighed, "Ah, youth! Ah, love!"

Alphonsine had never been gentler. She let Édouard caress her, every touch inflaming his blood, but she would not yield to other endearments. "Afterward, Edouard, afterward. It seems so wrong now, somehow." And he, respecting the delicacy of the woman who was about to be his, curbed the turbulence of his youth and contented himself with a chaste kiss, while Alphonsine tried to check the thought: "Not in Franz's bed!"

# 19.  The Secret Marriage

THEY said it was the narrowest part of the Channel but to the passengers on the boat to Dover it might have been as wide as the Atlantic for all they could see beyond that haze of snow and sleet. The wind howled and the boards creaked, and high overhead the flags flapped like captive birds straining toward kindlier skies. Below, great watery mouths gaped and frothed as if each would engulf the vessel and its miserable human freight. But it was the wind that, like all invisible dangers, was the most terrifying. Now from the prow, now from the stern it heaved up the helpless craft and shook it and rattled it till it looked as if the nails would fly out of its seams and the disjoined boards scatter over the sea with their living wreckage.

Huddled in the captain's cabin Alphonsine Duplessis and several other ladies, distinguished from the rest of their unsheltered sex by the elegance of their clothes, were enfolded in their private misery. At first they had smiled wanly to one another but soon each wished to be alone. Whenever a particularly violent pitching jumbled them into a heap of shawls and furs, they no longer troubled to beg pardon but silently

216

disentangled themselves to seek again their circumscribed yard of deck, for it would have been unsafe to sit on a chair.

Outside Édouard de Perrégaux was keeping watch with another man whose wife was within. The shoulders of their coats were white with snow. Now and then they would brush it off. Long since they had stopped trying to make conversation but stood in readiness, if the worst should happen, to rush to their women.

"It's all my fault," Alphonsine accused herself at every perilous lurch, "and God is punishing me. Poor Édouard! He will die and these poor English ladies will die, all because of my sins."

From every part of the boat a wail rose to confirm her thoughts. How long had they been buffeted about? Hours ago they should have been in port and here they were, these ladies and herself and those others sprawled on deck, all in peril of their lives because of her. God was against the thing she was doing and was showing His wrath.

All of a sudden the vessel rolled like a dying whale, lurched forward and as violently bolted back, shuddering in all its timbers. "It has happened," thought Alphonsine and resignedly crossed herself. At the same instant Édouard stumbled in and clasped her about the shoulders. Always Édouard! Even in death Édouard, when the features she sought in his too familiar face were those of Franz.

"We're there, *mon ange*," he said.

There? In heaven? In hell? Why did Édouard always call her his angel?

"At Dover. Come, my love."

The chalk hills surrounding the low-lying town rose like glaciers on a dead world. It was bitter cold. Even in her voluminous wrappings Alphonsine trembled violently. But the trembling came from a chill within.

"Monsieur le Vicomte de Perrégaux?"

A voice as French as the pop of a champagne cork rose above the clipped tones of the English and a compact little man whose grizzled head blended with the astrakhan of his coat collar came hurrying toward them. Édouard stepped forward.

"Welcome, welcome to England!" the man greeted them with a bow and a flourish of his hands as if he were spreading a carpet for Mademoiselle Duplessis. "Roland de l'Orme," he said, "of the Embassy. Mademoiselle, Monsieur, your humble servant."

Alphonsine smiled gratefully. Before the man's warmth she forgot the wintry bleakness and even, for a moment, the inner chill. The two men conferred briefly. She saw an exchange and an examination of papers with now and then a glance of inspection and frank approval in her direction from a pair of youthful pupils under the gray brows.

Monsieur de l'Orme had overlooked no detail for their comfort on the journey to London, even to the footwarmer filled with embers at every stage for the exquisitely but lightly shod feet of Mademoiselle Duplessis. Édouard, sitting beside her, gave only the surface of his mind to the genial gentleman's informative conversation. Time enough later to learn the intricacies of the Embassy.

Discreetly observant from the seat opposite, Monsieur de

l'Orme saw the youth clasp Mademoiselle protectively at every jolt of the wheels and even when there was no threat to her comfort. He noticed how, in the middle of a sentence, he would lose himself in contemplation of her profile, and indeed, who could blame him when he himself, at his age, felt his heart cavorting with the impetuousness of twenty years? Ah, love, blissful delusion! How completely it blinds us to the fact that often the look in the beloved eyes is not for us, and that the little hand crushed in our own is quiescent only from indifference? Monsieur de l'Orme had begun by envying Perrégaux, but now—surely he was not pitying that lucky devil?

At Canterbury they stopped at the inn for refreshment. Mademoiselle Duplessis ate very little. Perrégaux did not do much better. The other guests, Monsieur de l'Orme noticed, ate not at all, at least not till they were recalled from Mademoiselle Duplessis by the mundane appeal of their roast beef.

"How real is the love of beauty in the heart of man," he remarked to his tongue-tied companions. "Look at our portly alderman there, holding that succulent morsel in midair, not tempted by it in the least while he devours you with his eyes, Mademoiselle. And that poet—he must be a poet, he looks so ill fed—pushing aside the plate his host is probably paying for! Look at him resting his head on his hands and feeding his soul on your beauty."

"The soul . . ." Alphonsine took up the word dreamily. "The soul is always trying to find on earth the beauty it once contemplated in heaven. When it finds it, it's love. That's what love is."

"You were saying?" prompted the startled de l'Orme. But Mademoiselle Duplessis, having uttered, retreated to her silence. Édouard darted an apprehensive look from one to the other. He was about to speak but he trusted more to his firm grasp of her hand to bring her back to himself.

It had stopped snowing but it grew colder as night came on. While the carriage drove toward Rochester Monsieur de l'Orme, if he made any reflections, kept them to himself. Certainly he would have had little response from the youth wholly absorbed in the girl beside him and from that silent being wandering alone in her invisible realm.

What or whom was she seeking there? By the light of the carriage lamp above her he could detect every emotion depicted on her face by that inner drama. She was leaning her head on Édouard's shoulder—he had put it there—but it might as well have been an inanimate pillow instead of the flesh and blood of a lover. Yet there was no mistaking the sensuality that would at moments convulse the statuelike calm of her face and bring the lids down over the too revealing eyes. He would then notice the thrill which Perrégaux, ignorant of the secret ecstasy, would feel. *"Mon ange, are you cold?"* The angel was too far away even to hear.

At Rochester they stopped for the night. De l'Orme was appreciative of the delicacy which made the lovers sleep apart but it also perplexed him. Ah, well, perhaps the blood of a race cools with age, like the blood of a man growing old. In his youth how differently he would have behaved. Next morning he was nevertheless unreasonably incensed with Mademoiselle Duplessis for having innocently deprived him

of his sleep, and in the carriage he made no effort at conversation.

What was the woman's allurement? She was quiet, almost
too quiet, and her beauty was of that ethereal order which
should elevate rather than incite. Yet its effect was of the
most *troublant*. She looked like ice and she was fire, like the
Sicilian Etna which in his youth he had seen, calm under its
crest of snow till one day, without warning, it hurled its heart
of fire into the heavens and poured its lava blood in terrible
destruction down the slopes. Alas for the victims in its way!
For the Perrégaux and, perhaps even now, for the de l'Ormes!

"You're an old fool, de l'Orme!" he told himself at a chance
meeting of her candid eyes. "An old fool corrupted by the
prevalent taint of Romanticism. She's just a simple girl
running off to England to marry an heir whose relations don't
approve."

Chance had drawn him into the romance when Perrégaux,
with whom he had been corresponding on the Embassy post,
took him into his confidence and begged his assistance. He
had engaged for them a house in Brompton Road and staffed it
with discreet servants. There, in the gray February dusk, he
left them with the promise to call on them the following
morning.

It was a very different house from the mansion on the
Boulevard de la Madeleine. The high-ceilinged rooms were
paneled in a dark wood that gave them a cold austerity. They
were overfurnished with large pieces which made the fires
in the hearths seem inadequately small.

"It's so cold, Édouard," she said, drawing her furs about her.

"*Cher ange,* I'll warm you with my love," he said, embracing her.

She pulled away. "Not before the servants, Édouard," she said. Seeing his hurt look, she added: "Not yet, I mean."

But it was not only before the servants, who took it for granted that since the two were living under the same roof they must be married. What perplexed them was the mistress' order that they should make up the bed in the room adjoining the connubial chamber, after they had taken such pains to make the master bedroom so attractive! They did as they were told, however, but not without varied comment on the ways of those peculiar people, the French.

Alphonsine herself would have been at a loss to explain why she refused to sleep with Édouard. She had given him a ready enough answer and, to his unquestioning adoration, a convincing one. "When we marry it must be a real marriage, Édouard. I must come to you as your bride on our wedding night."

In spite of his constant desire, sharpened to agony by her proximity and her new gentleness, he obeyed. She knew, however, that the true motive was too deeply hidden within for her to uncover.

"It's true, it's true! What I told Édouard is true," she tried to convince herself. "I must come to him as a bride. *Mon Dieu!* How could I go through with it otherwise? Poor Édouard! I do love you, even if it's not in the same way as—I must not say the name. I've been honest with you. Didn't you say, Only let me love you—that is all I want? Perhaps some day I may love you as I love—*Seigneur!* What am I saying! I could never love another as I love—*Seigneur! Seigneur! Aidez-moi!"*

Why then was she marrying Édouard? "Because the poor boy cannot live without me. Ah, that's not the truth! It's because of that Forestine. Madame Elmyre, Madame Elmyre! Why did you tell me about her? No, no, it's not the Forestine! It's Weimar. It's because of Weimar. But what has a dull little German place to do with it? It's because Édouard is le Vicomte de Perrégaux. Yes, Alphonsine Plessis! That's the true reason, Madame la Vicomtesse de Perrégaux!"

Meanwhile Édouard went daily to the Embassy not only to be initiated to his post but to act as a spur on Monsieur de l'Orme, who was in charge of the marriage negotiations.

"Patience, patience!" de l'Orme chided him. "Youth! Because it has a devil in the flesh it can't understand that bureaucracy has lead in its shoes. I'm doing the best I can. Another week—"

"A week!" came the agonized cry.

"Well, a few more days."

Alphonsine patterned the long hours after those at home. In the afternoon she would drive to Kensington Gardens. At the Broad Walk she would get out, as carriages were not admitted into the park, and join the promenaders. They were not so numerous as at the Bois, nor were they as sociable. Each group remained as isolated as if enclosed in a glass bell, like the Chelsea figurines on the mantel in Brompton Road. Even the dogs shared the aristocratic aloofness. "Dash! Dash! Do you miss me, Dash? Do you wish you were back in England?

No, lucky Dash! You have the Bois. I wish I were with you at this moment."

One day she varied the route and drove through Queen's Gate to Hyde Park. At the Serpentine she stopped the coachman and got out. There were many more people here, all the London fashionables, riding, driving or walking. The trees looked like the trees of home. The alleys too, if one closed one's ears to the language, were like the Allée des Acacias. At least this one was, with its glimpse of the Serpentine beyond. "Dash! I wish you were here, Dash." Vividly she saw the dog bounding toward her, with *him* just behind, while she held Dash's colored ball ready to throw. But she must not think of *him* or she would go mad.

Nevertheless, think of him she did. Every day she counted the hours, waiting for the one that would lead her to the alley which reminded her of the Bois and of their first meeting. Detail by detail she relived it as, during the solitary nights, in the great English fourposter, she relived every moment they had spent together.

Even when she was with Édouard *he* would come between them, drawing her to him with his compelling look, and she would respond with swooning eyes—to Édouard's, adoring and bewildered. In all her fantasies she was careful not to call *him* by his name. It was as if saying it aloud would act like magic on time and space and summon him here, to London, where he must not come. The waiting became as intolerable for her as for Édouard.

At last one evening Monsieur de l'Orme appeared with a beaming, unofficial smile. "*Eh, bien, les tourterelles!* Tomorrow is the day," he said. They both cried out with almost desperate relief. "Tomorrow, the twenty-first of February, at the Kensington Register Office."

"Oh, a civil marriage?" asked Alphonsine.

"The church ceremony follows. I have already arranged with the minister. There will be no spectators."

That night in their separate rooms neither could sleep. Crazed with visions of anticipated bliss Édouard got up and knocked at her door. "Darling! *Cher ange!*" he said softly. "Please let me just—just lie quietly beside you. I—I can't rest! I can't close an eye. I promise—"

"No! No! Édouard!" she cried, and veiling the panic in her tone went on, "Be good now, *cher enfant*. Don't spoil everything by your impulsiveness. I won't open the door."

"Then I'll lie across the threshold and—and all the servants will see. Just let me told you in my arms. I promise."

She tiptoed barefoot to the door. "Édouard?"

"*Mon amour!*"

"Be good and go back to bed. Do you want to rob us of our wedding night?"

"Then just let me kiss you and—and I promise I'll go."

She opened the door. In his need of her he crushed her so passionately that for a moment he might have been *the other*.

"Go! Go, now!" She tore herself from him, breathless and quivering from his kisses on her lips and throat. "Go or I shall cry," she said.

"*Mon ange! Mon amour!* Forgive me. I'm—I'm going mad."

"Go, please."

"Am I forgiven?"

She leaned her cheek against his. "I know what you have been suffering, Édouard," she said. "Go, *cher enfant.* Try to sleep."

The following morning Monsieur de l'Orme, with a flower in his buttonhole called for them in a sumptuous diplomatic carriage. He had with him two young gentlemen whom he introduced as Mr. Perry and Mr. Blackwell. "Our witnesses," he said.

Alphonsine held out her hand. The two men, staring at her, could only utter a joint gasp.

"Are you nervous, *mon enfant?*" Monsieur de l'Orme twitted Édouard. Alphonsine frowned at that *mon enfant* addressed to the man she was going to marry. He did look such a boy in his pride and embarrassment.

The servants, watching the masters go out at that hour, wondered but did not question. Some official function, no doubt, for my lady to be so richly dressed in the white gown with rosebuds under the sable cloak.

It did not take long to reach the Register Office though Perry and Blackwell could have wished it longer, and that both sides of the road were lined with their friends to see them riding with such a "stunner"—a new word in the London vocabulary.

When they arrived they were shown to a private chamber where the Civil State officials were already waiting. Mr. Strother and Mr. Samuel Cornell unbent their dignity enough to bow, and even to smile, to Mademoiselle Duplessis. Monsieur de l'Orme and the witnesses drew up to a small table and, while they were conferring with the Civil State,

Édouard pressed Alphonsine's hand so hard that he did not notice how it had been trembling.

The Civil State, for now Strother and Cornell were invested in their official impersonality, called the lovers before them and began to fill out a document. The two witnesses signed it. Édouard and Alphonsine signed it also. The Civil State then added its august signatures. When the party left the Kensington Register Office, after the civil marriage formality, they were man and wife in the eyes of the English law.

As the carriage was making its way toward the church, Alphonsine found herself suddenly wishing for Julie, or even Madame Elmyre. She could think of no other friend. Delphine? Delphine was hardly a friend, only her agent who would quit without scruple the moment there was nothing more to gain. No one else. With a pang Alphonsine realized how alone she was.

"Édouard! Édouard!" she found herself calling.

"Yes, *cher amour*? What is it?" Dash's eyes looked out apprehensively from his face.

"It's—I don't know, it's just that I was frightened. We're going too fast."

Monsieur de l'Orme cautioned the coachman.

At the church they entered a flower-decked chapel. Alphonsine, in her white gown now, was carrying a bouquet of lilies provided by Monsieur de l'Orme. Except for the witnesses and the flower girl who had brought the bouquet and whom neither threats nor bribes could have shaken in her resolve to see the ceremony, the church was empty. Alphonsine shivered in the cold and longed for her furs. The girl, in her amorphous wrappings, wished she could touch for luck the beautiful bridal *gownd.*

The minister, very fair and very young, was so shy that he hardly lifted his eyes from the church slabs. On her part Alphonsine thanked God for it. As she listened to the solemn charge from the Book of Common Prayer the words, more awesome for being only partly understood, augmented the guilt in her heart and the terror that she might betray herself.

"I require and charge you both, as ye will answer at the dreadful day of judgment, when the secrets of all hearts shall be disclosed . . ."

"(*Aidez-moi, O Seigneur!*)"

"That if either of you know any impediment why ye may not be lawfully joined together in matrimony . . ."

"(*Seigneur! Seigneur! Aidez-moi!*)"

"Ye do now confess it."

The words pierced her brain in jagged lightning. The blood rumbled like thunder in her ears so that she barely heard what followed. As through a haze she saw the minister addressing Édouard, whose lips moved in an inaudible answer. Now, for the first time, level and stern, the eyes of the man of God sought hers. "Wilt thou . . . forsaking all others, keep thee only unto him, so long as ye both shall live?"

There was a hush, prolonged and tense, finally broken by the "Ooh!" of the flower girl and Monsieur de l'Orme's whisper: "*Répliquez,* Mademoiselle. *Répliquez,* 'I will.'"

"I will," breathed Alphonsine.

After that she heard nothing over the clamor of music in her head, eight notes over and over, in every key, over and over. Vaguely she was aware that Édouard took her right hand and pressed it. The ring. Where was the ring? Somebody found it.

"With this ring I thee wed . . . with all my worldly goods . . ." Worldly goods . . . Why were they all kissing her? Who was this ragged girl who looked so like Julie?

"The bowkay, Miss—I mean, Mum. It's lucky for the girl as gets it."

Alphonsine delivered it into the outstretched hands.

"God bless you, Mum. Law', now I can sell it for money."

The lamps, discreetly shaded, were burning in the master bedroom when they returned home that night. It was late and the servants had retired. Alphonsine was about to go into her room when Édouard restrained her. "Have you forgotten so— so soon?" he said, the gentle reproach at once canceled by a kiss.

She tasted the wine on his lips. They had both drunk, perhaps too much, of the generous champagne at their wedding supper given by Monsieur de l'Orme. "Besides, you can't go in," said Édouard. "This morning I—I locked the door and threw the key in the Thames."

"But my toilette, Édouard! All my things are in there."

"You won't need your things. Not—not tonight, dearest."

He felt her start in his arms. "Come, my love," he said. "The fire has died down. O dearest! How long—how long I've waited for this night!"

In spite of herself she thrilled to the grip of his arms. Dropping her cloak on a chair she went into his dressing room where, to her amazement, she found all her lavish frivolities neatly arranged. She began to undress, scarcely aware of what she was doing except when the hooks caught or the ribbons refused to untie.

"Dear God, help me! *Aidez-moi, Seigneur!*"

All day long the prayer had tolled in her brain like a despairing buoy in her soul's storm. *"Seigneur! Seigneur!"* Her dress and her petticoats swirled like the spume of waves about her. She stood, looking round for something to throw over herself. She found nothing. How long had it taken her to undress? The lamp, burning low, began to smoke. She blew it out and went into the bedroom.

Édouard, half uncovered, was in bed. He held out his arms. "Come, my love!"

One by one she put out the lamps. "Leave this one," he said when she came to the bedside. "I want to look at you when—I want to see you my—my bride!"

Frantically she struggled with the clasp of the necklace which she had forgotten to take off. It would not open.

"Come, dearest!"

The violence of his long pent-up longing clashing with the storm in her brain whirled past and present, identity and reality, into a wild confusion till suddenly and excruciatingly the senses were pierced as by a sword of light.

"Dearest, you are mine," he whispered.

"Franz! My Franz!"

At her cry his whole world crumbled.

# 20. Love and Conscience

CAMILLE, heart of my heart! Another week and we shall
be together. Six long days, but on the seventh I shall
mount your stairs and you'll be in my arms. Ah, first I shall
gaze into your eyes to recover the soul I left there, and I
shall run my fingers through your hair, then kiss your cheeks,
your throat, and finally that lovely mouth where always there
is plenary indulgence for all my sins, my Camille! You will
be wearing *il velo greco* which covers you like the ripples of
the sea and it will remind us of that first time. . . . Then a shaft
of moonlight, piercing through the blinds half-drawn for love,
will fall upon you and the sight of your face in immortal
rapture will make my blood surge, and the second wave will be
vaster than the first, and those that follow will have the
urgency of the first. I am now counting the days. Then it will
be hours. Then in your arms I shall forget all time. Your
Franz."

She knew the letter by heart and yet she spelled it out with
slow deliberation to feel for the hundredth time the sensual
incitement of those words. Franz was coming back! Another
night, another day and they would be giving life to those

thoughts that inflamed her. Yet she dreaded his coming. While counting the seconds bridging the time to his return, she would have pushed the bridge back beyond that dreadful night, three weeks ago, when God had punished her for her sin.

Poor Édouard! Could she ever get his insane sobbing out of her ears, his look of anguish out of her eyes? That crazed, horrified, pitying, yes, pitying look, with which he held her close to the lamp whose heat she could still feel burning her cheek, yet not so stingingly as her own shame. Had he heaped upon her all the opprobrium of his hurt and humiliation she could have blotted out the memory as one blots out in forgiveness the injuries done to one. But he pitied her! "My poor angel, how you must love—love him to do this thing!"

He pitied but he would not forgive. "I am not God," he said. "Ask God to forgive you!"

He had risen from the bed and unlocked the door which he had so carefully secured to keep her with him on their wedding night, and until morning she could still hear him trying to check the hurt which exploded in wordless, inhuman cries. She would have thrown herself at his feet and bathed them with her tears and promised—ah, could she have kept her promise?—never again to see Franz. But he would not open. The door which she had locked against the lover he locked against the wife.

Finally, spent and despairing, she had sunk into a sleep that was more like a stupor. She recalled with a sad smile how cheerfully the afternoon sun had been picking out the overblown roses of the hideous carpet when the maid awakened her. "His Lordship was suddenly called away," said the girl. "He begged me to give you this."

The packet, addressed to the Vicomtesse de Perrégaux contained money, her passage across the Channel and a ring with the Perrégaux crest. "If you have pity for me, since I can never hope for love," read the note, "I implore you *never* let me see you. I shall remain in England. You now have what you want. May my name give you the happiness which its bearer could not give. I shall never cease loving you. Édouard."

The unstammering directness of the writing revealed a strength that made her feel lost.

"Where did His Lordship go?" she asked the girl who stared at such a question. "Oh, it says here it is a secret mission," she caught herself.

That evening Monsieur de l'Orme, more courteous than ever, had come to offer his condolences and his services. "I am desolated that England should lose you so soon, Madame la Vicomtesse. But sickness and death spare no one. I trust you will find Madame your mother still alive on your return. The sight of you would restore her. Will you be ready by ten tomorrow, Madame la Vicomtesse? You should have seen Monsieur de Perrégaux's distress at having to leave on his mission at such a time!"

Those dismal hours of waiting, the endless night alone in the bed where in bitter penance she forced herself to lie, living over again the horror of the night before, and yet perversely allowing herself to indulge the unshakable fantasy that the *other* had possessed her there. Always the *other*. As long as she lived she knew he would come between her and any other love. Ah, Franz! Franz!

As she set the letter down on the *prie-dieu* a rush of blood brought drops to her forehead which the next moment was as cold as ice. When was Korff coming? Somehow he must cure her, by medicine, by sorcery, she did not care how. But he must undo the disastrous effect of the last few weeks upon her health. She blamed the English climate, she blamed her spiritual anguish, all the while trying to blot out of her mind the increasingly frequent danger signals of her unforgiving disease.

But what did it matter? What did anything matter? Franz was coming back in spite of the very beautiful Forestine. Franz! My Franz! She passed her hand over a freshly gilt design on her *prie-dieu*. It was repeated on the mirror of the dressing table and also on the head of the bed, above the painting of the maiden captured by Eros. It was the crest of the Perrégaux.

However, she did not use the title. She had no right to it in France, as Édouard's relatives were quick to inform her through their lawyer, the very morrow of her return. Oh, the scandal, the panic of the Perrégaux! Now they were starting proceedings to annul the marriage. The lawyer, a gallant old gentleman not impervious to the Duplessis charm, spoke of the advantages that would still be hers, however, not the least considerable of which was a substantial sum for damages.

"Let the Perrégaux found a house for lost girls," she said scornfully.

"But will you give your consent in writing?" asked the lawyer.

"Does Édouard agree to the annulment?"

"Here is the Vicomte de Perrégaux's letter, Mademoiselle."

It was a formal lawyer's letter to which Édouard had merely added his signature. His name, shakily written, had filled her with such a sense of loss that she had to turn away to hide her tears. "I shall consider it. I need time," she said. "I must consult my own lawyers."

"They can only urge you to agree, Mademoiselle. Although the marriage is legal in England it is illegal here. You are both French subjects. You are Catholic. Unless you were remarried in France you could not claim either title or—"

"You have told me all this before, Monsieur. I do not want to hold Édouard to anything he does not desire. If I have it from Édouard himself that he wishes this annulment I—I—"

Somehow she could not go on and the lawyer left before she could retract her half promise. The legal mind, however, had misinterpreted her emotion. While talking she had glanced at the jewel tree. The toy bird had summoned up the nest she had destroyed. In the tangential ways of the human psyche that childhood incident had become associated with Édouard, whom she had so cruelly hurt.

As it was, Édouard and her guilt now obsessed her as much as Franz and her love. She had married Édouard in order to hold Franz and God had visited her with terrible punishment. Indeed, she felt so deeply the divine disfavor and her soul so trembled with terror that she could no longer address herself to the Almighty. One day soon after her return, when she had endeavored to distract her guilt-laden mind by visiting her favorite shops, she came across a statuette at the antique dealer's. Its presence there at that moment of her wretchedness struck her as a sign from on high. She bought it and had it placed in her boudoir.

It was a large gilt sixteenth-century Virgin whose heart, pierced with arrows, brought the Mother of Sorrows close to her own human suffering. She now prayed to the Virgin to intercede for her with her Son. As a woman the Mother would understand. As a Virgin she would take pity on the fallen one who had sunk through her marriage to even deeper sin.

The torment of her conscience made her more beautiful as her face took on spiritual suffering like a veil. Her long, slim hands, now so often joined in supplication, were like a pale flame. In the white garments that she preferred she looked like a girl whom heartbreak had made a nun, but whose passionate eyes betrayed the hungers that still bound her to the world.

This was the woman to whom the lover returned, and his ardor, after a season with the fleshy Fürstins, leaped to new lambencies. Their union was indeed a meeting of two fires, consuming everything earthly till their spirits merged in an exultant death. But after each death came a resurrection of desire and the barriers of flesh melted in the burning till Franz, gazing upon the transfigured face upon the pillow, believed himself a god.

The Jockey Club waited for the *cher maître* in vain. Korff waylaid him only to have the captive coat-tails slip through his fingers. Marcel could tell them nothing except that when Liszt was not with the Duplessis, Madame la Vicomtesse du Plessis as she now called herself, he was at the piano in an inspired trance from which he awakened only to dash off to the Boulevard de la Madeleine. "He's possessed by two demons, his music and his love," said Marcel. "I don't know which is stronger. Perhaps they're one and the same in different forms."

For weeks there had been much speculation about Alphonsine's disappearance at the same time as Perrégaux. Some, like Korff and Ronceval talked of a romantic elopement, perhaps even a marriage. "That English post was only a ruse, dust in the eyes," said Korff. "Wait and see the rocket they'll shoot off from England. *French count marries his mistress* blazing across the skies."

"Where's your rocket now?" asked Ronceval when the Duplessis returned alone.

"I was mistaken," said Korff. "She went off to consult some quack who promised a marvelous cure. Poor girl, she doesn't know how lost she is!"

For the lovers no one, nothing, existed except themselves and each other and Franz's music which was like the eternalization of their love. They did not go out as often as before, but wherever they were seen it was always as the apparition of two pilgrims from another sphere. Liszt was called away more and more. During his absences the Duplessis lived like a nun but for her drives with Dash to the Bois and her evenings at the theater. Her doors remained obstinately shut to all her admirers, who began to seek solace elsewhere. Even Prince Stacklyn, disheartened from his many repulsions, withdrew his patronage, to the dismay of Delphine, who cried bankruptcy.

"A beautiful woman who belongs to the world has no

business falling in love," she warned. "It's suicide. Worse than that, it's poverty."

Alphonsine only smiled abstractedly. For her the days and weeks flowed by in a blissful dream which succeeded in obliterating, at least while Franz was with her, the shadow of her guilt. One cloud persisted, however, as yet only a speck on the horizon of their love: his extended tour through Europe, perhaps even to Russia.

"Franz! Take me with you, Franz!" she begged him with the insistence of an importunate child each time the tour was mentioned. Always he had some excuse—the hardships of the journey, her health, the inhuman demands of his work. "Is that the real reason?" she would ask, searching his eyes for the truth.

One day she called to his unobservant gaze the new silver service at her dinner table. "A coronet. Very charming, my fairytale princess," he said.

"There's nothing fairytale about it, Franz," she said earnestly. "It's my device. I have every right to use it. At least in England," she added after a pause.

"But this is the crest of—why, of Perrégaux! I've seen it on his seal. Can it be true, then, the gossip of the Club that Marcel reported to me? Is it true, dearest?"

At the evenness of his voice she stared at him in amazement. There was no shock, no anger, not the least trace of jealousy on his face, only a gentle, almost pitying wonder.

"You are silent," he said with the same mildness. "Then you did marry Perrégaux as it was rumored?"

He might have been asking whether she had worn a blue

dress rather than a white. "You are not jealous! You are not even angry!" she cried astounded.

"*Ma pauvre petite,* my adorable child!" he said, laying his hand on hers.

She drew sharply away, rose and ran to her boudoir. He followed her there, took her in his arms and kissed her but he could not still her trembling nor the dry, sharp cough that mingled with her sobs. "Camille, my dearest," he soothed her. "Why should I be angry that you married Édouard? Why should I be jealous? Will that alter my love for you or yours for me? You married him for my sake, I see that clearly—"

"Then you'll let me go with you?" she broke in hopefully.

"In the autumn, my love. Then we'll go away together as I promised."

"*Seigneur!* And how shall I live without you till then?"

"It will be only a few months. We'll keep our love alive in our hearts, dearest."

"You'll stop loving me when I'm not with you."

"Camille, beloved! How vain are all our words! We've said so much, I more than you, my lovely silent one. But all our words have been absorbed by the ineffable harmonies within us, and whether or not we are together there will be a divine, a melancholy echo, a wonderful vibration always, immense and infinite. We may not be happy, my love—"

"I shall be wretched, wretched!"

"But we shall attain something better than happiness."

"No! No! There is nothing better than happiness. I need it. I want it!"

"Our love is too great to be content with the possible. There are inaccessible raptures for souls thirsting for the absolute. For them, for us, love is an ecstasy without end."

"Franz! Take me with you, Franz! I can't follow you in your flights. I know nothing of your absolutes. Only let me go with you. You needn't be ashamed of me now. I am still a countess. You went away with Madame d'Agoult. My title is as good as hers."

"Camille! *Ma pauvre petite!*"

He took both her hands and pressed them against his heart.

"I shall take you with me as I promised," he said huskily.

"Ah!" she gasped.

"In October. You will go to the spa while I am away. You will get well and strong. And then, our wonderful months in Constantinople."

"I shall never see Constantinople," she said tonelessly. "It is not in my destiny."

Going to the statuette of the Virgin she lighted a taper from the one that was sputtering out.

Despair deepened in her eyes as the days passed and her mournful beauty roused desires that were more of the soul than of the flesh.

"Franz! My Franz!" The oft-repeated name was now a cry of anguish.

Liszt lived in a state of exaltation such as he had experienced in his youth when at the feet of Lamennais he had dreamed of dedicating his art to God and humanity. Something in Camille had the same kindling effect. Was it that purity which, like a hidden pearl, she had kept inaccessible to corruption, or her evocative quality which made her become all the women he had loved through his imagination? Or was it perhaps the allure of sin and desire that surrounded her?

Somehow Camille and his music, with all its associations, had become inextricably identified. His "Dance of Death" was all but finished. The Concerto, developing from the love theme and embracing all the color and conflict of living, was shaping into a masterpiece. So far it was only a beginning and a progression, like his life and Camille's. The linked themes sang of their longing and fulfillment, but the work still lacked the resolution.

What was it to be? The lady gazing with sorrowful eyes on the prey of Death could not herself escape. All living ends. All joys as all sorrows must die. That was the Romantic credo. There could be but one resolution. Liszt waited for life to create it for his art, though he already knew what it would be.

Meanwhile in the time that remained he could not tear himself away from Camille. He spent day and night with her and for the last week they scarcely left the house. Often they would sit silently, hand in hand, her head against his shoulder and his face leaning on hers. At the flutter of her lids he would draw away a little and plunge his gaze into her eyes to communicate the thoughts too deep for speech. Only once she broke the silence. "Franz! My Franz! It's my soul speaking to yours. Pray God your soul understands."

She no longer asked to go away with him, and her silence saddened him more than her earlier importunity. He knew it was not resignation but something nearer hopelessness that made her refrain. More than once, in pity of that face, as contained as a martyr's in its suffering, he found himself on the point of saying: "Pack up your things, Camille. You're coming with me now." But the whole Weimar galaxy would suddenly appear before him, lifting patrician hands in horror, to a chorus of *"Ach, nein! Ach, nein!"* At that operatic prohibition he instantly changed his mind.

Sometimes as he held her in his arms it seemed to him that she had no substance but was really the shadow from the Campo Santo. He could find no words for this troubling delusion and sought to dispel it by crushing her to him so that her pain would assure him of her reality. But she, the taciturn, found the words for him. "Franz! Franz! It's not me you possess. I am jealous of what you think I am." She would then woo him with frenzied caresses which, rousing the man, made him for the moment forget the artist.

They parted when the chestnut trees along the Seine were sending up their white tapers toward the sky of so clear a blue that it seemed as if no cloud could ever flaw it. They had devoted the previous day to a pilgrimage, to the Allée des Acacias, to Les Halles and the Fountain of the Innocents, to that other fountain where the students had crowned her Goddess of Love and Beauty and, in the evening, to the bench at the Madeleine from where they had discovered their star. That night they could not find it.

"Because it will not look on our parting," she said.

He sealed her lips with a kiss.

"No man will ever kiss my lips again," she said. "Until you come."

Not a word about Constantinople. Not a tear. Her reserve affected him more than any outburst of emotion.

She drove with him in his carriage to the border, her coupé
with Marcel and Dash following. They sat embraced, their
lips joined, their eyes closed to everything outside of themselves. When the carriage stopped they started awake. Another
embrace, another kiss and he led her staggering to the coupé
which Marcel was leaving. Still without a word he kissed her
lips and eyes and backed away as from a queen.

She gazed after the carriage till she could see it no more.

"We did not say good-by, Dash," she said. "That brings
good luck."

# 21.  A Death at the Spa

"LA DUPLESSIS! La Duplessis!"

The usual rustle of admiration greeted her as she came forward in her box and threw off the ermine wrap she was wearing though it was early June. Her gown caught the shimmer of the lights, suffusing her with a quivering incandescence which emphasized the dead pallor of her face. She wore no adornment but a camellia in its nest of leaves at the division of her bosom, and a circlet of pearls far back on her parted hair.

"She looks just like her portrait," whispered those who had seen the painting at the artist's studio. "They say Monsieur Leets paid a fabulous sum for it."

Lithographs of it were selling in the shops along the Seine and many a youth who had lost the original solaced himself with the effigy. Since Liszt's departure her doorbell seldom rang and when it did it usually announced some shopkeeper luring her with new baubles or a creditor presenting a bill. The sovereignty of the great Monsieur Leets had been too powerful for any man to challenge. Besides, no one would have been admitted beyond the antechamber.

Throughout this last performance of the season, though the glasses were pointed more often on her than on the stage, no one entered her box. A liveried lackey was posted outside to guard her privacy.

Against the red plush of the loge she looked more than ever like a rare Italian cameo but that at frequent intervals her stillness was convulsed by a fit of coughing heard above the voices of the actors. The people would then turn in her direction and shake their heads pityingly. Korff, leaning toward Ronceval after one of these interruptions, said in an undertone: "I'm at my wits' end. I can't do anything with her. She thinks I can work miracles and quarrels with me when the medicines do no good. But she refuses to go to the spa though I've warned her that a summer in Paris will kill her. Franz might suddenly come back, she says!"

"Franz? Who but a woman in love would dare call him that? Ah, love! Even *lèse majesté* sounds charming on its lips," said Ronceval. "Any news of the great man lately? My column is languishing for some appetizing morsel."

"The letters don't come so frequently now," said Korff. "Not that she ever shows them to anyone. But Delphine tells me."

"Would the gentlemen kindly retire to the foyer if they wish to carry on a conversation?" a bearded gentleman interrupted.

The two men stopped talking of their own accord, however, at the sudden start of the Duplessis, whose glasses, pointed at the box opposite her, dropped out of her hand. Without waiting to pick them up she rose hurriedly and left.

Korff and Ronceval focused their glasses where she had been looking. Far back, half enveloped by the draperies, was Édouard de Perrégaux, his countenance still fixed in pain and adoration. A moment later he shook himself like one dispelling a dream and passed his hand over his eyes. Soon he too had left the theater.

June turned suffocatingly sultry yet Alphonsine remained in Paris where the very leaves curled up and died in the merciless sun. Most of the fashionables had hurried out of the city and still she lingered. For what? She herself could not have interpreted the vagueness of her longing. Julie, who watched her growing more and more silent, more and more withdrawn, tried to amuse her with her chatter but Mademoiselle only smiled wanly and turned away. Once when Julie wound up the jewel tree and the bird began its heart-free caroling Mademoiselle started up with such a cry that the girl fell on her knees asking forgiveness.

"I only wanted to distract you, Mademoiselle," she said.

"You mustn't! You must never touch that bird again!" said Alphonsine in a voice harsh with anger. But at the girl's tears she threw her arms about her. "I am not well, dear child. Everything agitates me. Everything cuts deep into me and it's as if my soul were bleeding. There, you may take the *joujou* into your room if you wish, but never play it for me again. Do you understand? Never."

For days at a time she would not leave the house nor even the bedroom to which she had the statue of the Virgin moved. Then, unpredictably, she would order her carriage and go shuttling from one end of Paris to the other, buying everything in sight till the coupé was piled high with gaily colored packages like a holiday float.

It was hurry, hurry, hurry. No, she did not want the new hat delivered, nor the Aubusson rug, nor the Ming vase. She must have them at once, at once. She must wear the hat, and ride with her feet on the Aubusson roses—so beautiful, so different from those horrors in the English house! She must put roses, red roses in the Ming—and off she would go to buy them at Madame Barjon's. "All you have, Madame. Hurry! Hurry!"

During those periods she would not go to bed but visit her old haunts, the casinos, and gamble on borrowed money. Nobody refused credit to Mademoiselle Duplessis, the protégée of Prince Stacklyn, the friend of Monsieur Leets. The creditors, therefore, accumulated their bills, investments that would pay off handsomely.

Nothing availed to make Alphonsine forget Franz. He was with her in everything she did. The more infrequent his letters the more his presence gained reality. Nevertheless the one hounding her like a materialization of her own conscience was Édouard, everywhere Édouard, except in her house, which Franz wholly possessed. There she relived with him their every moment.

She counted the hours and the days and the weeks and now the months, and she rejoiced as they passed, bringing nearer the promise of October. Yet sometimes she regretted the flowing away of her days in this hurried, sterile activity which only stressed the wasting of her life. With childlike faith she kept alive the hope that he would surprise her by coming back before autumn. That was why he scarcely wrote now. At every opening of the door her heart cried: "Franz!" and whenever she left the house she gave the porter orders to admit Monsieur Leets at any hour of the day or night.

When Franz's letters no longer came she was so certain of his return that she refused to go out and spent hours at her toilette, changing her gowns to suit the hour so that no matter when he arrived he would find her beautiful. Then, still as a statue, she would sit near the balcony with Dash at her feet as she keyed her ears to the sound of the wheels that would announce Franz. But the carriages that stopped, more and more infrequently, brought only Korff or Madame Elmyre, or someone from the Perrégaux family, tenacious of their scheme to annul the marriage.

One day when the conviction of Franz's arrival was so strong that she expected him to come rushing in at any moment, Delphine brought her a letter. Franz! Surely from Franz saying that he was on his way to her. It came from Édouard.

It was the first communication she had had from him since her return to Paris and his boyish handwriting reawakened the conscience she had been trying to lull. It also brought him back to the world from which she had been endeavoring to exorcise him. Then she had really seen Édouard that time at the theater and at those other places where she had persuaded herself her imagination had summoned him. Édouard still loved her, then! Perhaps he had even forgiven her. Poor Édouard, so good, so faithful. "Like you, Dash. Whatever happens I can always count on Édouard."

When she read his few impersonal lines, however, she gave a sharp little cry. Édouard writing so coldly! Édouard asking for his release in the words she had heard so often from the Perrégaux lawyers. It was as if Dash had suddenly turned and bitten her. Deep within she felt something give way. An unseen prop, taken for granted in the security of her life, had suddenly collapsed.

She reread the words, hearing in them more clearly than the first time the echo of the law. But the signature was Édouard's. There was no mistaking that. He might have expressed the wish differently but the wish was there. Édouard demanded his freedom.

"You shall have your freedom, Édouard," she said softly. "I shall write the words and sign them with my name, and your lawyers will free you from me, Édouard—if they can!"

At the escritoire she wrote hurriedly: "Dear Édouard: In your letter I can see only one thing for which you demand an answer. Here it is. You wish me to state in writing that you are absolutely free. You are free, Édouard. I repeat it and sign myself, Marie Alphonsine Duplessis."

She folded the sheet and sealed it. The smell of the sealing wax made her think of incense and of churches. It also made her cough. When the spasm ceased she avoided looking at the handkerchief she had pressed to her lips but let it fall to the floor, where it lay, like a brighter flower, on the carpet.

How long could she go on disregarding Korff's advice and letting her life ebb away? The Paris heat was deadly. She was deluding herself that Franz would come before October.

"Delphine! Delphine!" she called.

Delphine found her with feverish eyes and flaming cheeks and pacing about the room in agitation.

"Delphine, send this note at once to the Vicomte de Perrégaux," she said. "Then have my trunks packed, but quickly! Quickly! Korff will be coming soon. Show him in immediately. And tell Julie to get her things ready. I'm taking her with me."

"Where are you going, if I may know?" inquired Delphine.

"To Baden, maybe Wiesbaden. Or Ems."

"Or maybe to all three? And pray, Mademoiselle, what money will be left for me to pay the bills?"

"Monsieur Leets left you enough for six months."

"Which you spent in six days, Mademoiselle."

"But I charged everything."

"Yes, but the bills had to be paid."

"There will be more money. But hurry, hurry! Get my things packed. We leave tomorrow."

"Not tonight?" asked Delphine, sarcastic.

"Why not tonight? It'll be cooler. Yes, yes, tonight."

She hated the life at Baden. The sanatorium, the doctors with their false joviality, the long hours of enforced rest, the glasses of nauseous goat's milk, the association with other victims of the same disease pretending to be well, oh, so well, and only there on a holiday! They all suffered from the same restlessness, the same alternation of euphoria and dejection, the same life-hungry eagerness, and they all had that pre-destined look of those doomed to die young.

Julie, like a poppy in her blooming health in this hothouse of cankered humanity, drew all eyes. Emaciated youths had a flicker of resurrection in her presence and clustered about her like hungry bees, while Alphonsine, reclining on a chaise longue on the terrace, roused no interest because she was one of them, the health-seekers.

Through her lowered lashes which gathered a flicker of rainbow motes in the sun, she watched this daily drama of life and death. For the first time another woman was drawing the admiration that had always been hers. The shock unnerved her.

What if she should never get well, nor even better? The strange, terrible symptoms she had been having, those reddened handkerchiefs, her melting flesh—such signs did not point to recovery. In her rooms she would study herself in the glass. Oh, she was beautiful, with the kind of beauty Franz loved. "The ultimate refinement," he once said, "where soul pierces through flesh."

Franz always made much of the soul, even in those moments when he was chained to the flesh. The others had sought her body, caring little for anything else. The soul was nothing but a ghost and the men who paid for their pleasures wanted flesh and blood. All but Édouard, who loved her for whatever she cared to give him.

As time passed she realized that Baden was not doing her any good. Panic and restlessness drove her to Wiesbaden. It was only the setting that changed. She went from doctor to doctor, demanding miracles. When they performed none she set off for Ems.

"Hurry! Hurry!"

The carriage jolted, the miles sped and the autumnal countryside rushed past in the somber glow of the dying year.

"Mademoiselle, you are wearing yourself out," said Julie. "It would be so much better if we went back home."

The warning and the innocent confirmation of her own fears deepened Alphonsine's despair. Ems was only another Wiesbaden. She was never going to get well. With morbid fascination she watched in others what she knew was happening to herself. Still, gloomily resigned, she submitted herself to the cure—ironic name!—waiting for the weeks to pass till October and Franz. He would come. In Constantinople, in the happiness of their love, she would regain her strength.

The regimen affected her nerves, always acutely sensitive. She could not sleep and spent the hours longing for the familiar noises of Paris which had at least lulled her restlessness. Here the stillness of the nights made the hollow coughing of the "guests" sound like a summons to the grave. The walls of her room became the confines of a vault. She could not breathe. Wrapping the blanket about her she would go to the window to reassure herself by the solidity of the buildings across the gardens that she was still of this world.

One night as she was peering out across the moonlit shrubbery she heard the postern gate open and saw, a black silhouette in the greenish haze, a covered cart making for the entrance just below. Who could be arriving at this hour?

She opened the window and leaned out through the tangle of vines. The horse's hoofs sounded muffled as if wrapped in cloths. The cart, long and low, had no passenger, for only the driver descended. He gave one low cautious knock at the door which opened instantly. Who could be leaving at this hour?

The coachman went to the back of the cart and opened a low door. Immediately behind him hurried two men, one at each end of a stretcher covered by a sheet. The moonlight picked out the hills and hollows under it, and the shape was the shape of a body. Stifling a shriek Alphonsine drew back and banged the window shut.

The scene returned to her throughout the night as if, in the poignancy of horror, it had etched itself upon her eyeballs as on her brain. Someone had died. How stealthily they had smuggled the body away in the dead of night, like a shameful thing! Whose was it? Which of those youths or girls whom she had seen on the terrace, all as self-absorbed and as remote in their private affliction as the stars in the heavens? It might have been herself those men had spirited away. Sudden and appalling, the specter of Death reared itself before her.

Her mind reeled. She might die here among strangers and be carted away in guilty secrecy like the thing she had seen. What if Death did not wait for the priest and she should die with her sins upon her soul? The words of the nuns, about damnation and eternal fire, rang in her memory and she trembled as, when a child, she had trembled at the awfulness of the word sin, the more terrible for not being understood. She had so many sins—for every lover she had ever had, for every pleasure and luxury she had coveted, for her selfishness and for her cruelty.

"Édouard! You must forgive me, Édouard, before I die!"

Her cry re-echoed night long in her brain with her whispered:
"O Holy Virgin, pray for me!"

Now the image of her gilded Virgin became as tangible as
the figure of Death. She must go back to Paris at once to
throw herself at the feet of the Mother of God. But what if
she should die on the way? Then her sins would remain
unabsolved. She would burn in hell forever, but the worst
torment of all would be that she died without Édouard's
pardon. In the breaking dawn she sat down and wrote him:
"On my knees, dear Édouard, I beg you to forgive me. If you
still love me enough to answer my prayer then send me just
two words, your pardon and your friendship. I am here alone
and desperately ill. So, dear Édouard, my pardon. But
quickly! Quickly!"

Ems was now a place of horror. She needed the reassurance
of her own familiar things and the benevolent nearness of the
Virgin. Before her letter could have had time to reach Édouard
she was on her way to Paris.

October was half over. Although she had been as aware of
each passing hour as of the gnawing thought of Franz, still
she had prolonged her stay at the spas. To make herself
strong for Constantinople, she told herself, but really to delay
her return to Paris and the dreaded certainty that Franz would
not be there.

Her premonition was too soon confirmed. Ah, but there
were still twelve days to the end of October! Why had
Delphine left her and taken another place in her absence? The
trayful of creditors' bills could have told her, but she never
troubled herself about such matters. There had always been

someone to pay. Someone would take care of the bills again. Besides, Franz would be coming back.

But where was Édouard? Why had he not flown to her at her urgent prayer? Had she lost him too? The thought gave her such a sense of being abandoned and alone that for the first time she felt frightened in the city suddenly become a desert.

Korff found her in such an alarming state that he omitted the jocular hint he had rehearsed on his unpaid services.

"Rest, complete rest for at least a fortnight," he prescribed.

She answered him with a peal of laughter that had nothing of gaiety in it. "Will you then bury me at the end of the fortnight?" she asked. "Where's Delphine? Where's Édouard? Where's everybody?"

Korff replied to that most important question about everybody. "Monsieur Leets, according to Marcel, has left Weimar for Hungary."

"Then he'll soon be here. Well, won't he?" she prodded his silence.

"After another tour."

"Ah? It can't take too long. Even if he didn't come back till the end of the month. . . ."

Korff tactfully left the suspension unresolved. "As for the Vicomte de Perrégaux, he's at present in England," he went on.

"That's why he hasn't come to see me," she said. "I thought it strange he didn't answer my note."

Korff's interest had an avid glint. Whatever the mystery of the English flight, whatever the quarrel, here was surely the promise of a reconciliation. His bills would be paid. Heartened by the prospect he poured out the latest Parisian gossip to amuse her, but he could see that her thoughts were far away. She said no more about Liszt, but she did ask, with a concern that had in it something of panic, whether Édouard would be long away.

"He comes and goes," Korff replied vaguely.

He comes and goes . . . but her conscience was always with her. "I must see him," she said, clutching the doctor's hand with both of hers. "I can't wait. What if I wrote to the Embassy?"

"A good idea, except that he's often abroad on his missions. Perhaps there is something I might do for you?"

"You? Not you, Korff! You can't even make my body well. How could you cure my soul?"

# 22.  Concerto

FRANZ did not come. In the Allée des Acacias the fallen leaves scurried from the wind and the pods hung like dead things from the branches. The fountains no longer played and at night the stars gazed down with a cold, pitiless look. The first snow had already fallen, bringing out the joyful children, but from the dark doorways of Saint-Antoine anxious eyes peered, and fear seized the heart at that white terror falling with the softness of summer petals.

Édouard did not come. Against the dark tree trunks across the street there was no longer his faithful shadow. At the theater to which Alphonsine still dragged herself she looked in vain for those adoring eyes.

Nor did the others come. She had cast them off in her dedication to Franz and now they had abandoned her. But she did not want them. Her life of sin was over, she assured the Virgin. "I know I am going to die. Édouard's forgiveness, that is all I beg, dear Mother of God."

She never spoke her other thought before the pure Virgin: the hope that with Édouard's forgiveness would come the

257

pardon of the Almighty Who would no longer punish her by keeping Franz away.

On mild days she would still dress herself and go out in her carriage, but now the admiration which people gave her tried not to betray pity. The real Duplessis, vital and radiant, was no more. This was her ghost lingering among the places where she had passed her few enchanted years.

As December drew to a close she lived in a renewed hope that gave bloom to her cheeks and the old fire to her eyes. The New Year would bring back Franz and her happiness. He could not stay away, remembering, just as she could not keep her heart from bounding at every thought of him.

The night before New Year's Day she had Julie lay out the clothes she had worn for Franz and it distressed her that she had discarded the slippers. Their very dust was precious to her, and she grieved over their loss as if they had been living things. Somehow, because of them, the good augury of New Year's Day was marred.

It dawned, a gray morning, flecked with soggy flakes that melted as they fell. Alphonsine looked out of the window and shivered. "Happy New Year, the happiest year of your life!" The words made her start and turn quickly. There was Julie, her lips still heavy with sleep, standing at the door in her nightgown, her arms round an overflowing of fronds and flowers. "They've begun to arrive, Mademoiselle! *Les étrennes.*"

Alphonsine searched eagerly for the card, found it, read it and let it fall to the floor. "Put them in the other room, like last year," she said.

The flowers were not from Franz. Their beauty pleaded with her in vain.

The bell rang at intervals all morning, but not so often as the previous year. As each gift was brought in Alphonsine's cheeks flushed and her heart palpitated with hope. Prince Stacklyn remembered her with a purse filled with banknotes —a kindness and an insult. But neither her pleasure nor her hurt lasted beyond the moment. What did they all mean to her, these shadows from a world to which she no longer belonged?

There was nothing from Franz, nothing from Édouard. For her the New Year died before it was born.

"Put away my gown, Julie," she said. "Put away my jewels. I am not going out."

"But, Mademoiselle, it is New Year's Day! You must be happy, then the whole year will be happy."

"I have had my happiness, dear child," she said. "Take the day off. The porter will receive whatever will come."

"I'll just go to mass, Mademoiselle, and come back at once."

From behind the casement Alphonsine watched the snow. The flakes were falling less thickly now, revealing a brightening sky. Dash, whom Julie had let out, came bounding in, his coat flecked with glittering drops. He shook himself and came to sit at her feet. She laid her hand on his head and felt an overflowing of pity for this free creature which, in its devotion, preferred her solitude to the promptings of nature. "Good Dash, good Dash," she said.

She watched the people passing back and forth across the street—parents with their children, gray-haired couples arm in arm in the secure oneness of joys and sorrows shared. They were perhaps visiting children and grandchildren, or they were going to the Church of the Madeleine to thank God for their blessings.

She too should be going to church. But what if *he* came and, not finding her, would go away and never return? She listened for the bell, but it had long since stopped ringing. How few in comparison with last year had remembered her this day! And no one, no one at all, had come to call.

"Ah, Dash!" she sighed. "The heart has many friends, but sorrow is alone."

Julie, returning from church, found her as she had left her. "Oh, Mademoiselle," she said. "You should have been there. The priest said such beautiful words about a lily coming out of the dust and about new hope and new life for everybody, even the beggar in the street. He had us all crying and I think he cried himself. It would have done your heart good. Wouldn't you like to go out? It has stopped snowing."

Alphonsine shook her head. "We've already been all round the city, Julie. We gave the poor people their gifts and then we went to the student quarter and they crowned me queen. It was all so gay we were laughing like children!"

"Did the porter go with you, Mademoiselle?"

"The porter? No."

"But you're wearing the gown I left you in. You didn't go out in that light dress, Mademoiselle?"

"For the journey we made it didn't matter what I wore. Don't be distressed, dear child. My mind isn't wandering. . . . Quick! Someone's at the door!"

She started to her feet but reeled with dizziness and sank back into her chair. She had grown so weak that the least unaccustomed sound threw her into nervous agitation.

"Who is it? Tell me, quickly! What is it?" she called after Julie. "Hurry! Hurry!"

The seconds seemed like hours before the girl returned followed by a liveried messenger carrying a painting covered with a draw curtain of white satin. He placed it against the back of a chair and pulled the cords.

Julie gave a delighted shriek. "Why, it's you, Mademoiselle! You'd think it could speak, it's so real."

Alphonsine turned as pale as if the blood of her body had been drained by her double so glowingly alive in the frame of gold. "Who sent it?" she asked.

"It is from the gallery, Mademoiselle Duplessis." The man handed her a card.

She thanked him and dismissed him. She tried to read the card but could make out nothing but a dancing blur. "What does it say, Julie?"

The girl wrinkled her brow and spelled out: "To Camille from Franz. *Hommages.*"

Alphonsine took back the stiff little square. The words were in Franz's hand. So much she could see. The rest she guessed at. "You may go now, Julie," she said.

Franz must be in Paris, then. He had ordered the portrait sent to her because he would soon see her. Surely that's what it meant. But what if he were still in Hungary or even in Russia? Might he not have enclosed the card in a letter to the gallery? Suppose it meant that he sent back the portrait because he no longer loved her? He had coldly written *hommages* and not *love*.

Ah, no! Franz, who felt pity for the least living thing, would not have been so cruel to her whom he loved. She heard his words of love even now, as when he had uttered them in their moments of closeness. She felt the ecstasy like lightning through her at the memory. Franz was coming! He might be on his way to her even now.

"Julie! Julie! Quickly! Help me dress!"

Night came and she was still sitting at the casement in the dress and the jewels she had worn that other New Year's Day. The pale square of light from the street lantern, falling aslant, made an insubstantial background from which she emerged like a spirit. She sat so still that she seemed scarcely to breathe except when some street noise, or the striking of the hour, made her start.

Ten o'clock. Eleven. Still she hoped. Midnight and the end of New Year's Day. But Franz had often come after midnight. She remained there, waiting.

"Mademoiselle, isn't it time you went to bed?" Julie asked uneasily.

"You go to bed, dear child. You're young. You need your sleep. Can't you see how quietly I'm resting? Go to bed. I'll call you if I need you."

Seeing only the outward calm Julie left her. In the street the night noises gradually ceased. The city was falling asleep after its happy day.

"No one has come," she said when two strokes from the church clock echoed with finality in her heart. She got up, seeing the darkened room spin about her, and tottered to the window which was becoming her only outlet to the world. "No one will ever come except Korff. Good-by, Franz. Good-by, Édouard."

The sky arched an unfathomable blue, almost black, over the city. There was no moon nor could she see any stars. Ah, yes, there, directly above her as she leaned against the balustrade, shone a solitary star. The discovery thrilled her. "He will return," she said. "You will guide him back to me."

The star cast its light upon her as on all things, impersonal, implacable.

When she threw herself wearily upon the bed she read another meaning in the presence of the star. She was as alone on earth as it was in the heavens. "Franz! Franz! Why have you forsaken me?" she sobbed into her pillow.

That bitter January her health grew so much worse that Korff feared he would not find her alive from one visit to the next. Yet she refused to remain in bed. "I'll have time enough to rest in the grave," she told him.

For long hours she would sit by the window in a lace negligée, one arm about Dash and her eyes fixed mournfully on the life she was so soon to leave. Then suddenly she would stagger across the room and sink upon her knees before the Virgin in a paroxysm of self-accusation and tears. "I know Franz will not come. I know my eyes will never see him. But O Virgin Mother of God! My pardon! My pardon from Édouard. Do not let me die with that sin upon my soul!"

She knew the Virgin had answered her prayer when late in

January the bell clanged as in the happy past and eager foot-steps resounded on the stairs.

"Édouard! Édouard!" she called even before he appeared.

He flung open the door and would have come headlong into the room but that the ghost crumpled at the feet of the Virgin held him. He took the intervening steps on tiptoe as in a church and would have knelt had not Alphonsine lifted up her arms for him to help her rise.

How light she was! So light that by comparison her portrait seemed to be the living being and she the shadow. How was it possible in a few short months? Why had they not told him?

"Thank God you've come at last, Édouard," she said, breathing with difficulty. "But cruel, cruel! You might at least have answered my note."

"Your note? When—when did you send it? I've been abroad for months."

"I wrote to you from Ems, Édouard, when I thought I was dying."

"Dying! Don't say that word, *mon ange!* You'll live—live and be happy with me. We'll forget everything but our love. For I love you my—my dearest. More than ever, I love you. We'll live in Italy—anywhere. I'll marry you again in France and—and—"

"Faithful Édouard! My Knight of the Sunflower. That's what Delphine used to call you. She has left me too. Every-body has left me."

"I'll never leave you. I love you, *mon ange!* Oh, if you knew what these—these terrible months have been without even the sight of you. I was hurt and jealous and—and I thought I

—I hated you. I thought I could forget you. Ah, dearest, dearest!"

He threw himself at her feet and buried his head in her lap. When he lifted it he could not understand the long look she gave him, no more than in the past when desire would overwhelm reason. Perhaps it was a mercy that in those burning eyes he did not read the thought: "Édouard! Always Édouard when it should be Franz!"

He felt her hands quivering in his like imprisoned fledglings. For a while neither spoke though he tried to recall her from her remoteness with soft kisses on her wrists. Suddenly she leaned forward so that her face almost touched his. "Édouard! Édouard! Can't you see I am not long for this world? I am dying, Édouard, dying, and I cannot die without your pardon. That is what I begged in my note. That is what I must have now. Your forgiveness, Édouard!"

The nearness of her made its appeal even more strongly than her anguish. He rose, lifting her up, and held her close. How slight she felt. There was no longer the sensation of flesh but of a phantom one clasps in a dream. In terror of a dissolution which seemed to be happening right there in his arms, he began to kiss her blindly, desperately. But she drew back, holding him off with all her strength.

"Not love! Not love!" she cried. "Your pardon, Édouard! Your pardon!"

"There is nothing to forgive, *mon ange*," he tried to calm her. "If there was I forgot it—and forgave it—long ago."

Instead of soothing her the words increased her agitation.

"No! No! You must not deny me, Édouard! Your forgiveness
before I die. I implore you!"

She was trembling so violently that his arm shook. "Well,
then, I forgive you. For whatever you did I—I forgive you."

"That is not enough. Say this after me. With my great love
I pardon your great sin. Say it."

He repeated the words while her eyes took them from his
lips like a tangible salvation.

"Ah, you are good. You are so good, Édouard! Go now,
dear. Good-by."

The tenderness in her voice stirred him. "One kiss, *mon
ange.*" He sought her mouth but she struggled away.

"Not on the lips!" she said. Not on the lips consecrated to
Franz.

She left the house once only after that, on the 3rd of
February to go to a concert where Liszt's music was being
played. She was so feeble that two attendants had to carry her
to her loge. There, still beautiful in the aura of death, she sat
with lowered lids, absorbing the sounds as a flower the light.
No one went to disturb her solitude. Besides, they knew they
would not have reached her.

When she returned home she had Julie sit by her as she lay,
in her evening dress, upon the bed. "Do not let anyone in,"
she said. "Unless—unless it should be—"

The young girl nodded. Always Monsieur Leets!

"Do not leave me."

Again Julie nodded.

"You are not afraid, dear child?" Alphonsine looked deep
into her eyes.

"I have seen it before," said Julie simply, "and I am not

afraid, Mademoiselle. It cannot be terrible or there would not be such peace after it comes."

Julie held Alphonsine's hand. They did not speak. The clock ticked the relentless rhythm of time, without beginning and without end. At last Alphonsine sank into so deep a sleep that the doorbell did not reach it.

Julie went out to receive Perrégaux. "It's useless," he said, laying on a chair a jacket of Alphonsine's which, in a final desperate hope, he had taken to the famous hypnotist, Alexis. "He cannot cure her, Julie. He said—he said it is only a matter of hours. Let me sit by her with you."

"I promised not to let anyone in," she said. "But you can sit here by the door as before. I'll call you if—"

It was too late. Three sharp, startled cries came from the bedroom. When Julie rushed in Death had already preceded her.

The final marvel of Alphonsine's life was her loveliness in death. Her head, haloed in point d'Alençon lace, was that of a pure young girl. In her hands she held a bouquet of camellias to which a crucifix lent the grace of final indulgence.

They buried her from the Madeleine where she and Franz had discovered the undying symbol of their love. Few followed her to the cemetery. Julie, weeping silently, was the only woman. There was Édouard. There was Prince Stacklyn, stooped and trembling, mourning his Annette whom he had lost for the second time.

The news reached Liszt in Kiev. He was stunned. Camille, who had reawakened the disillusioned man and kindled the artist was now the prey of Death. The girl of the compas-

268      THE LAST LOVE OF CAMILLE

sionate eyes gazing on dissolution was herself dissolution and
those pupils which had spoken more eloquently than her
ruefully smiling lips were now a liquefying horror in the
triumphant skull. "O symbol of human nothingness! O cruel,
inescapable Victor!" he cried, flinging from him the letter
from Paris.

Perhaps she had died in loneliness and abandonment. How
could he have let those months pass without a word to her?
Had she known despite his thoughtless silence, that she had
lived with him as closely as his music, the greatest intimacy he
could confer on any human being? But she was a simple girl.
Without some explicit word she would not have known that
he meant to return to her, that he had been waiting till the
final Russian tour to fulfill his promise. Had she understood
the gift of her portrait? That he had sent her likeness because
he would soon be coming to claim her? Now the picture alone
remained, the only visible memory of the radiant beauty which
had restored fire to his spent genius.

He went to the piano for release. The tentative fingers
touched the keys as one touches warm flesh. Suddenly they
beat out seven crashing chords that filled the room with the
ominousness of a *Dies Irae*, but bitter, mocking and rebellious, the theme that for a year had been echoing in his
brain. Again and again he sounded the titanic thunder till
the piano shook and the reverberations, going through him
like a galvanic charge, brought him down in a trembling heap
over the keyboard. At last he had the nerve-shattering opening
of the Concerto in E Flat Major.

He did not finish it till the following year. The memory
of Camille had been too intense. He exhausted himself with

recitals to forget his grief but he could not dispel her from his mind. Gradually the numbed heart awakened and a new love began to burgeon. It was at the Polish castle of the Princess Carolyne de Sayn-Wittgenstein that, with a small orchestra, he gave the first reading of the Concerto.

The feudal hall, hung with tapestries and decked with flowers, cast the glow of its hundred *torchères* on jewels and uniforms. The orchestra outnumbered the audience, but the Almanach de Gotha boasted fewer names for distinction. A smell of incense pervaded the air. Indeed, on either side of the improvised stage two bronze burners of Byzantine design were sending up clouds of propitiatory fragrance. The musicians sat, expectant. Only the pianist's bench was empty.

From a side door Liszt entered, tall, slightly stooped, his gloved hands twisting, his Florentine profile remote in its perfection. He was wearing neither decorations nor orders. In the unrelieved black of his formal suit he looked like some high priest come to officiate at a mystery. He kept the fire of his eyes veiled. Even when the applause broke at his entrance and he acknowledged it with a series of bows, he did not once lift his lids.

On his way to the piano he took off his gloves and let them drop to the floor. He surveyed the orchestra before sitting down, nodded and with motions of his head and hands began conducting the Concerto whose piano solo he was to play.

Like a burst of Mephistophelian mockery from the orchestra the bitter theme of waste and loss filled the hall's immensity, making it shudder a second later to a sardonic blare, a mockery of mockery, the defiance of the lacerated spirit against forces greater than itself. Again and again the crazed demonic cackle stormed the ear and stilled the heart, till calm returned to the spirit which, in the resignation of the piano, told of the fugacity of love and beauty and of all things born to die.

The audience listened in unbearable tension. But there was no pause between movements to make them draw breath. As one wave follows another, the second movement flowed after the first in a sorrowful, elegiac introduction of the love theme of Camille. It came first from the strings in the purity of its original statement, all aspiration and desire, but soon an ominous minor broke into the lyric serenity, the first intimation of Death. In exaltation, against flowing arpeggios, the piano took up the theme of love. Flesh and spirit merged in melodic ecstasy, but the foreboding chords rumbled and exaltation drooped its wings at the imminence of Death.

But if the beloved dies does all love die? The will-o'-the-wisp of the triangle tinkled its musical denial. Yes, life had its pleasures still, sweetly consolatory to the flesh, for what could quench the thirst of the heart? Life was as eternal as Death, and Love shared their eternity. In martial tempo the theme of love triumphed through the majestic closing movement.

Nevertheless, when the music ended, tears were streaming down the pianist's cheeks. He clapped the piano shut like a coffin lid.

"It was wonderful, Franz! Wonderful!" sighed his hostess.

She was not beautiful, like Camille, but her eyes held inspiration. Besides, she was a princess.

# Historical Note

THE LAST LOVE OF CAMILLE

THE WOMAN who for more than a century has been variously known to fame as Marguerite Gautier, Camille and the Lady of the Camellias, not to mention the later Violetta of Verdi's *La Traviata*, was born Alphonsine Plessis in the department of Orne, France, on the 15th of January, 1824. Her origin was obscure, her childhood sordid. In her early adolescence she was left to fend for herself in Paris by her unprincipled and degenerate father who had already exploited the girl's beauty for his profit. Her rise was rapid, thanks to her loveliness, intelligence and an innocence of heart which her mode of life never affected. Within a few years she was the queen of fashion and the most sought-after courtesan in France.

Her story, as it is popularly known, derives from the novel and, later, the play, *La Dame aux Camélias* by Alexandre Dumas the Younger. It tells of the courtesan, Marguerite Gautier, who, when she experiences love at last, is willing to sacrifice her happiness and, as it happens, her life for her lover's sake. The elements of fact in the novel are the following: in 1844 Alexandre Dumas—the Armand Duval of the story—

then a young dandy of twenty, fell in love with Marie Alphonsine Duplessis, as she then ennobled her plebeian name. The relationship lasted until August, 1845. In February, 1847, Alphonsine Duplessis died of consumption and her things were sold at auction. Moved by both events Dumas wrote his novel shortly thereafter, almost at fever heat, and created the romantic prototype of the "lost one" with a heart of gold.

Reality was less sentimental. Alphonsine Duplessis did find love, her first and her last, in Franz Liszt. The two met in the autumn of 1845 when each, for different reasons, was ripe for a supreme experience. They were together, except for his concert tours, through the autumn and winter and all Paris thrilled to the great romance. Yet at the very height of it Alphonsine went off secretly to London and there, on the 21st of February, 1846, married the young Vicomte Édouard de Perrégaux.

The two, however, parted the day after their marriage and Alphonsine rejoined Liszt in Paris. Why did Alphonsine marry Édouard when she was in love with Liszt? Why did she part from the young count? *The Last Love of Camille* is the outcome of these questions.

Alphonsine Duplessis, Perrégaux and Liszt are the components of the human triangle, but love itself is the protagonist in three different aspects: the love of a man for a woman for his art's sake; the love of a woman for the man who has awakened her to spiritual as well as sensual exaltation; the dedicated love of a youth for love's sake only.

*Set in Linotype Fairfield*
*Format by Katharine Sitterly*
*Manufactured by The Haddon Craftsmen, Inc.*
*Published by* HARPER & BROTHERS, *New York*